POINT
BLANK

POINT

BLANK

Jayson Livingston

St Martin's Press   New York

This novel is a work of fiction. Names, characters, places, and incidents are either the product of the author's imagination or have been used fictitiously. Any resemblance to actual events, locales, persons, living or dead, is entirely coincidental.

POINT BLANK. Copyright © 1990 by Jayson Livingston. All rights reserved. Printed in the United States of America. No part of this book may be used or reproduced in any manner whatsoever without written permission except in the case of brief quotations embodied in critical articles or reviews. For information, address St. Martin's Press, 175 Fifth Avenue, New York, N.Y. 10010.

Design by Judy Dannecker

Library of Congress Cataloging-in-Publication Data
Livingston, Jayson.
  Point blank.
    p. cm.
  "A Thomas Dunne book."
  ISBN 0-312-05143-3
    I. Title.
PS3562.I943P65   1990   813'.54—dc20   90-37278

First Edition: December 1990
1 3 5 7 9 10 8 6 4 2

ACKNOWLEDGMENTS

I would like to express my appreciation to the following people for their help and support.

Sacramento County Deputy Sheriff Officers David Clegg and Daryl Jackson: Their knowledge was a tremendous help, and their tolerance of my many questions is gratefully appreciated.

Mike DeGray: His help with the tough spots brought the book together, allowing me to see daylight when there seemed to be only night.

Yvonne Walton: A lady who never minded listening to my constant babble and ideas, and who took the time to read my material. Her support was genuine.

Georgette Livingston: My mother, whose professionalism and encouragement made this book possible.

Also, a special thanks to my family and friends for their continuing support.

POINT BLANK

PROLOGUE

Surprisingly agile for a man his size, he moved across the damp grass on monstrous feet, slithering from shadow to shadow like a large jungle cat stalking its prey.

Ahead of him, bright lights reflected from the window of the room where ten women followed their blonde aerobics instructor's gyrations. He watched, unimpressed, until his gray eyes settled on the instructor. His heart quickened then, as anticipation grew. Even in the icy cold of the night, sweat quickly formed on his brow.

When class was over and the women began gathering up their things, the man walked into deeper shadows, where he could watch and wait and plan every detail.

Finally, after the last vehicle had driven off, he carefully made his way to the door. It was unlocked. *That's very unsafe, lady*, he thought smugly. *That's how murders happen.* He laughed to himself.

In the darkened room now, the smell of it attacked his senses. Perfume, body sweat, the sweet smell of a mingling of women. He picked it all up as his excitement grew.

Slowly, he walked through the aerobics room and into the back. He could hear heavy breathing—or was it his own? No. He could hear her breathing and moaning. The sound came from the locker room on his right. The door was open. He made no noise as his rubber-soled shoes glided across the tile.

He found her between the fourth and fifth row of lockers, sitting on a bench. She was naked but for her panties. He watched, fascinated, as her left hand worked at her crotch and her right hand caressed her nipples. Her moans grew louder as her body quivered. He bit his lip, tasting blood, as he slowly advanced toward her.

She was shaking now, head back, eyes closed. And then he was behind her. Nice legs. Flat stomach. Firm tits; his face dripped sweat. She opened her eyes and he smiled.

She tried to scream, but he had the plastic bag over her head, his big, meaty hands around her throat. Soon, the twitching stopped and her body fell limp.

He left her on the bench, but rolled her over on her stomach. With his pants unfastened, he crouched down and entered her, reaching ejaculation almost the moment his member touched the moist tissue. And then it was over, though his excitement had started to flow again.

He looked down at the motionless beauty, fished into a pocket, and pulled out a shiny coin. He flipped it onto her back and smiled. It was going to be a good year.

In his car now and hungry, the blonde bitch forgotten, the man headed for the nearest twenty-four-hour convenience store. He was pleased to find one without customers, and strolled inside, giving the young punk behind the counter a toothy grin. He headed for the pastry section, snatched up a dozen assorted fruit pies, and deposited them unceremoniously on the counter. "Put 'em in a bag, ya fuck," he ground out.

The young man was clearly nervous about the man with the pies and quickly reached down to grab a small sack. He laid the sack on top of the pies and asked, "Is that going to be all, sir?" His voice crackled with fear.

"No! I'll take whatever you've got in the register, too."

The clerk started to raise his hand to hit the panic button, but the man's hand was around the back of his neck with incredible speed. He quickly slammed the clerk's head into the counter, snapping cartilage. Blood pooled on the counter and the clerk slumped to the floor.

The man reached over the counter, popped open the register, and pulled out approximately forty-eight dollars. He then bagged the pies and threw the money on top. On his way out, he glanced up at the clock in the corner. It was 11:37.

CHAPTER 1

Tuesday, December 8, 1988: 2337 Hrs.

With the constant drizzle and the temperature hovering around thirty-eight degrees, Sacramento's early December weather was getting to seem downright cold. Wondering if they were going to luck out and have a white Christmas, Robert Hollinger checked his watch. It was 11:37, almost midnight.

He looked over at the detective sitting in the driver's seat and said, "This really sucks!"

Neal Jessop, a fourteen-year veteran of the Sacramento Police Department, and Robert's partner for the last twelve months, grinned. "You got a problem?"

"Yeah, I got a problem. It's the friggin' turd hunt we're on. I'm on my eighth hour of overtime, for one thing. And I've been sitting in a cold, unmarked squad car in the rain for nearly five goddamned hours, watching the front of this run-down hotel, waiting for two fluteheads to show up, who probably won't, when I could be home, giving Dana the high hard one. Other than that, things are just fine and dandy."

Neal laughed. "Jesus, you're a punk." He switched the headlights on and off twice.

The radio squawked to life. "Yo, Neal?" came the response.

"I've got me a full-grown pussy in the car, here."

"No kidding? Is it loose?"

"Yeah. This punk is whining about our little stakeout detail."

"Well, we want sloppy seconds when you're done."

Robert grabbed the microphone from Neal. "You couldn't handle it, Dalton. Way too much meat for you."

Laughter filled both unmarked cars.

The stakeout Robert was complaining about was actually a bit more serious than the detectives wanted to admit. The two subjects had several felony warrants for their arrests and were wanted in connection with at least a dozen armed robberies of liquor and convenience stores that also included several cold-blooded shootings. It was amazing that none of the clerks had been killed.

The four detectives knew that these shitsacks were heavy duty bad guys and had to be stopped.

The Robbery Division had been working on the case since the second holdup, just before Thanksgiving. Fortunately, a break had come down just this morning, when a street person wandered into the police station with some solid information, pinpointing a location. Armed with a search warrant, they had converged on the room in the hotel, but had come up empty-handed. But the room had been full of personal stuff, so their quarry hadn't checked out; it was just going to be a matter of time.

Robert saw the suspects' vehicle first, quickly identifying it as an '84 Camaro, white on white. "Show time," he muttered through his teeth.

Neal watched the Camaro pull up in front of the hotel. One male subject got out, carrying a travel bag. He hurried up to the door, where he was joined by a tall blonde woman. Immediately, they walked into the hotel.

At that moment, the Camaro raced away, careening up the street. Neal grabbed the microphone. "Dalton, take the vehicle. We'll take the home boy and the blonde."

"Got it," Dalton replied, wheels already rolling.

Neal switched the radio back to channel one, Central Dispatch. "Five-eight-six."

A smooth female voice repeated, "Five-eight-six."

"The suspects have arrived at our location. Roll patrol cover."

"Five-eight-six, ten-four."

The detectives left the squad car, crossed the street, and entered the hotel. Robert wore Levis, a UCLA sweatshirt, a military field jacket, a scarf, and a ball cap. Neal was dressed similarly, but their attempt at undercover apparel didn't fool the old man behind the desk. He looked up, decided they were cops, and went back to the magazine he was reading.

Room 407 was on the fourth floor. No elevator. The detectives hit the stairs, moving carefully and quickly. Stairs and hallway reeked of urine and other questionable odors—that alone would have kept them moving.

They reached the fourth-floor landing. Found the room at the end of the foul-smelling hallway, and moved, sliding up to the door. They could hear voices inside—one male, one female.

Robert pulled his Bren 10 10 mm auto from his pancake holster. Neal had his Smith and Wesson 645 .45 cal auto out and ready. A glance passed between them, and Neal banged on the door. "Police officers!" he shouted. "Open up! We have warrants for your arrest!"

They heard the pump of a shotgun rack and jumped aside as a frying pan–sized hole exploded in the door and buckshot blasted into the wall across the hall. Down on his haunches, Robert grabbed his portable radio. "Five-eight-six. Shots fired. Need backup now!"

Up now, Neal plowed into the door with his shoulder, busting it off its hinges.

Robert stayed low, peering into the room where red, blue, and yellow lights from the bar across the street flashed off and on through the window.

In a quick volley of shots, Robert heard Neal's cry, and the thud as he hit the floor. Another shotgun blast rocked the room. Robert could see the shape of the man with the gun, who was racking up another shell. He cut loose three rounds in that general direction and heard the shotgun clatter to the floor. The man who had been holding it slammed against the dresser and fell.

The woman began to scream. Robert hit the light switch and looked down at Neal. He lay on his back with a gaping hole in his chest. He seemed to be trying to form words, but blood gurgled up in his mouth.

Robert's heart pounded up in his throat as his mind raced. *Jesus Christ! Focus! Get control!*

The suspect lay motionless and the woman stood in the corner, screaming. Robert approached the suspect slowly, kicking the shotgun under the bed.

The woman's screams became words. "You fucking bastard! You motherfucker, die!"

A gun roared to life as a round whistled by Robert's left ear, ripping into the mirror above the dresser. He dove to his left, squeezing the trigger three times. The barrage of bullets hit their mark, shattering bones and vitals. Three uniforms entered the room, guns drawn.

Robert slowly approached the woman's motionless body. Two uniforms also advanced, guns aimed. The third uniform squatted on the floor at Neal's side. With a groan, he grabbed his portable radio. "Baker fourteen, officer down. Room four-oh-seven, Carlon Hotel. Need code three, ambulance!"

"Baker fourteen, ten-four."

* * *

Dalton Casteel positioned his unmarked vehicle three car lengths behind the suspect's white Camaro, convinced the scum had no idea he was being followed.

Mike Clegg grabbed the radio microphone out of the glove box. "Five-eight-seven," he said.

"Five-eight-seven," the dispatcher's voice returned.

"We're following suspected two-eleven vehicle. We'll wait for cover units before executing a felony vehicle stop. We're southbound on Twenty-second Street." Mike chuckled to himself. Oh, how he loved felony stops. As he held the microphone in his hand, it came to him again just how much he loved his job.

"Five-eight-seven, ten-four," the woman's voice responded. And then, "Charles seventeen, Charles eleven, Baker twelve. I need you to start for Ivy five-eight-seven's location."

The sound of the three units acknowledging their call filled the radio.

Mike keyed the radio again. "Charles seventeen. We're still southbound on Twenty-second, just crossing P Street."

Dalton had a very hard look on his face, his mind filled with different scenarios about how this bust could go down. None of them were pleasant.

The radio suddenly came to life again, Robert Hollinger's voice yelling, "Five-eight-six. Shots fired. Roll back up now!"

Mike looked at Dalton. "Shit! . . ."

"Don't say it, Mike. Let's just stay with the Camaro. We're out of position to help anyway."

The radio crackled, as Dispatch advised all units to stay off the air until advised. With this order came a loud "beep" every ten seconds.

Edgy, Mike squirmed in his seat and listened to the familiar beeping sound.

The radio squawked again. "Baker fourteen, officer down. Roll code three, ambulance room four-oh-seven, Carlon Hotel."

"Christ!" Dalton swore. He looked in his rearview mirror. A unit had pulled in behind them. He listened as the dispatcher announced to resume normal traffic. "Light 'em up, Mikey," he muttered, gripping the wheel.

Mike pulled back the sun visor, exposing a round magnet. He reached to the floor and grabbed a softball-sized light, also equipped with a magnet. He stuck the two together and turned on the switch. The light began an intense red glow. Immediately, the Camaro came to life, sliding sideways onto V Street as the driver fought for control.

Mike was on the microphone. "Five-eight-seven. We're in pursuit of two-eleven vehicle, eastbound V Street."

"Eastbound V Street, ten-four. Twenty-one Baker, can you start?"

There were now two patrol cars behind them. The streets were still wet from the earlier rain, but the pursuit reached speeds of eighty, then ninety miles an hour.

The radio air was cleared again. "We're now northbound on Twenty-eighth Street."

"Northbound Twenty-eighth, ten-four."

Dispatch seemed cool. Mike didn't know who the lady was, but she was very good. Stability in a time of crisis.

The vehicles were now hitting speeds of one hundred miles an hour. Mike watched the cars, houses, and businesses whizzing by, and thought to himself, *I trust you, Dalt, but I think we're gonna die.*

But Dalton had complete control of the Monte Carlo. "Still northbound on Twenty-eighth," Mike panted.

"Roger. Northbound Twenty-eighth."

The street was one way. The Camaro sailed along the bike lane, still at high speed. They were approaching J Street now, and the Camaro suddenly slammed on the brakes, skidding up on the sidewalk. It careened off several newspaper stands and pushed into a glass-encased Regional Transit bus stop, where it came to a stop sideways, jammed against a pole.

Dalton slammed to a stop thirty feet from the Camaro.

Mike was the first to exit the unmarked, his Smith and Wesson 659 9 mm extended. He moved quickly in a military crouch to one of the fallen newspaper racks for cover, the gun still trained on the vehicle.

Dalton used the open door of the Monte Carlo for his cover, his Sig Saurer 9 mm in his left hand. With his right, he grabbed the microphone off the console. "Five-eight-seven. Suspect vehicle nine-oh-one'd at the corner of Twenty-eighth and J."

"Five-eight-seven, ten-four."

He tossed the microphone on the seat. Both following patrol cars had now come to a stop, one on the sidewalk behind Mike, the other in the middle of the street. The red and blue light bars bounced off the building and cautiously passing automobiles. Dalton could hear other units responding to the location, code three.

Mike, who was still crouched behind the newspaper stand, barked out orders to the suspect in the Camaro. "Exit the vehicle now, with your hands in the air!"

The suspect slowly climbed out, arms up.

"Now turn and face your vehicle," Mike ordered. "Put your hands on top of your head. Lock your fingers and start moving backward. If you so much as turn your head, I'll shoot you where you stand."

The suspect slowly moved backward, pleading, "Don't be shootin' me, Officer."

A uniformed officer moved up. "I'll cuff him," he said, holstering his gun. As he approached the suspect, he grabbed the man's fingers, bending them backward to trip him to the ground, where he cuffed him.

Dalton and Mike watched, guns still trained on the man. Another uniform helped his partner put the suspect in the back of the patrol car.

Mike then crept up on the Camaro, checking to see if the suspect had been alone. The vehicle was empty. He nodded at Dalton.

Dalton holstered his gun and picked up the microphone. "Five-eight-seven. Go ahead and resume. Suspect in custody."

"Five-eight-seven, ten-four. Units resume normal traffic at

oh-oh-one-seven hours. Suspect in custody. Any units still responding to Twenty-eighth and J Streets, code four. KMG five-hundred clear."

Dalton walked up to Mike. "Let's get to it."

Mike looked at Dalton. He was talking about searching the vehicle. "Let me radio Captain Sweeny first, and let him know we got the other half of this bullshit."

Dalton nodded, but his thoughts weren't on the vehicle search. They were on the earlier call of an officer down.

One of the patrolmen walked up to Dalton. "Want us to book him?"

"Yeah. Start with the arrest report. Before you leave booking, I'll give you some more charges."

The patrolman nodded and walked back to his vehicle. He shone his flashlight into the backseat and said, "You are one ugly sumbitch, aren't you?" The suspect hung his head.

Robert sat in the hotel lobby, the adrenalin still pumping through him. He didn't think the full impact of Neal's death had hit him yet, and he wasn't looking forward to the moment when it did.

Several patrolmen had sealed off the first and fourth floors. He hadn't seen anybody from CSI, the coroner, or the shooting team, which would consist of a couple of investigators from the district attorney's office and maybe a couple of homicide detectives. It wasn't going to be pretty, no matter how it was cut. The media would have a field day, for one thing. Odds on favorite they would call it a racial shooting. No doubt.

Two groups of paramedics came down the stairs. They met Captain Sweeny in the lobby.

The captain said, "Well?"

"We've got three dead bodies up there," one of the medics said.

Sweeny did not look happy. His twenty-plus years with the department hadn't slowed down the aging process. He sighed. "What's the status of my officer?"

The medic shook his head. "If one of those bodies up there belongs to you, I'm sorry."

The captain grimaced and walked over to Robert. "How are you doing, Rob? Are you hurt?"

Robert shrugged. "Depends on what you mean. Physically, no. I'm okay."

Sweeny patted Robert on the shoulder. "Why don't you give me your weapon now, and then head for Internal Affairs? Homicide will want your statement, too. The sooner you get it over with, the sooner you can go home."

"Neal's dead," Robert said woodenly.

"I know." Sweeny took out a cigar and lit up. "Clegg radioed me just a few minutes ago. They got the other half of this shit."

Robert nodded and started to walk away. He stopped, and looked back at the captain. "Captain Sweeney . . ."

"Yeah?"

Robert opened his mouth, and then said, "Forget it. It's not important."

Sweeny watched the detective leave the building, as the knot in his stomach became a ball of fire.

CHAPTER

2

Wednesday, December 9, 1988: 0130 Hrs.

Robert walked out of the Internal Affairs office, sighing his relief. The interrogation was over, and it hadn't been nearly as bad as he'd thought it would be. The three detectives who had talked to him had actually been pleasant, almost understanding. They were the way they should be, not the head- and badge-hunting shitheads they were rumored to be. The last thing a cop needed was to have a fellow officer tell him he was a piece of scum. Taking it from John Q. Public was bad enough.

Robert rode the elevator to the Homicide Division on the eleventh floor. His head was beginning to feel like an overripe melon, but at least here the guys waiting for him were sincere.

The office was deserted, but for homicide detectives Tom Runyo and Steve Taylor. And from the look on their faces, this was the last place they wanted to be, too, at 1:30 in the morning.

Tom Runyo, a big, lumbering man, shook hands with Robert. "You know Steve?"

Robert nodded and shook hands with Taylor. "Mind if I sit down?"

Tom nodded toward a chair. "You okay?" he asked.

"I've been better," Robert said. But he was starting to relax. He hadn't realized until just now how tired he was, how drained, how fucked up.

"You've already been to IA?" Tom asked.

Robert nodded.

"Okay, then just tell us what went down tonight."

Robert went into the story again, but he had trouble when he got to the part about Neal.

Runyo picked up on it immediately. "What's bothering you?" he asked.

"I don't know..." Robert paused.

"Go ahead and get it off your chest," Taylor offered. "You're among friends here."

"Well, it's just that I've been working with Neal for the past year, and I've never known him to do anything stupid or act without thinking."

"And you think he didn't realize the danger?" Tom asked.

Robert shifted in his seat. "No, he knew the danger. We'd been tracking those two suspects for the last week. Everybody in Robbery knew how dangerous they were..." Robert paused again and took a deep breath. "It was like Neal committed some sort of..." He let his words trail off.

Taylor finished Robert's sentence. "Suicide?"

Robert's eyes connected with Taylor's. The detective knew the answer. "Yeah, suicide. That's the first time I've been able to say that word since the shooting. That's fuckin' stupid, huh? The whole premise is stupid."

Tom shook his head. "Not really. We've had other cases where officers have committed suicide in the line of duty, because they just couldn't bring themselves to eat their guns."

Robert felt sick to his stomach. "I don't understand it. Everything seemed great, just dandy."

"He didn't mention any problems he might be having?" Tom asked.

"No."

"Neal was married, wasn't he?"

"Yeah. Cindy is a real sweetheart. If there were any problems there, I sure didn't know about them."

Taylor was scribbling on a pad. "I've known Neal for ten years, and it doesn't add up. How about those final moments before the two of you went into the hotel? Did Neal seem okay? Did he still have his sense of humor?"

"Just like any other night," Robert replied, looking down at the floor.

Taylor stopped writing. "Well, Neal never was much on talking about his problems, no matter what was bothering him. It was just the way he was." He cleared his throat. "Okay, Rob. Everything seems to gel. We'll submit our report to IA. They should release their findings in a couple of weeks. You do know you'll have to be on a mandatory five-day administrative leave."

"Yeah—"

Tom interrupted, obviously trying to put a smile on Robert's face. "Did we mention that it's with pay?"

Robert forced a grin. "Yeah, I know all about administrative leave. This is my third shooting."

Steve smiled. "We have a celebrity in our midst."

"Will that sway IA's verdict?" Robert asked.

Tom shook his head. "Not if the shooting falls under the city's guidelines, under the shooting policy." He stood up. "That's about it, Rob. Why don't you blow this pop stand and try and get some rest. I'm sure your lieutenant will want you to come down tomorrow."

"Yeah, okay. And thanks." Robert shook both detectives' hands and walked out the door with his head down. The only thing he knew for sure was that it was going to be a sleepless night.

* * *

The ringing of the phone woke Stu out of a deep sleep. He focused his eyes on the illuminated dial of the clock. It was 3:40 A.M. He groaned. The phone was still ringing. He finally picked it up.

"Detective Redlam?"

"Yeah," he said, trying to shake the cobwebs from his brain.

"This is Bonnie Short, Central Dispatch. Sorry to wake you."

"Cut the crap and get to it," he grumbled.

"We've got a body at two-six-four-oh Fair Oaks Avenue, at the Free Spirit Spa and Fitness Center."

For the last seven months the graveyard shift in Homicide had been scratched; instead different detectives were working on an on-call basis. This was supposed to save all the city taxpayers lots of money. What a crock of shit. Every time a Homicide dick was called out to a crime scene, he ended up on overtime, double time. Well, that was city politics for you.

"So why call me? Runyo and Taylor are on call this week."

"Runyo and Taylor caught an officer involved in a shooting about three hours ago," came the reply.

"Swell." By this time, Redlam had his feet on the floor. He reached for his notebook. "What's that address again?" She gave it to him and he wrote it down.

Stu Redlam, a fifteen-year veteran with the Sacramento Police Department, had spent the last five-and-a-half years as a homicide detective. Supposedly, they were the elite of the elite detectives, so he wondered why every time he was pulled from his bed to look at another corpse, he didn't feel particularly elite. He guessed the movies and TV had something to do with average street-tough, hard-working cops coming to be considered as an elite crime-fighting network. The term "crime fighting" had always made him laugh. Most homicides were solved with a lot of legwork, stupid bad guys, and snitches, not because of great insights like those of Steve McGarrett on "Hawaii Five-O," or Thomas Magnum seemed to think. That made great copy, but didn't solve murders.

Stu walked out of the bathroom, a towel wrapped around his waist. He passed the mirror and stopped, studying the ugly scar across his left shoulder. It was still highly visible, even with all the hair growing over it. He touched it, almost tenderly, remembering the night he took the bullet. He twisted to the left. The knife scar on his side was pretty noticeable, too. He shook his head. *Jesus, what a beat-up piece of shit you are!*

He hung his silver St. Michael's medal around his neck. He wasn't a religious man, but the patron saint was supposed to protect all law enforcement officers. So far, the medallion had done a pretty good job.

By the time he left his house, wearing 501 Levis, sweatshirt, and heavy jacket, thirty minutes had gone by since his rude wake-up call. No big deal. ETA was ten minutes away from the town of Carmichael where he lived.

Stu pulled into the parking lot at the fitness center, squeezing the Blazer in between the two black-and-whites. He ducked under the crime scene tape and walked up the path, boot heels clacking on the cement. God only knew what he would find. The body could be in tiny pieces. It never got any easier.

He opened the door, then looked at his darkened fingers, cursing. CSI, the crime scene investigator, had already dusted. That might be Grant Coogan, and Stu hoped it was. Grant, one of twelve crime scene investigators in the city, was one of the best. He had an uncanny sense of knowing just what was needed beforehand, saving the detectives a lot of work. And he was young. Stu liked that. Crime scene investigators were also patrol officers when they weren't up to their elbows in bodies and mayhem. Stu had heard that Coogan was an excellent street officer, too.

The patrolman who was supposed to be covering the door was nowhere around. Stu saw him standing off to the side of the building, head down, throwing up. It gave Stu an indication of what was waiting for him, and he knew it wasn't going to be pretty.

Inside, Stu made a face. The place smelled like dirty socks and strong perfume. He swallowed deeply.

Before he reached the hallway leading to the back of the building, a patrolman popped out. "You from Homicide?"

"I'm from Homicide," Stu answered.

"Well, she's in there. In the locker room. Hope you don't mind if I stay out here."

Stu found Grant Coogan taking pictures of the naked body and the surrounding area. Her knees were on the tile floor, while her torso, face down, was draped across a bench. A plastic bag lay near her head, but the creep had strangled her, too. Deep purple bruises circled her neck.

He looked at Coogan and managed a smile. "So what have we got?"

"We've got shit," Grant muttered. "Runyo and Taylor still on that shooting that went down earlier?"

"Yeah, I guess so. At least I think that's why I'm here. Have you any info on what happened down there?"

Coogan reloaded his camera. "Big shoot-out, I guess, involving a couple of Robbery detectives. Neal Jessop and Robert Hollinger. You know them?"

"I've seen them around."

"Neal Jessop was killed. Hollinger dumped two."

"No shit?" Stu grabbed the body's cold wrist, looked at the fingers and under the fingernails. "Did you go to the scene?"

Coogan shook his head. "I missed out. Freddy and Lewis got it."

"Real mess, huh?" Stu was looking in the open locker. He pulled out a radio, extending the antenna. He used it to prod around in the locker.

"What I hear, a real blood bath," Coogan said.

Stu reached into his back pocket and pulled out a pair of surgical gloves. He slipped them on and then went fishing in the purse at the bottom of the locker. He unsnapped the wallet and looked at the driver's license. Her name was Mary Kay Attwater, and she lived in the American River Canyon area near the town of Folsom.

Stu grabbed her head by the hair and lifted it up, peering into her face. "I'd say it's her."

Grant stepped over the bench, studying the picture and the woman. "No doubt about it, it's her."

Stu let the head fall back to the floor, and looked at the coin that rested in the middle of Mary Attwater's naked back. "Did you get a shot of this?" he asked, pointing at the coin.

"I did."

"You gonna print it?"

"Doubt it would do much good. I'll save it for my scrapbook."

"Really awesome body," Stu said. "Nice ass."

Grant chuckled. "Are we as sick as we sound, or is it just me?"

Stu smiled. "Sicker, pal, sicker."

Stu picked up the coin, grasping it by the edges. "It looks foreign."

"Probably is. Put it back. It looks good against all that tender flesh."

"You fuckin' guys are really something!" a voice said out of nowhere.

Stu and Grant turned and looked at the young patrolman who had led Stu to the locker room.

"What did you say?" Grant asked.

"We've got a dead officer downtown and a dead woman right here, and you two goofs are telling jokes and laughing as though you were out on the town. Why not show some respect for the dead!"

Stu stood, dumbfounded. "She's dead, so she could give a shit less about respect. Neal Jessop was a good man, and now he's dead. I feel for his wife or his girlfriend, and his family, but he doesn't care if we laugh or cry, either. So my advice to you is, go outside, blow your nose, and come back and see me when you're all grown up."

The uniform quickly left the locker room.

Stu sighed. "The kid has a lot to learn."

Grant nodded. "And he'll probably learn just like we did, the hard way."

Stu cleared the locker room at 7:55, after CSI and the lab people had finished. The body was on the way to the coroner's office, and the business had been released back to the owner, whom they had finally managed to locate.

The janitor who cleaned the fitness center each night, and who found the body, had been questioned and released. There was nothing left to do now but tackle the paperwork while waiting in the hope that somebody would come up with something significant.

Stu and Grant walked to the parking lot, weary and hungry and very much aware that this was a new day.

"Want to go to breakfast?" Stu asked.

Grant shook his head. "I'd better get to the office or I'll never get home."

"Catch you later then. And oh, Grant, whatever you get, it's for my eyes only."

"It's a deal," Grant said, getting into his car.

Stu was about to pull out of the parking lot when Sergeant Nick Scofield waved him down. He was out of breath. "What happened in there, Stu? I've got an officer who is pretty shook up."

Stu looked at the hard-as-nails sergeant, who was also a good friend, and smiled. "Good old Nick. Still the softy inside."

Nick turned red around the ears. "Don't be too hard on the kid, Stu. He hasn't had much time with this homicide stuff, and he's only twenty-two. Shit, I remember a couple of snot-nosed rookies who thought they knew everything about law enforcement. That was some fifteen years ago."

Stu laughed. "I also recall a couple of sorry assholes who couldn't even execute a friggin' vehicle stop correctly."

"Yeah, that was us." Nick's smile started to fade. "How are you really doing, amigo? Have you heard from Gail?"

"Nope, and I don't suppose I will." He hastily changed the subject. "I've got to get to the office and get the press release out, ASAP."

"Right. Let's go to the watering hole soon. It's been a long time since we've been out drinking together."

"We'll make it soon, I promise. I'll even buy the first two rounds."

Stu watched Scofield walk off and opened his clipboard. He needed a standard dead body form, the homicide sketch form, the witness statement form, and physical evidence form.... He closed the clipboard and started the Blazer. *Yeah, the elite. That's us, the fucking elite.*

Jack Smitovich was sitting behind his desk in the study when the call came in at 11:20 A.M. He had just finished reading the paper, and scanned it several times before angrily tossing it aside. There wasn't one goddamned thing about a dead aerobics instructor. Just some stuff about the city police in a big shoot-out at a crappy downtown hotel. This, he concluded, had better be good news.

He picked up the receiver and barked, "Yes?"

"Phase one completed," the voice said in his ear. The voice was very deep and lacked emotion. Almost haunting.

"I didn't see it in the paper," Jack spouted angrily. He then chastised himself. *Play it cool. Don't upset him. Change your tone!* "Ah, well, I didn't see it in the paper."

"It went down late," came the husky reply. "Watch for it on the evening news. Trust me. Mary Attwater is no longer among the living."

Jack suddenly felt a chill, the teeth-chattering kind. This gorilla took a genuine delight in killing. Well, if nothing else, he had hired the right person.

"You sound kind of shaky," the voice went on. "How come? You afraid of me?"

Jack couldn't believe his ears. There was a long pause before he said, "Phase two starts when you're ready." He cleared his throat and continued. "The file will be at the same location, locker two-seventeen, downtown bus terminal."

"Is this one gonna be as pretty as Mary Attwater?"

Before Smitovich could answer, the line went dead.

He was relieved that the animal had hung up. And he was going to be even happier when this whole mess was over!

CHAPTER 3

Wednesday, December 9, 1988: 1140 Hrs.

The Robbery Division was cramped with bodies and paperwork. To put it mildly, the office was a solid clusterfuck.

After the shooting at the hotel the night before and the word that Neal Jessop had been killed, everybody had gone a little nuts. Not Neal! Not in Sacramento, where it was rare for an officer to be killed in the line of duty. Not when it was only sixteen days until Christmas, and Jessop's desk drawers were filled with unwrapped gifts he hadn't wanted to take home until the last minute. Everyone had felt his own kind of pain, but for Mike Clegg, the shock had been numbing; Neal had been one of his partners.

Mike sat at his desk in silent rage. Why? What the fuck had happened? Neal and Robert were both excellent combat situation officers, and had faced much worse. Now one of them was dead.

Mike remembered the night two years ago when he had

taken a .357 slug, and Neal had pulled him to safety despite a bullet lodged in his own shoulder. And he had still managed to dispatch the bad guys.

Mike hadn't spoken to Robert since the shooting, and the way things were shaping up, he wouldn't get the chance today, either, with a monumental mountain of paperwork on his desk.

Mike looked around the office. Everybody was busy, but somber. Annie Pankrow, the Division secretary, looked to be the worst of the lot. He had never really noticed Neal and Annie together, but the way she was taking it... *Enough of those thoughts, Mikey,* he thought, glancing down at the report in his hands.

The top page was the arrest report on Reginald Max, the 211 suspect they had apprehended the previous night. The search of the Camaro had turned up three weapons possibly used in the 211s and the store clerk shootings. They had also found several grams of crack.

The booking slip had been copied and attached to the report, with charges for the 211 (armed robbery), two other counts of armed robbery, and a 11550 (possession of a controlled substance). Mike would bet the house that the DA would be filing additional charges and thought that if there was one shred of justice out there, anywhere, the DA would file charges of 187 (homicide), for the murder of Neal Jessop, too. And if that happened, Mr. Reginald Max would be going away for a very long time.

Dalton walked up to Mike's desk. "Just got the rest of the reports covering last night back from word processing."

Mike took the reports from Dalton glumly. "We're up to our asses in reports."

"That we are. You okay?"

"I've been better. You?"

"Pretty shitty. Have you seen Robert this morning?"

"Not yet. I heard Sweeny called him in, so he should be here soon." Mike shuffled a stack of reports.

Lieutenant Quentin Cray walked out of his office then and headed for Mike and Dalton. "The captain is getting heat from upstairs," he told them, "and wants the reports ASAP, so don't go taking any moonlight strolls together." He laughed at his own little joke and went back to his office.

Dalton made a face. "God, what a nipplehead."

Quentin Cray didn't have one ounce of common sense, even though he had been with the department seventeen years. There were times when he was tolerable, even a decent guy, but that was only when he stayed out of everybody's hair. His decision-making was lousy. He really had no business being a cop; everybody thought he would have made a great beach bum.

Standing about five eleven and weighing about one-seventy, blue-eyed, dark-haired Quen, as he was called, wore suits that belonged in a courtroom, not in a detective squad room. He looked like a high-priced shyster.

Dalton thought back to the time about six years ago, when everybody thought that Quen might turn things around and actually become an effective cop. Off duty, he had found two thugs rolling an elderly couple in a shopping mall parking lot and had taken down the perpetrators quickly and efficiently. Unfortunately, the transformation hadn't happened. Once a bozo, always a bozo. Quen was an administrator, and that was all he would ever be.

Dalton watched the lieutenant disappear into his office and wondered if he gave a fuck about Neal. "Who contacted Neal's wife?" he asked Mike.

Mike sighed and signed the last few reports. "Sweeny, I think."

Dalton was organizing the reports as Mike handed them to him, putting them into a large manila envelope for the lieutenant, when Robert walked through the room and on to the captain's office. Dalton checked his watch. It was noon. "Robert's here," he said.

Mike looked up. "Where?"

"Just went in with Sweeny."

Mike shook his head. "What a lousy way to get a five-day vacation."

Robert sat down across from the captain, trying to deal with four-and-a-half hours' sleep. When he had finally gotten home last night, he had found a note from Dana saying that if she was going to have to sleep alone, the least she could do was be in her own bed with her cat.

Feeling let down, though realizing that Dana probably hadn't heard about the shooting, he had gotten into bed and fallen asleep instantly. At nine-thirty this morning, when he finally got around to listening to his messages, Dana's voice had come across clear, but shaky. She had just heard about the shooting and wanted him to call her at work as soon as he could.

Robert thought about calling her as he dressed for the day. With his mind going in twenty different directions, he wouldn't know what to say.

Now, in Sweeny's office, he found himself just as tongue-tied, as though all that needed to be said had already been said, and the rest of this was superfluous.

Sweeny's medium-sized office was decorated in blues and grays. A leather couch sat along one wall, with two padded chairs in front of his oversized desk. The walls were covered with departmental plaques, citations, awards, and photographs. Pretty blissful career, Robert thought, taking one of the chairs. He looked out the window. It was raining again. Perfect weather for his mood.

"Have you finished all your interviews?" the captain asked.

"All of them except with the DA. I have a meeting this afternoon."

Sweeny nodded. "I went ahead and made an appointment for you with the psychologist. Tomorrow morning, ten o'clock."

"Swell," Robert muttered, reaching into his back pocket to pull out a can of Skoal. He did not get along with psychologists. He'd had his first encounter with them during his preemployment days, and twice since. And that was three too many.

While Sweeny took a call, Robert mulled it over in his mind. In the event of an officer-related shooting, it was mandatory to see the department shrink. This was to, quote unquote, see if shooting a human being had scrambled your brains, and to determine if you were still stable and sane.

Robert hadn't met an officer who hadn't felt some kind of remorse after a killing, and it was human nature that it should bother some more than others. It was the psychologist's job to sort through that and decide who qualified to continue in the job.

Since the shooting at the hotel and Neal's death, Robert had given the subject some heavy-duty time. And he had finally realized what he was feeling. In most shootings, it happened fast. So basically the adrenalin was released after the fact, and lasted about an hour. And then came the letdown. Not actually remorse for the goon you dumped, but a rather cheated feeling. You expected to have changed the world somehow, hoping you had made a difference. But you really hadn't. No one cared about the bag of shit who lay dead on the ground. But *you* cared. You had just survived the most dangerous aspect of your job, and felt nothing but relief that *he* was the one down and not you.

After the academy, you were told by officers with more experience that being involved in a shooting was something great because you got the bastard. But after your first shooting, you realized it wasn't great at all. And this was when the cheated feeling surfaced. It was hard to explain. He had tried to explain it once to a former girlfriend, and she had just stared at him with a blank look on her face. Her puzzlement was typical of anyone who wasn't in law enforcement, and even of some who were.

So Robert thought, fuck you, people, and all you department shrinks. My job isn't to try and explain what goes through the head of a police officer in the middle of a crisis, especially to somebody who doesn't have a clue as to what the hell is going on out there in the cold, hard streets.

Captain Sweeny was off the phone now, and Robert asked, "How is Cindy doing?"

"As well as can be expected. She asked about you."

Robert nodded. "When I'm finished at the DA's office, I'm going over to see her."

Sweeny looked at Robert. "If it means anything to you, I think the shooting went down by the numbers."

Robert met Sweeny's eyes. "Did either Dalton or Mike mention the possibility of . . ."

"Suicide? Yeah, they mentioned it."

Robert took a deep breath. "Can it be kept out of the papers?"

Sweeny got up and walked to the window. "The rain out there will have to freeze into a wall before I let them print something like that about Neal."

Robert sighed with relief.

The captain turned and faced Robert. "I want you here on Monday morning. We have a shitload of cases building up, and Cray is dragging his ass. On top of that, we're now one man down." He lowered his eyes.

Robert stood up. "I'll be here."

Sweeny walked around his desk and put a hand on Robert's shoulder. "You're one hell of a cop, Hollinger. I'm very sorry about Neal, but we're all going to have to let him go."

Robert nodded, shook Sweeny's hand, and walked out of the office.

Grant Coogan walked into Homicide, hoping he hadn't missed Stu. He turned to the man behind the first desk and asked, "Excuse me, you ugly piece of shit. Is Stu around?"

Bryan Houser looked up, put the new issue of *TV Guide* aside, and replied, "Well, well, well. If it isn't Sherlock Holmes. Sorry, haven't seen him."

Coogan continued through the squad room and caught up with Lieutenant Stanfield. "Have you seen Redlam?" he asked.

"He's down in ID. You have something?"

"Only time will tell." Coogan hurried out and quickly made his way to ID. He rang the bell, flashed his department identification, and was buzzed in. He found Stu sitting in front of one of the many California state ID computers. The system tied in with all statewide law enforcement agencies. It was formally called CAL ID, but thought of as God.

Stu looked up at Coogan and grinned. "What be happening?"

"Have you been to Attwater's apartment yet?" Grant asked.

Stu shook his head. "Why? Do you want to go along?"

"I'd like to print the apartment. You never know what might pop up."

"You're more than welcome," Stu said, turning back to the computer screen. "Not a damned thing on Attwater here. Just a couple of parking tickets." He turned off the terminal and stood up. "Let's hope we have more luck at the apartment."

"Any next of kin?" Grant asked.

"Not that I can find."

"Things are looking really peachy."

Stu gave Grant a crooked smile. "Yeah, real fucking peachy. Let's hope the apartment turns up more than we found in her car, or in her locker at the spa, or in her purse. We found a three-eighty semi-auto in the glove box of her BMW, money and jewelry in the locker, and money in her purse, so the motive sure as hell wasn't robbery."

"She should have had the pistol with her at the spa. Could have saved her life."

"And the killer could have used the weapon to blow her brains out, too."

"If you're ready, let's get this show on the road."

Mary Attwater had lived in a cluster-home complex out in the American River Canyon area. Stu's brother owned a house not far from the address, and his brother had paid around three hundred grand. But when they pulled into the visitor's parking area, he realized he had probably fallen short of the figure. It looked like something out of "Lifestyles of the Rich and Famous," and it wasn't an apartment complex at all. The word condominium came to mind, but he really wasn't at all sure what that really meant. One you rented, he guessed, and the other you purchased.

He had the key to Attwater's unit but thought it would be best to tell the manager what they were going to do. They didn't need Folsom PD hauling them in as common house burglars.

They found the sign spelling out MANAGER in big, bold letters, and after knocking on the door, Stu looked around, and found himself suddenly envious. Everything was beautiful and green, with creeks and ponds and waterfalls. The pond closest to them had been stocked with koi carp, which he knew to be exotic Japanese fish.

Grant seemed equally impressed and whistled through his teeth. "If you're thinking what I'm thinking, forget it. We'd never make it on a cop's salary."

A woman in her late thirties finally opened the door. She stood there, staring up at Stu and Grant as though they were a couple of bothersome mosquitoes.

Stu reached into his coat for identification. "I'm Detective Redlam, and this is Officer Coogan, Sacramento Police Department, Homicide Division. Are you the manager?"

The woman just stood there, wide-eyed, face vacant.

"Hello, there."

"I heard you. What do you want?"

Personable, Stu thought. She had shoulder-length blonde hair, big, brown, bedroom eyes, and wore a loose-fitting top and skintight pants. "Are you the manager?" he repeated.

"Yes."

"We would like to search Mary Attwater's apartment, or condo, or unit, or whatever it's called."

The woman glared at him. "It's a cluster home, and I would think that Mary might have something to say about that!"

Stu didn't like this lady, and gave her his professional glare, though she clearly hadn't heard about Mary Attwater's death. "Well," he drawled, "it might be kind of tough for her to protest, ma'am. Miss Attwater was murdered last night."

That did it, Redlam. The good old spear through the heart. Show no mercy. Use tons of tact.

Miss Manager started to shiver. "Murdered? Mary? Are you sure? H-has anybody identified the—the body?"

Oh, good. And she watches TV, too. "No, not yet, but we're positive it's Mary Attwater. Of course you could always come down to the morgue and take a look for yourself."

"Dear God!" She put a hand over her mouth.

"Look, Miss . . ." Stu waited for a response.

"J-Julie Clark . . ."

"Look, Miss Clark, we have to get with the program, here. Would you please direct us to Mary Attwater's unit?" Stu really didn't have time for this hostile bitch or her moans and groans. He was beginning to lose his patience.

Julie Clark struggled for control, but nodded. "Yes, of course." Her attitude seemed a bit more hospitable now. She brushed by them. "It's this way," she said.

They walked along the well-landscaped pathway beside a meandering stream. Stu looked at the water and the trees and winter flowers, at the overcast skies. Anywhere to keep from looking at Julie Clark's drawn-in body as he followed. She looked as though she were freezing to death, although it really wasn't that cold.

She stopped by a unit near the pool. "This is it," she said.

"Thanks," Stu said. "And, oh, Miss Clark, I might need to ask you some more questions, later."

She shivered. "I'll be home."

Stu nodded and put the key in the lock.

CHAPTER

4

Wednesday, December 9, 1988: 1150 Hrs.

Robert left the DA's office and headed for Neal's house, out in east Sacramento County in the unincorporated town of Rancho Cordova.

All day long, he had been asked to reflect on the events of the previous evening. Now, everything seemed a total blur. He was surprised that his statements had made any sense at all. Maybe they hadn't; he didn't care. His only concern was the nagging thought that if he had handled things differently, a little more professionally, his partner might still be alive. And thoughts like that, he knew, could kill a man.

And then there was the suicide thing, smacking him right between the eyes. Yet if it had been professional suicide, a suicide committed in the line of duty, he wanted to know. He would want to know what had caused it, and hope to help keep it from happening to someone else. He had the feeling that Tom Runyo and Steve Taylor would be looking into it.

They were good men. Maybe they could find the answers. But one thing was certain: he couldn't mention it to Cindy, because it would kill her. He loved her like a sister, and wanted to protect her at all costs.

It was going to be tough, and it was something the academy couldn't teach you. All those classes in search and seizure, using deadly force, and investigation couldn't prepare you for something like this.

Robert pulled onto Neal's street with his heart in his throat. *Well, just get it done, Robby,* he told himself, parking in front of the house.

A couple of cars were parked in the driveway, and one blue station wagon sat catty-whompus in the RV space. He guessed the vehicles belonged to relatives. It was good Cindy had someone to help her through this.

Robert got out of the car, but before he reached the porch, Cindy had opened the door. She was looking at him with eyes full of anguish. He could tell she had been crying all day. And then she was in his arms, sobbing, "Oh, Rob, why did this happen!"

Robert stood there stupidly, unable to do anything but hold her. Finally, he reached out and touched her face. "I don't know, babe. I just don't know."

Cindy grabbed Robert's hand and pulled him into the house. He could hear voices in the kitchen, but she was leading him to the bedroom. She motioned toward the bed where she had laid out all Neal's police articles. Ribbons, uniforms, pictures, citations, the works.

Robert picked up a snapshot taken of them when he had been in Robbery only a couple of months. Both men were smiling into the camera, happy and carefree. Robert replaced it on the bed, feeling Neal's presence stronger than ever.

Cindy stood beside him, arms folded tightly to her chest. "He loved working with you, Rob. He always said you kept him young."

Robert pointed to the snapshot. "Do you remember when that was taken?"

"Yes. Back when Neal thought you were a cocky young punk."

Robert nodded, and laughed a bit. "I don't think he ever changed his opinion of me. He was always calling me a punk. . . . Come here, girl."

They sat on the bed, hugging and remembering, until Cindy pulled away. "He left you something, Rob." She pulled open a dresser drawer. "After you two were together for about six months, he told me that if anything ever happened to him . . ." She returned to the bed and handed him a small black case.

Robert took the case and opened it. It was Neal's Silver Star and Purple Heart from Vietnam. Robert felt winded. They were beautiful. He had been too young for Nam, but his older brother had gone. He remembered holding his brother's Bronze Star for hours, feeling the same kind of wonderment that touched him now.

Cindy watched the unashamed tears roll down Robert's cheeks, and her own tears began again. "He always said you were like a very special friend he had lost in Southeast Asia, and it was really important to him. He loved you like a brother."

She sat down beside him. "God, I'm going to miss him, Rob. . . ." She had started to cry in earnest, and he felt new tears on his own cheeks. He sat there, holding her, loving her, wondering why the good people had to suffer so much.

Stu walked into Mary Attwater's home and gasped. "Holy Christ! Would you look at this place!"

Grant followed him into the spacious foyer and shook his head. "As I said, not on our salary!"

The living room was sunken, plush, white, and expensive. Stu stepped the three steps down into it, knowing instantly what Mary Attwater had been all about. Lots of show, and who cared about comfort? In a place like this, you wouldn't be able to sit on the couch, you wouldn't be able to read a magazine, and you'd probably have to take off your shoes before treading on the whiter-than-white carpeting.

"All this on an aerobics instructor's salary?" Grant said, examining some of the elaborate objets d'art placed around the room.

"Ha, ha. Not on your life. This little cookie was into more than that."

Stu climbed the three steps up to the dining room, noting that the cabinets held find china and crystal and sterling silver. On the sideboard were muave silk napkins.

"What are we looking for?" Grant asked, poking into the silk flower arrangement on the table.

Stu headed for the kitchen. "Anything to help us solve the case. Shit, I don't know. The only thing I can be sure of, the lady had money."

In the stark white kitchen, everything was too neat, too organized. Too sterile. Stu shook his head. *Nobody lives like this.*

Grant walked down a small hallway, while Stu took the spiral staircase that led upstairs. Grant found only one room, and opened the door. It was an office, or was it called a study? Didn't matter. One large desk took up the corner, and the walls were lined with file cabinets. Grant felt a twinge of regret as he went through the folders. Stock market stuff. Nothing to help them. Wonderful!

Upstairs, Stu found three rooms. Two had been used for storage, the third was the master bedroom. Stu stared at the room, which was bigger than his house, and at the bed, which was bigger than his living room. Miss Attwater could have held an orgy with the San Francisco 49ers and there would have been room left over for the cheerleaders.

The room had been decorated in peachy colors, and the bed was made up with a satin comforter. "Awesome," Stu muttered.

One wall was filled with shelves, holding more objets d'art, expensive perfume bottles, and large vases filled with colorful silk flowers. At the end of the shelving, Stu found a row of buttons and pushed the first one, feeling like James Bond. The top section of wall raised up, exposing a stereo system. Stu kept pushing buttons. Lights dimmed, and the room filled with a deep, earthy jazz.

"Fuck nuts," Stu said, heading across the room and into a walk-in closet. He wasn't at all surprised by the selection of expensive clothing, the furs and leather. But the small door at the back of the closet took his eye. He opened it, and discovered paradise. Racks of filmy undergarments and sexy dressing gowns. He felt suddenly hot. In a small dresser drawer, he found a collection of crotchless panties, sexy bras, garters, and black nylons.

"What were you into, little lady?" Stu said, chuckling to himself. He then poked around in the bottom drawer, and his chuckle became a hoot. He feasted his eyes on the flesh-colored vibrators and crazy-shaped dildos. All this, along with porno magazines, self-help sex manuals, and some sex toys Stu had never seen before. He sat back on his heels and shook his head. What they had here was either a bitch goddess or Miss Hose Monster herself.

Stu heard Grant's voice in the upstairs hallway shouting, "Where in hell are you!"

"Master bedroom!" Stu shouted back. "You won't believe what I found!"

"Likewise," Grant said walking into the bedroom. He stopped and groaned. "Oh, God, you gotta love this room!"

Stu walked out of the closet. "You'll like what I found in here better."

Grant gave Stu a shifty smile and followed him into the closet. He looked at the array of goodies and grinned. "Well, I'll be damned."

Stu shrugged. "I have the feeling we'll all be damned before this case is over."

Out in the bedroom now, with the music turned off, Stu asked, "You said 'likewise' earlier. What did you find?"

"Some names and numbers, and this." He handed Stu a little black book.

Stu opened it, glancing at the pages filled with numbers. "What the hell is this?"

"Don't know. Might be in code."

"Where did you find it?"

"In the safe." Grant walked over to the dresser against the far wall.

"In the safe. Care to explain?"

"I found it behind a Chinese watercolor. It was open."

"Ransacked?"

"No. It was full of money, jewelry, and gold bars."

"Crapola," Stu muttered. "Well, let's hope Miss Manager, Miss Clark, can give us some answers." Stu stopped, deep in thought. So far, they had a rich bitch who sure as hell hadn't made all her money teaching acrobics. They had a woman who had expensive tastes and a voracious appetite for kinky sex. The cause of death was either suffocation or strangulation—the coroner's office would determine that—and the big question, with robbery out was, had she been sexually assaulted? Had she been killed during a rape?

Stu knew he would find the answers to those questions after the autopsy, and when he located her source of extra income. The whole case was as shady as an unpruned tree.

He looked at Grant. "You say you've got a list of names and numbers?"

Grant closed a dresser drawer. "Yeah. Nothing in here but your basic undergarments."

Stu lowered the wall to its original position, concealing the stereo system. "Let's go downstairs, Grant. I want to see the safe."

In the study, Stu popped the answering machine and pulled out the cassette. He then walked to the open safe and started listing the contents. He was on the last bar of gold when his portable radio squawked to life. "Ivy two-two-six from Ivy two-two-two."

Stu acknowledged the caller, Tom Runyo. "Ivy two-two-six, go ahead."

"Channel five."

"Ten-four." Stu turned the radio to channel five. He looked at Grant. "He's close." He then rekeyed the radio. "Two-two-six on five."

"Hey, Stu, can you copy?"

"What's up, Tom?"

"Where the hell are you?" Tom asked. "I'm in the complex but I might as well be on Mars! This place is huge!"

Stu smiled. "We're at one-oh-three-five-one, northeast corner, by the pool."

"Check," came the reply. "See you in two."

"What's he doing out here?" Grant asked.

"Beats the hell out of me. Guess we'll find out soon enough."

While they waited for Tom, Grant prowled around. Stu sat in the living room, on the white couch, and studied the little black book. But his mind was on other things.

He had been working solo for the past three weeks, while his partner, Joey Pandoza, was out on stress-related leave. Joey had been the detective who had taken Stu under his wing when he had first arrived in Homicide, four years earlier. As the youngest detective in the squad, he had been very aware of the resentment from the other detectives. Most of them believed that time and experience made the cop; it was a matter of paying dues.

Well, he had put in his time, first with Metro detail (misdemeanors and other related bullshit); that had been the first step on the way up to detective. Then on to Auto Theft, not much of an improvement, Bunco, Rape/Sex Assaults, Narcotics, and finally Homicide. By this time, Stu had observed, you were older, lazier, and just waiting for retirement.

But he had beat the system. He had worked for Metro only six months before being assigned to Narcotics. His patrol training officer was now the sergeant in HIP, the Heroin Impact Program, a task force put together in the early 70s, and well respected.

Stu worked HIP for two years until somebody upstairs took a liking to the aggressive thirty-two-year-old, and within a matter of months, he was in Homicide.

Joey said right up front he had a lot of potential, and took him as his partner. Pandoza and Redlam. Joey had announced to the whole squad that he had one hell of a detective on his hands, that Stu had hidden powers, that he could see beyond the physical. Those kinds of comments had always flustered Stu, but deep down, he had appreciated the compliment. He had appreciated Joey.

Joey had also said that Stu was the beginning of a new generation of cops, the beginning of a weeding-out process. He hadn't been wrong, because now, they were looking for younger, more aggressive men. Joey had no problems with that. He was forty-three, but had the heart and mind of a much younger man.

Now, four years later, the "youngster" in the bureau was without a partner.

Stu had seen the change in Joey coming, as his heavy drinking became a daily event. The older man had also developed a negative attitude about everything and no longer seemed to care. And then he had lost his father to cancer, his older boy had gotten busted in Reno on drug charges, and things had really gone downhill from there.

It was on a gloomy Thursday afternoon that Joey finally snapped, doing a most convincing Nazi stomp on his kitchen, taking out the appliances, cupboards, and most of the dishes. Sheila Pandoza had called Stu in the middle of it, begging for help. Stu had dropped everything, but by the time he arrived, Joey had settled down and was sitting out on the redwood deck, drinking Jack Daniels straight from the bottle.

Stu had walked out on the deck, not knowing what to say. Joey just sat there, looking down.

"Tell me about it," Stu had said finally.

"I don't know, amigo. I think I need a break."

Stu could see it was the whiskey talking, but it was more than that.

"I'm done being a cop," Joey had said then, "at least for the time being."

Stu hadn't answered him; what could he say?

Two days later, Joey Pandoza went out on stress-related leave for an undetermined time.

Stu knew he wouldn't be flying solo for long. It would be just a matter of time before the department transferred someone in.

Now that he thought about it, Homicide was three officers down. Two would be replaced, but they would never see the third. That was city politics.

Runyo and Taylor arrived then, bringing Stu out of his reverie. Runyo exclaimed, "Jesus H. Christopher Columbo! Would you look at this place!"

Stu grinned. "Kinda makes you want to call it home, doesn't it?"

Both men nodded, but neither advanced into the room.

"What are you doing out here in the boonies?" Stu asked, heading for the door.

"Checking out a couple of leads from that dead transient we caught last week," Runyo replied, "and because we are now lucky enough to have a computer in our vehicle and wanted to track you down. We need to run something by you."

Stu smiled. The city was just now getting vehicle computers; the County Sheriff's Department had had them for fourteen years. "So what's up?" he asked.

The detectives were outside now, and Stu locked the door. He studied Runyo, who looked uneasy. "Well?"

Runyo walked along beside Stu, hands stuffed into his jacket pockets. "You know about the shooting last night?"

"Yeah. Because of it, I got called away from my beauty sleep."

"Did you know the officer who was killed?"

"Jessop, wasn't it? No, I didn't know him. At least not personally."

"How about Robert Hollinger?"

"The other officer involved? No. Why?"

Runyo cleared his throat and lowered his voice. "Well, Robert said that it looked as though Jessop had committed professional suicide. Of course, that's not what was released to the media."

Stu knew where Runyo was heading. "Ahhh, I don't think I want to hear what you're about to tell me."

"We want to look into the possibility. Neal was a pretty straight guy. Mr. All-American Cop, if you know what I mean."

"And Lieutenant Stanfield will cut off your nuts if he finds out about this."

Runyo shrugged. "We're supposed to look into all officer-related shootings, right?"

Stu nodded.

"Well, we'd just be doing our job."

"Pretty thin, Tom. Pretty thin."

"Hell, thin is my middle name."

"With your wife's cooking, I'm not surprised," Taylor chuckled.

Runyo scowled at Taylor. "With comments like that, you're not going to get invited to Christmas dinner."

Taylor chuckled again.

Stu smiled. "I can see where you guys have seen *Lethal Weapon* a couple of times. Seriously, I don't see a problem with a little off-the-record investigating, but I don't know a dick about it. If it comes back on you, you're on your own."

Runyo nodded. "We just have the feeling that Neal Jessop was into something over his head."

"Let me know if I can help," Stu said.

Runyo and Taylor were heading for the parking lot, when Runyo called out, "See you at Toomie's tonight?"

Stu nodded. "Bring money. You're buying." He then turned to Grant. "Let's talk to Miss Manager."

CHAPTER 5

The bus depot was crowded at five-thirty in the afternoon, with people bustling in and out of the glass doors that led to the terminal.

The man came through the doors, smiled at a pretty blonde, and then surveyed the lobby. When he found it to his liking, he made his way toward the lockers on the far wall.

With the key to locker 217, he opened the metal door and removed the large manila envelope. He then closed the locker and walked into the coffee shop.

Seated at the far end of the counter, he gave the dumpy waitress his order.

"One Michelob, no glass," she repeated and hurried off.

He opened the envelope and pulled out the 8-by-11 glossy of a strikingly beautiful redhead. He smiled at the photo, noting that her skin looked very pale, her eyes very green. He continued to stare at her, and then he was with her, touching her, caressing her breasts, kissing her, licking her neck. Her breath was coming in short, soft puffs. His hand was on her nipples, slowly moving lower. Her breath became uneven, growing louder. Soft screams, then whimpers.

His forehead was beaded with sweat as his hands worked faster. Her back arched, her body quivered.

Suddenly, they were not alone. Someone was with them. *NO!* Who? Her breath was accelerating, but he was slowing down.

"No, don't stop," she cried.

"I have to. Someone is fucking it up."

He opened his eyes, feeling the presence of the intruder. It was the fat fuck sitting down the counter from him. He turned his head toward the fat man. "If I ever see your eyes fucking me again, I'll clean you out and eat you." He turned back to the photo, but this time, it was just a photo.

The fat man stood, threw several bills on the counter, and scurried away.

The waitress placed the beer on the counter. "You just get into town?" she asked.

He stared her down with his vivid gray eyes until she scurried away, too.

On the back of the glossy, he found a data sheet. Name. Phone number. Address, both home and work. Also a vehicle description and a list of places she frequented.

He smiled. Smitovich had picked some real beauties to snuff.

He downed his beer in two gulps, got up, and walked out.

The waitress began to protest. "Hey! You didn't pay—" She stopped herself. Hell, she would pay for it. It was worth it to be rid of him.

Stu sat on the leather couch while Grant stood against the far wall.

Miss Julie Clark sat in a wicker chair, holding a cup of coffee.

"How long had Mary Attwater lived in the complex, Miss Clark?" Stu asked.

Miss Clark took a sip of her coffee. "Please call me Julie."

My, my, how things change, Stu thought, and repeated his question.

"Just about from the beginning," Julie said. "I mean, when we first opened up."

Stu looked at her. "And when was that?"

"About two years ago."

"Was she renting or buying?"

"Leasing," Julie replied.

Stu was scribbling notes in a pad. "By the way you acted earlier, I take it you knew Miss Attwater fairly well?"

Julie's face grew hot. "Always be tough with the law." That was what her mama had always told her. "Be tough, and they'll back off." But this man was bullheaded and strong. He was also very attractive.

"I'm really sorry about the way I acted before," she said finally. "That was my mother talking, not me."

Stu frowned. "Beg your pardon?"

Julie rushed on. "We weren't very close, if that's what you mean."

"Miss Attwater? Or your mother?"

"Miss Attwater."

"Did she have any boyfriends?"

"Yes, she did, but . . ." She flushed again. "Hmmm—well, sometimes she had boyfriends, and sometimes she had . . ."

Stu waited for a few moments, then said, "Yes, Julie?"

Julie hesitated. She didn't want to sound stupid. Even with all this murder conversation going on, she found herself attracted to the solid-looking detective. He had hard blue-gray eyes, but they could be soft, too, and his brown wavy hair was touched with gray. He didn't look that old. Maybe thirty-six? Weren't homicide detectives supposed to be older than that? They were on TV.

Julie swallowed. "Well, one time, she did say that she liked the company of women."

"Was she propositioning you?" Stu asked.

Julie shook her head.

Stu looked at Grant and winked. "So are you saying that Mary Attwater like both men and women?"

Julie took a deep breath. "Yes. You know. Don't they call that being AC/DC?"

"Or acey-deucy," Stu chuckled.

"I think what Julie is trying to say, is that Mary Attwater was a woman in comfortable shoes," Grant said.

Stu's smile faded. It was suddenly back to business. "Did you meet any of her boyfriends, or girlfriends?" Stu asked.

She thought for a moment. "No. I met some of her close friends, but they weren't her lovers." Julie paused. "At least I don't think they were."

"Men or women?" Stu kept writing.

"Women. Business partners, I think." She was studying the detective harder than ever. She suddenly found herself wondering what he would be like in bed.

"What kind of business partners?"

"I'm not really sure. I know she dabbled in the stock market."

Dabble, huh? Was that what it was called? From what Stu had seen on Mary Attwater's desk, it was a bit more than dabbling.

"When was the last time you saw Mary Attwater?"

"Yesterday afternoon. She dropped by to give me the name of her hairdresser."

"Did you ever go to the Free Spirit Spa and Fitness Center?"

"No, I work out at home."

Stu cleared his throat and looked over his notes. He thought about bringing up what they had found in Mary Attwater's closet, but decided against it. He was sure that Julie Clark knew nothing about her ex-tenant's kinky ways.

"That should do it," Stu said, standing up. "Thanks for your time."

Julie walked with them to the door.

"By the way," Stu said. "Is there a number where I can reach you?"

She gave him the number and said, trying not to sound eager, "I'm home most evenings."

They left, and she closed the door behind them, reluctantly.

Stu climbed into the driver's side of the unmarked Blazer, stuffing his notes, the little black book, other paperwork he'd picked up, and the answering machine cassette into a manila envelope.

"Boy, that woman sure had a thing for you," Grant said, getting in the seat beside him.

"Naw. Just your overactive imagination playing tricks on you," Stu said, though he was very much aware of Julie Clark's candid flirting.

"Shit, Stu, I didn't just fall off a cabbage truck. That Julie Clark was showing serious fuck-me eyes back there."

"I think that's supposed to be turnip truck," Stu said. "I'm married, Grant," he added. "Well, sort of . . ."

Grant laughed. "So there you go. Call the lady. Come on, Stu, this is America."

"Won't happen," Stu muttered, though he found himself thinking about his wife, Gail, somewhere in the Midwest, doing her thing without a care in the world. Now *that* was one hell of a grim picture.

"You'll call her," Grant said. "And it won't be about business. I can see it in your eyes."

Stu was now pulling out on Madison Avenue. "All you see is shit."

Grant laughed. "Okay, smartass, we'll see."

Stu shrugged, but he was thinking about Julie's big brown eyes. *Oh, Redlam, you putz!* "Yeah, we'll see."

Mike Clegg was at the water cooler when Leon Pullman asked, "You seen Robert yet?"

"No. He's probably been busier than a one-legged cat trying to cover shit on a frozen pond."

The older, black detective chuckled. "Well, you let him know we're all concerned, if you do hear from him."

Mike patted Leon on the back. "Will do."

Dalton sat at his desk rubbing his eyes. He pulled a bottle of Visine from his top drawer and put several drops in each eye. He had been looking over two other case reports they had been working on; both seemed to be leading nowhere. He looked up, eyes watering, as a tall, leggy blonde hurried into the office.

Mike perked up. "Yes, ma'am?"

"These are your latest case files," she said, depositing them on the nearest desk. "Enjoy."

As fast as she had walked in, she walked out.

"Oh, that hurts," Mike said to Dalton. "Love 'em and leave 'em."

Dalton nodded.

Mike picked up the reports, sorting them into even stacks. He then distributed them on various desks, including his own.

"As if we don't have enough to work on already," Dalton grumbled.

"Well, pard, it's a shit storm out there, and unfortunately, we're the weathermen."

Dalton smiled, the first genuine smile he had managed all day. "Yeah, that's for sure. Let's leave this bullshit until tomorrow."

Mike nodded. He checked the duty roster. Four men still in the field, so all he had to do was sign out, and he was gone.

The phone rang. Mike took the call: "Robbery. Detective Mike Clegg."

"Hey, Mikey. How you doin'?"

"Question is, how are *you* doing?" Mike looked at Dalton. "It's Robert."

Dalton picked up his phone and punched the blinking line, so they had a three-way conversation. "Rob. Are you okay?"

"I'm hanging in there. I just got back from seeing Cindy."

"How is she holding up?" Dalton asked. He had so many questions, he didn't know where to begin.

"She'll be okay. She's tough."

Mike asked the biggest question of all. "What happened out

there, Robby?" He knew that Robert must have answered that question at least a hundred times today. And he hated putting it to him again, but he had to know.

Robert took a deep breath. "When we knocked, we were answered with gunfire. Then . . . Then Neal blasted through the door, running full tilt into another barrage of bullets."

Mike thought for a minute. "But that would be suic...." His words trailed off.

"Is that what happened?" Dalton asked, looking at Mike. A lump was forming in his throat. "Was it suicide?"

Robert didn't speak right away, and both men gave him all the time they had.

Robert finally spoke. "Yeah, it sure looked like it to me."

Mike sucked in his breath. "Jesus, why?"

Dalton suddenly felt sick. All this was such bullshit. First, losing a friend and partner, but losing him to suicide? He felt the pain of it in his heart.

"Was he having any problems at home?" Mike asked.

"None that I know of. As far as Cindy is concerned, Neal went down in the line of duty."

Mike quickly ran it around in his mind. Had Neal been in some kind of trouble without letting on? He sighed. These last two days had been the most fucked-up days of his career. "You need anything?" Mike asked then.

"No, I'll be fine. How are you guys holding up?"

Mike replied, "We're troupers. You just get some rest and we'll see you soon."

Dalton spoke for the first time in several minutes. "Anybody looking into this?"

"Not officially."

That was good enough for him. Somebody was doing something.

Mike said, "Well if you need anything, let us know."

"Thanks," Robert said, and hung up.

Mike closed his eyes. He had heard of officers committing suicide that way, but this time, his mind ran the "not-one-of-my-friends" routine. God, what a mess!

* * *

After Robert had hung up, he found himself shaking, knowing that things would probably get worse before they got better.

He dug a beer out of the refrigerator, popped the top, and walked into the living room. Whether they wanted to face it or not, it was all coming together. But the visit with Cindy had helped more than he would have thought possible.

He turned on the stereo and put on a Dwight Yoakam disc. As the music washed over him, he sat back in his recliner and closed his eyes.

Minutes, maybe hours, later, he heard the front door open. Dana had walked into the living room.

He stood up. God, she was beautiful. She wore a red skirt and a white blouse, topped with a red blazer. Her long legs looked sleek in patterned hose, and her feet tiny in spiky red pumps.

"Hi there, stranger," she said, walking into his arms. "You didn't call, but I forgive you."

He hugged her and kissed her, burying his face in her hair. It seemed like weeks since he had held her this way.

Dana pulled back, looking up at him. "Are you okay?" she asked pensively.

"Yeah. As good as can be expected."

"I should have waited for you last night. I'm sorry."

He looked into her clear, green eyes. "You had no way of knowing what happened, and I didn't get home until after four...."

"But I should have been here for you."

Robert smiled and hugged her again.

"How's Cindy?" she asked.

Robert sat down on the sofa. "She's handling it. Take a look on the kitchen counter."

Dana peeled off her blazer and walked into the kitchen. When she came out, she was holding the black case containing Neal's medals. "God, they're beautiful," she whispered. "Neal's idea to give them to you?"

Robert nodded. Dwight Yoakam was still belting out some serious country lyrics.

Dana sat down beside Robert and said, "Talk to me, Rob."

Robert took a deep breath, wondering if he could tell her what he really felt.

She had her shoes off, feet tucked under her, wanting to help, not knowing how. He was tough, he had been through a lot, but something like this . . .

Her throat constricted. Right after their first month together, now almost two years ago, he had been involved in his second shoot-out. He had killed three teen-age boys, all members of the Crips, a dangerous street gang. It had been a rock house bust gone sour, and two officers had been seriously injured. Robert and his partner had chased five gang members into an alley, and Robert had taken a .25 caliber bullet in the thigh. More shots had been fired. When the investigation was over, it was determined that it had been the bullets from Robert's gun that had killed the three kids.

She remembered the media running with it, and how they had persecuted him, calling it a racial shooting. The NAACP had asked for an independent investigation. No one had seemed to care about the two officers who were in the hospital, fighting for their lives.

Weeks later, people were still asking whether the police could have taken them alive, the youngsters/students/teenagers/kids, or whatever sounded good that day. Was it necessary to strike them down in the prime of their young lives?

The fact that the victims had all done substantial time in Juvenile Hall or at the California Youth Authority had been conveniently ignored. And that all the victims had been shooting at the police at the time of their deaths. And that they had all carried high-powered weapons.

The district attorney's office had eventually cleared the shooting, but then the lawsuits began, with each family suing the city for the wrongful deaths of their sons. Nobody had thought to ask the mourning, loving families why their children had been caught in a rock house bust, or why they were carrying powerful weapons and shooting at the police. Or, more important, why the kids hadn't been home where they belonged, in the care of their loving families, at three o'clock in the morning.

Dana had really helped Robert during that trying time, because she understood what it was to be a cop. Her father was a cop, and two of her brothers were cops, and she had her own career as a records officer with the California Department of Justice.

"Come on, Rob, talk to me," Dana coaxed, rubbing his neck. He looked at her and smiled. "I love you," he said softly.

Dana kissed his cheek. "And I love you. I also have the perfect cure, something to make you forget all about this mess." She stood up and walked into the bedroom. When she returned a few minutes later, she was naked and carried a towel. Blonde hair covered one shoulder and breast. She winked at him. "Last one into the hot tub is a rotten egg."

Robert finished his beer and went to join her.

CHAPTER 6

Wednesday, December 9, 1988: 2000 Hrs.

Stu walked into Toomie's Bar and looked around. It wasn't fancy. Just a friendly place that suited the local law enforcement brigade. Small, intimate, a place where you could either quietly drink yourself into oblivion or talk about your troubles. Somebody was always around to listen or make sure you got home without wrapping yourself around a tree.

Tom Runyo and Steve Taylor were already seated in a corner booth near the juke box. A slow country song pulsated throughout the room.

Stu joined them in the booth, noting from the assortment of glasses that they were several drinks ahead. It was also apparent they had been arguing. Serious or not, he couldn't tell.

"What's up?" Stu asked.

Steve frowned. "You can tell this dildo that all this crap on the juke box is just so much redneck noise."

Stu winked at Tom. "Gee, Steve, I kinda like this song."

"Oh, swell, another one! I'm fuckin' surrounded!" Steve stumbled out of the booth and over to the juke box.

Stu got up and walked to the bar, waving at the bartender.

Jimmy Cook, the owner and bartender, grinned. "Hey, Stu. It's been awhile."

Jimmy was the faithful ex-cop turned businessman, a deputy sheriff for seventeen years until a bullet in the shoulder forced him into retirement. He was good people, and he ran a first-class establishment. "Too long," Stu replied.

"What'll it be?" Jimmy asked.

"How about a simple Tom Collins."

Jimmy smiled. "You've got it. Hey, how did Runyo get out from under his pretty young wife?"

"Every man needs his space," Stu replied. "Or maybe he got a kitchen pass."

Jimmy placed the drink on the bar. "Want to run a tab?"

Stu nodded and walked back to the booth.

Steve had returned to the booth, too, and flashed a toothy grin. "This next song is a classic."

"Shit," Runyo spat. "It's probably some jerk yelling out, 'I want some pussy, I need some pussy.' Your taste in music sucks, friend."

Stu laughed. He had never been much of a music lover, though occasionally he heard something he liked. But if he had to make a choice, he would rather listen to the country stuff. It was a clean, honest kind of music that told an honest story.

Runyo downed his drink and carefully made his way to the bar. He, too, was showing definite signs of inebriation.

A few minutes later, as Runyo staggered back to the booth, Steve's selection came up on the juke box. A very heavy guitar, followed by a guy screaming his head off. When you could make out the lyrics, suggestions of all kinds of horrors assaulted the ears.

Real nice, Stu thought. Jesus, and our kids listen to this!

Now it was Runyo's turn to look strained. "Who the fuck is that?" he grumbled.

Steve seemed offended. "I dunno, somebody called the Blasted Dead, or the Dead and the Maimed, or maybe it's the Putrid and the Fucked. Whatever, it's good stuff."

"Oh, Christ, give me a break! It sounds like two chain saws having sex."

Runyo got up and walked to the juke box.

"Whatcha gonna do, Tommy?" Steve asked.

Runyo looked back at his drunken partner. "Just watch." He reached behind the juke box and unplugged the power cord. The music wound down and stopped. Runyo looked more than satisfied. He then replaced the plug, waited for the machine to reset, and deposited a handful of quarters, programming several songs. He smiled and walked back to the booth.

"Oh, hell!" Steve growled. "You goddamn cowboy clown!" He put his head down on his arms on the cluttered table.

Runyo's first selection started to play. A soft guitar, good stuff.

Steve's head snapped up. "How many songs did you program?"

"Eight."

"Oh, Christ!" Steve downed his screwdriver and climbed out of the booth, muttering, "I'll probably eat my gun before this night is over...." He stopped and looked down at Runyo, misery all over his handsome face. "I-I didn't mean that," he said bleakly.

Runyo nodded. "We know what you meant."

After Steve had gone to the bar for another drink, Runyo shook his head. "This whole thing has him kinda crazy. He was closer to Neal than I was."

Stu sighed. "I know how he feels. It's touched the whole bum lot of us, and I've decided that this friggin' job is going to kill us all someday, one way or the other."

Runyo leaned back and tried to relax. "Have you heard anything from Joey?"

"He's in Arizona visiting relatives. Should do him good."

"Hmmm, you just don't know anymore, do you?"

"No, you don't," Stu replied. "Just about the time you think you've got life all figured out, it smacks you in the nose."

Steve returned with his fresh drink. "Well, one thing is clear," he said, sliding into the booth. "After tonight, it's going to be one hell of a Nuprin morning."

Stu sat back and began to relax, too, or maybe it was just the alcohol killing his brain cells. He thought about Gail, wondering if he cared, and he thought about Julie Clark. Grant Coogan had been right all along; he would call her soon.

The crisp morning air had been washed clean after the earlier rain, and the sun was bright, shining on the houses along the quiet street.

The man sitting in the car pulled out his data sheet and checked the address. It was just up ahead, the white house with all the trees and the Santa on the roof.

Her name was Leah McVey. Red hair, green eyes, five feet eight, 120 pounds. Healthy, and very beautiful. As anticipation grew, he looked at the glossy print of her. Soon, she would be his.

She was coming down the walkway now, heading for her black Corvette convertible. Top down, red hair whipping in the wind. *Welcome to sunny California.* He had heard the weather forecaster predict snow before Christmas. It didn't seem likely, not that it mattered. In the snow, in the sunshine, in the darkness of night, Leah McVey would be his by dawn's early light.

He laughed at his little rhyme as he pulled away from the curb to follow her.

When the alarm went off at eight-thirty, Stu lay in bed wondering what kind of a truck had collided with his head. He tried sorting through the events of the previous evening and came away with only bits and pieces, like Runyo's love for country music, Steve's drunken antics, and the fact that the number of drinks he could consume without falling flat on his face was definitely limited. He vaguely remembered driving home, taking all the back streets, praying he wouldn't run into a black-and-white. It had been stupid, and dangerous, and not the thing to do the night before an autopsy.

He groaned, rolling out of bed while the cymbals clanged and trumpets roared in his head. He was due at the coroner's office at ten-thirty; it wasn't going to be a good day.

He barely made it, pulling into the parking lot with only a few minutes to spare. He hurried into the building and confronted a long counter encased in glass. Behind the glass, a tiny prune of a lady looked up. No smile. Just curiosity. Stu pulled off his sunglasses and spoke into the circular speaker. "Stu Redlam for Mary Attwater's autopsy." He held up his badge and ID card, and cursed the whole procedure. It was worse than getting into an X-rated movie when you were twelve years old. And it was stupid. Who would want to hang out in the coroner's meat locker unless he had to?

After the woman had buzzed Stu in, he took a flight of stairs down and walked through double doors into the examining room. It was bright, sterile, and smelled of all those questionable things that made him want to gag.

Mary Attwater's body lay naked, face up, on a steel table, while the coroners took pictures. After a thorough examination, they would wash the cadaver in preparation for the autopsy, chart any visible trauma sites, swab the mouth, vagina, and anus, and photograph it again. At that point, one of a team of seven medical examiners would get down to the good stuff. Stu felt the pounding behind his eyes increase.

He hated this place. It was definitely the last stop on your way to hell.

A solid metal door opened, and Freddy Jenkins walked into what most homicide detectives called "the Parts House." Freddy and Stu had worked together before, and although the medical examiner had worked with dead bodies for more than twenty years, he hadn't lost his sense of humor. Stu supposed that humor was about the only thing that kept these guys sane.

"Howdy, Stu," Freddy said. "You here for the party?"

Stu nodded.

Freddy raised a brow in Stu's direction. "You look like shit."

"I feel like shit."

"I know how much you hate this place, so I'll try and make your stay pleasant."

"If that's supposed to be a joke," Stu said, "I'm not laughing."

Freddy looked at him. "I'm offended. You don't like my jokes."

Stu pressed on a smile. "Well, under the circumstances . . ."

Freddy chuckled. "I understand."

Stu decided that Freddy Jenkins would never understand.

A young woman walked into the room, dressed in the customary green smock.

"I want you to meet one of my college assistants," Freddy said. "Stu Redlam, Darcy Johnson." He smiled at the girl. "Stu is the detective working on the Attwater case."

Stu studied the college kid. Cute. Big blue eyes and blonde hair rolled in a bun.

"Darcy, what in God's earth drew you into this line of work?"

She looked at Stu, blue eyes twinkling. "It's a fascinating field, and it's just something I always wanted to do."

Stu shook his head and shuddered.

"Does this bother you?" she asked, motioning around the room.

God, and she's straightforward, too. "Yeah, it does."

"Then why do you stay in Homicide?"

Stu thought for a minute and said, "Because I like a challenge."

"Does the gore on the streets bother you?"

"Sure, but not like in here. This is so . . . so . . ."

"Clinical?" she answered for him.

"Well, that's one way to put it. In here, it's never-ending. Bodies in and out and in again. On the streets, I see it for a few minutes, deal with it, and then walk away. And my bodies usually have clothes on."

Darcy's eyes were bright. "But not all the time."

"No, not all the time."

Freddy Jenkins went up to the table and Darcy Johnson positioned herself across from him.

Stu pulled himself up to sit on an empty table near the examiner. This sucked. It was a bitch, and worse, all he could think about were Mary Attwater's crotchless panties.

Freddy pulled the microphone down to mouth level so his findings could be recorded on cassette tapes. The county wanted records of the entire procedure. A copy would also go to the district attorney's office, in the event the case went to trial. The tapes would then be put into evidence.

Freddy started off by saying, "December 10th, 1988, 1030 hours. Doctor Freddy Jenkins in attendance, along with assistant Darcy Johnson and City Homicide Detective Stuart Redlam.

"Subject's name, Mary Attwater. Female. Sixty-seven inches, one-hundred-and-ten pounds. On first visual examination, the apparent cause of death would seem to be strangulation."

With great precision, Freddy Jenkins made a sweeping incision in the shape of a Y on the woman's body.

Stu knew what was coming next. The chills had already started moving up and down his back.

The tip of the incision began at the base of each clavicle, meeting at the sternum. A single cut then extended down to the pubis. The chest cavity was now open. Freddy used a simple mallet and chisel to break off the breast bone. The sound of it cracking was sickening.

Stu thought about songs, and nursery rhymes, and his mother's pot roast, and about dogs and cats, and Julie Clark.

The ribs were being cut with heavy-duty shears now, and they snapped like tree limbs. Freddy was inside the chest cavity, and although he still spoke into the microphone, Stu didn't hear a word he said.

Each lung that was being pulled out would be weighed. Same for the heart, kidneys, and liver.

Darcy was taking tissue and fluid samples as Freddy moved toward the head.

Stu closed his eyes. He could feel rivers of sweat running down his chest.

Freddy sliced and then peeled back the scalp before picking up the saw. When Stu finally opened his eyes, Freddy was putting the bulk of the brain into a black plastic baggie. Darcy handled the small sections of brain that would be kept for further examination.

As Freddy shoved the organs into the body cavity, Stu felt faint. He seemed to be having trouble breathing. He got off the table and moved around the room; he was covered with sweat. All he could think about was Mary Attwater's carved-up body, and how beautiful she had been, and the total horrors she must have faced at the hands of a madman. And the worst thought of all was knowing the killer still walked the streets.

Unable to get a grip on himself, Stu quickly left the examining room and walked down the hallway to the little lounge used by the medical staff. He ran a hand through the water fountain, splashed cold water on his face, and concentrated on taking deep breaths and ridding his mind of all its ugly thoughts. At the refrigerator, he got out a seltzer, took a long drink, and sat down heavily on the tweed couch. He realized that he had just made a complete fool of himself. He wanted to think his actions had been caused by his hangover, but that was only a lame-brain excuse. It was everything, one after the other. Gail, the job, cases he hadn't solved, cases he would never solve, Neal Jessop committing professional suicide, and Mary Attwater's murder.

"You okay?"

Stu looked up into Darcy's bright, shining face. She wore regular street clothes now, topped with a white medical jacket.

He felt like an asshole. "Yeah, I'm fine. You guys finished?"

"Yes. Doctor Jenkins said you can go into the examining room when you feel up to it. He'll fill you in on the details then." She sat down beside him. "You weren't kidding when you said it bothered you."

"Yeah, but I've never pulled a boneheaded maneuver like that before." He tossed the empty seltzer bottle in the trash. "I've seen things on the streets that would make a billy goat puke, but in there . . ."

Darcy's little mouth turned up in a smile. "It just proves you're human, Detective Redlam."

"Yeah, I guess. And ain't that the shits."

The drive to headquarters cleared Stu's head and allowed everything Freddy Jenkins had told him to come into focus. First of all, Mary Attwater had been strangled to death, though they had found traces of plastic in her windpipe and nostrils. But the plastic bag hadn't killed her. Somebody's fingers had wrapped around her neck. . . . Stu shook his head and rolled down the window.

The killer had been strong, and she had been sexually assaulted. The semen samples taken from the vagina, anus, and mouth would give them the killer's blood type later in the day.

And then Freddy had dropped the bomb, his words burning Stu's ears like a hot knife through butter. The sexual assault had happened after Mary Attwater was already dead.

CHAPTER 7

It was dark by the time Leah McVey pulled into her driveway on Crestview Way. From his vantage point down the street, the man watched her get out of the black Corvette and heaved a sigh of relief. He was beginning to think he had misjudged her, and that she wasn't coming home at all. And that would have ruined everything.

He had already checked out the house and had found it neat and clean and empty. It was perfect. It sat back from the street, and that was perfect, too. He chuckled to himself, wondering what the pretty lady would say if she knew he had been following her around for the last couple of days, checking out her schedule. Or what she would say if she knew he had gone through her things. Or if she knew he was watching, waiting to make his move.

He wanted to be big about it, give her some time to unwind after a hard day at work. Maybe a drink, a little dinner ... Was she the type who stripped off her clothing the minute she walked through the door? He thought about the soft, silky undergarments he had found in her bottom dresser drawer, and sweat popped out on his brow.

Finally, when he knew he could wait no longer, he began the ritual. First, he smeared black camouflage makeup on his face, and then slipped on a pair of rubber surgical gloves. After he checked the magazine on the Browning Hi-Power 9 mm, he got out of the car, tucked the gun into the holster that rested against the small of his back, and started toward the house. The all-black clothing he wore would make him invisible on the dark street. He was one with the universe; the time had come to kill. Adrenalin began to pump through his body, keeping his steps quick and light.

As he entered the front yard, he could see her through the kitchen window. Lots of red hair, bright under the lights. *You should pull your shades, lady. Somebody could be watching.*

But she's mine, he thought, moving even closer.

A car ...

Slowing ...

Pulling into the driveway, now ...

Move!

He stepped into the shrubbery along the pathway to the house and slid the silencer out of his pocket, quickly screwing it on the end of the gun. This was a development he hadn't counted on, but he was in control.

The motor had stopped, he could hear the door open and close. Footsteps coming in his direction.

The footsteps were now in front of him:

Now!

He reached out with lightning speed and grabbed the man with his left hand, punching the gun into his chest as he pulled the trigger in rapid succession. The chest exploded, bullets ripping through soft skin and bone.

The body fell limp and he let go, the weight of the man smashing to the cement. He looked down. The visitor was young, well dressed. Perhaps a boyfriend?

He unscrewed the silencer and put the gun in the holster. *He* was now the boyfriend.

He opened the unlocked door and stepped in. *Leaving your door unlocked is a good way to get murdered, lady.* He could hear the shower running in the back of the house.

He strolled down the hallway, taking his time. In the bedroom now, he looked at the clothing tossed casually over the end of the bed. He walked over and picked up a pair of white panties, rubbing them across his face. Nice.

Smiling, he stepped into the steamy bathroom. He could see her silhouette behind the glass shower door.

She sensed his presence, undoubtedly thinking it was her boyfriend, and said, "Be out in a minute, Jerry, unless you'd like to join me."

Don't mind if I do.

The shower door shattered as his fist slammed through the smoke-colored glass.

She tried to scream, but his large hand stopped the sound at midthroat. He had crushed her windpipe.

Her eyes rolled back in her head as he pulled her from the shower. And when the last breath had finally gone out of her, he propped her on the closed toilet lid. She was now his.

Excitement flowed through him. The body was pale, but perfect.

He licked the blood off the rubber glove, oblivious to the cut on his hand. He smiled, unfastening his belt.

Jack Smitovich sat back in his easy chair, holding a snifter of brandy. He had hoped the alcohol would relax him, but he was still edgy and worried. The maniac hadn't called in a couple of days, and that in itself was like a double-edged sword. He wanted the job done, but God, how he hated talking to him, even over the phone.

A few minutes later, when the phone rang, Jack jumped a foot, splashing brandy all over the carpet. He took a deep breath and picked up the receiver.

"It's me," the husky voice said. "Read about it in the morning paper."

"Number two?"

"Yeah, plus an added bonus."

Smitovich tried to hold his rage. He had been afraid of this. "Shit, what did you do?"

"Got Leah McVey's boyfriend, too."

"Goddammit! Don't fuck this up by killing everybody you meet!"

"Well, I haven't killed you, yet."

There was a long pause. Finally, Smitovich spoke, trying to keep his voice calm. "The last thing I need is for you to be killing everything that moves."

"Hey listen, fuck-face. If you don't like the way I work, maybe you should be doing your own killing."

Silence.

After a moment, Jack said, "Are you still there?"

"I'm here."

"Okay. Look, just don't get careless. I don't want you getting popped before you finish the job."

"Never happen."

Smitovich waited a few seconds and then said, "Same location for the drop. You'll also be picking up some money."

"That's what I like to hear. Keep the cash flowing and I'll kill the president."

"I can believe that."

The man laughed and hung up.

Bloody bastard, thought Smitovich, pouring another double shot of brandy with shaking hands. All this crap had started five years ago. Five goddamned years out of his life. He couldn't lose it now, not when he was so close.

He thought back to the beginning, and decided one bottle of brandy wasn't going to be enough.

Jack had been on top of the world that hot summer in New York City. He owned several strip joints on both sides of the bridge and had his fingers into just enough on-the-side stuff to keep a positive cash flow that allowed him to live in luxury, but not so much that the big boys were trampling his face. The money, the cars, the penthouse, and all the pretty ladies had helped make up for the black hours in his life when his wife had walked out with his best friend and for the fact that he had a daughter who wouldn't speak to him, and probably never would.

Short, fat, and ugly, with a boring personality and a pessimistic attitude, Jack had never drawn the winners or had control of his life until he had become the boss and the money had started to roll in. Money had made it happen.

And then Jack Smitovich had learned that his accountant, Rubin Sanchez, had embezzled over three million dollars and taken off for Miami. He had found this out from his good friend, Johnny Spivey, who was also the manager of one of his most profitable clubs, by way of a strung-out stripper who had loved the guy and been left behind. Ratting on Sanchez had been her way of getting even.

He couldn't go to the cops because the embezzled money was filthy dirty. A week later, while he watched the bills pile up and wondered how long it would take the bank to start foreclosure procedures on his holdings, Jack had learned that eight of his prime, high-priced hookers had vanished, too.

At first, he hadn't made the connection, but then when the same little strung-out stripper announced that Sanchez had dropped her for one of the missing hookers, he began to get the picture. They had all been in it together. It had been a goddamned fucking sorority!

Jack had the names of the eight hookers, but the list was useless. They all used phony names, like Brandy and Tootsie and Passion. He did know where they were. Sanchez had packed them off to Florida and opened up his own little stable.

Jack's decision to head for Florida hadn't come as a surprise to anyone who knew him, considering what was left for him in New York. He cashed in what he could and took off before any more nails could be driven into his coffin.

And his plan had been a good one. After he was settled in Miami, he would find Sanchez and his eight back-stabbing whores and use every cent he had to buy a nine-way terminal contract. He didn't care how long it took. The "sorority" was as good as dead.

It had taken Jack several weeks to locate Rubin Sanchez, but what he found destroyed the picture he had so carefully pieced together. The slug was into prostitution in the sleaziest part of town; he had become a common pimp, with a stable full of hard-core streetwalkers. Hardly the trappings of a man with over three million dollars in his pocket.

And then the pieces had fallen into place again when Jack realized that Sanchez had received only a portion of the pie. Three million dollars split nine ways wasn't loose change, but it was far from the kind of money that would buy up Miami.

It also occurred to him that it was possible Sanchez hadn't received an equal share, that the hookers had taken off with the major portion. And that they might have masterminded the whole friggin' plot to destroy him. The thought of it boggled his mind.

He also knew by then that they weren't in Florida. He would bet the bank on that one. They had pulled one over on Sanchez, too, and left him twitching in the gutter. He could almost respect their black, conniving hearts. Almost.

Discouraged, Jack hired a cheap hit man to take out Sanchez and then spent the next year establishing a small call girl network. His goal was a big one. He wanted enough money to hire the best gumshoe in the country to find the hookers and enough money left over to hire the kind of cold-blooded killer who could take them all out. He didn't care how long it took. Or what the price. There was no price on revenge.

Within a year, he had realized the first part of his dream. He had become one of Miami's top escort runners, and with the deals on the side, the money had started to flow.

The break had come a year ago, when he had learned, from his personal private dick, that seven of the girls had been located in Sacramento, California, where one of them had family. So, for the most part, the "sorority" had stayed together, and Jack reveled in his good fortune. One was still unaccounted for, but it would be a start. A good start.

The time had come to arrange a meeting with the man called Walker Moon.

Jack had gone to the bar on Key Biscayne alone, expecting to see a man with a cold heart, cold eyes, and the kind of all-business demeanor that would make the meeting brief and to the point. Instead, he had found a kicked-back giant with shocking gray eyes and a wide smile.

But after they had settled themselves into a booth with a bottle of Tequila, Jack had realized that the man's fascinating smile didn't reach his eyes. The eyes had it. Cold, hard, unblinking. The man's reputation had preceded him, and Jack could see why. He was the kind of man who could rip off a head and eat the bones.

"You have a little job for me?" Moon had asked.

"It's more than a little job," Jack replied. "I want to put you on the payroll until my score is settled."

Moon took a swallow of Tequila and said, "How much money are we talking about?"

"Ten grand a pop, and when the contract has been honored, I'll give you an additional twenty grand as a bonus. I'll also pay travel expenses, because we're heading for the West Coast."

"We?"

Jack nodded. "This is too damned important to me to stay behind. We're temporarily moving to Sacramento, California."

Moon sat back and regarded Jack Smitovich intently. "How many bodies are we talking about?"

"Eight. All female. Seven are in Sacramento."

Walker Moon's eyes turned luminous. "And the eighth?"

"We'll deal with that when we find her. You have any objections to relocating out west?"

"On a temporary basis? None."

Jack felt the pounding of his heart subside. "Just remember, I pay the bills, and I call the shots. What you do in Sacramento is your business, as long as my business comes first."

The big man had agreed, and they had sealed it with a handshake.

Now, six months later, after settling into a routine with a couple of card rooms, a porno shop, and a few girls working the local hotels, the plan was in motion.

Surprisingly, Jack liked Sacramento, and decided he might stay on. Walker Moon could blow his brains out, just so long as it was after the job was done, as far as Jack was concerned.

In the back of his mind, he kept thinking about the hooker on the loose. The gumshoe was still working on it, and sooner or later he'd catch up with her. He would deal with it then.

Jack finished off the bottle of brandy and sighed. It was finally coming together, *if* the animal he had hired would just do his job and forget about ripping up everything that moved. The man was a fucking walking time bomb, ready to blow.

CHAPTER 8

Friday, December 11, 1988: 0830 Hrs.

Mike Clegg looked over the case files on his desk, ignoring the one with the bright yellow note attached. The number of files had now grown to twelve. Three cases had been solved, needing only the final paperwork, but as far as he was concerned, that still left nine too many, not counting the one with the note.

Dalton wasn't at his desk yet, but that wasn't unusual. He was always late. You could set a clock by his routine. "The last one in and the last one out," was Dalton's motto, and nobody complained.

Mike, who was always the first one in and first one out, finally looked at the note and groaned.

> CLEGG OR CASTEEL. PLEASE TAKE THE TIME TO LOOK INTO THESE 211S. THE ONE IN FAIR OAKS CONCERNS AN OFFICER'S SON.

Lieutenant Cray had signed the note in his large, heavy scrawl.

Mike couldn't believe it. With all the work piled up, they were supposed to drop everything because some officer's son happened to be in the wrong place at the wrong time.

He walked into the lieutenant's office, ready to do battle. "Excuse me, sir," he said, voice loud, forceful.

"What is it?" the lieutenant asked, without looking up from the papers on his desk.

"About the file and note you left me . . ."

No response.

Mike plunged ahead. "About the two-elevens and the officer's son. Well, we're kinda backed up, see, and . . ."

Lieutenant Cray finally looked up. "What's your point, Detective?"

"My point is, we're busy, with one detective dead and one detective out until Monday. Can't we just put this one aside for a few days until we get caught up?"

Cray placed his pen in the gold holder on his desk. "No way, Detective. I left my instructions, and I expect them to be carried out. Have a good day."

"Swell," Mike muttered, stalking out of the office.

Sergeant Nick Bell came into the squad room while Mike was still fuming. "What's up, Mikey?" he asked. "You look kinda down."

"Down?" He handed the sergeant the file and the lieutenant's note. "What is all this shit?"

Bell glanced at the file and grimaced. "Captain Reid's son works at a convenience store out on Fair Oaks Boulevard. Guess he was robbed and beaten up."

"Reid, over at Metro?"

"Yeah. So what's the problem?"

Mike sighed. "The lieutenant wants us to drop everything and start in on this bullshit."

"You and Dalton?"

Mike nodded.

The sergeant chewed on the end of his fat cigar. "Well, I

guess Captain Reid stirred up some shit and wants the guy who did this to his son, like a week ago yesterday. He called Sweeny this morning, demanding results."

"Wonderful!"

Bell patted Mike on the back. "Do the best you can. Look into the robbery, see if you can come up with anything, and go from there."

Dalton arrived at 8:40 carrying a box of miniature powdered doughnuts.

Mike was still upset. "You get that box of goodies from that convenience store on Fair Oaks Boulevard? The one near your apartment?"

Dalton nodded.

"Well, you're about to make a return visit." He handed Dalton the file and the note from the lieutenant.

Dalton looked at the note, crammed a doughnut into his mouth, and said, "What the shit is this?"

Mike watched powdered sugar fall like snow. "The kid who was robbed and beat up is the son of Captain Reid, Metro, that's what it is."

"And this happened on the night of the eighth?"

"You got it. Don't ask me to explain. It happened days ago, and now all of a sudden, we're supposed to pick up the trail and catch the creep."

Dalton snorted, powdered sugar blowing out of his mouth. "What it means is, we could be working on the goddamned crime of the century, and we'd still have to drop it."

"Jou god it, mon," Mike said, in a very convincing Jamaican accent.

"So tell me what we've got. My eyes hurt."

Mike managed a smile. "We've got two robberies with basically the same MO. The clerks were beat to shit, and the bad guy took off with some cash and a bunch of fruit pies."

"Fruit pies?"

"Fruit pies. Guess we could call this fucker the Berry Bandit."

Dalton couldn't help but chuckle. "Not much money taken, huh?"

"Petty cash."

"Well then, let's hit the road," Dalton said. "The sooner we can get some answers for the big boys, the sooner we can get back to the important stuff!"

When Mike pulled into the convenience store parking lot, he realized it was midmorning rush hour, when all the truck drivers were either unloading or taking a break, lounging around in the establishment with coffee cups in their hands. Trying to find a place to park was the pits.

It was Dalton's suggestion that they wait until things cleared out. And so they sat in the unmarked vehicle, talking about life, women, and how the whole department sucked.

Finally, after the last truck had pulled away, they walked into the store. A pretty girl was working the counter, and Mike smiled at her, pulling out his shield. "Detectives Clegg and Casteel. We're here to see Crispin Reid."

She returned Mike's smile. "He's in the back. Can't miss him."

Mike and Dalton walked into the back room and found the kid stocking beer into a cooler. He was even shorter than his father, though not nearly as wide.

"Hey, Mikey," Dalton tittered. "He's even shorter than you."

Mike gave Dalton a dirty look and headed toward the kid.

"Crispin Reid?" he asked.

The kid stuck his head out of the cooler. "Yes?"

"Jesus Christ!" Mike whispered. Crispin Reid's face was a mass of bruises. Tape covered most of it. Both eyes were black and almost swollen shut from the blow to his nose.

"Detectives Clegg and Casteel," Mike said, taking a deep breath. The kid had really taken a beating.

"Did my dad send you?" he asked, closing the cooler door.

Dalton opened up the file and said, "Well, sort of."

"Goddammit! I didn't want him giving me any help. I wanted it to go down just like any other robbery."

Oh, oh, problems between father and son, Mike thought. "Well, Crispin, without your father's help, it might have been a long time before we could get out here. I'm sure he was just trying to speed things up." Mike couldn't believe what was coming out of his mouth.

"I guess." Crispin sat on a stack of beer boxes.

"Why are you still working?" Dalton asked. "Wouldn't they give you a few days off?"

"They wanted me to take some time off, but I refused. I need the money. I'm only working a couple of hours in the morning, back here in the stockroom. I don't want to scare off the customers with my mug."

"What do you guys need from me?"

"We have the patrolman's initial report, but we want you to tell us about the night you were robbed."

Crispin collected his thoughts, trying to remember every detail. After a few moments, he went into the story, from the time the goon walked into the store until he had ended up on the floor. He concluded with, "I knew the guy was trouble when he walked in."

"Did you see a weapon?"

"Just his hands," he answered, touching his face.

Dalton read over the file to make sure the kid's story matched his first statement. It did.

"Okay," Dalton said. "How about a description?"

"Maybe six three or four. Maybe even six five. He looked like a giant coming through the door."

Mike wrote it down. "How much did he weigh? Give us a rough guess."

"An easy two hundred and fifty," Crispin said.

"Fat?"

"No. He seemed to be in good shape, though I couldn't see the upper part of him. He was wearing a heavy jacket."

"Hair?"

"Brownish." He thought for a moment. "Yeah, light brown, kinda tipped with blond. Sun-bleached, I guess you could call it. He had a healthy tan, too, like he'd spent some time on the beach." Crispin gave a short laugh. "I don't think I'd want to see him in a bathing suit."

"Why's that?"

"If you knew what I look like right now in a bathing suit, you'd understand."

"Back to the hair," Dalton said. "How long?"

"Short. Just barely covered his ears."

"How about facial hair?"

"He was unshaven, but no mustache or beard."

"How about his eyes?"

An odd look came over Crispin's face. "They were strange. Real spooky." He thought hard, trying to pick a color. "They were a real shiny blue, no, gray, that's it. I remember thinking they'd probably glow in the dark. But then just before he grabbed me, they turned sort of dark."

"Dark?"

"Yeah. Like I couldn't see any color. Weird."

Mike felt goose flesh on his arms. "Clothes?"

"Blue jeans and a jacket."

"The color of the jacket?" Dalton asked.

"Military. Like a military green." Crispin frowned. "There was something else along those lines, too. Yeah. He had some black stuff on his face. Not heavy, but like he might have had it on earlier and then wiped it off."

"Anything unusual about his features?"

Crispin shrugged. "The ladies might call him handsome in sort of a rugged, virile way. Sharp features with a square jaw."

"Any kind of an accent? Speech problems?"

"No. He had a deep voice, husky."

"Any deformities, like a limp?"

"No, but he had big feet. I remember looking at them as he was coming down the aisle."

"Shoes?"

"The regular running kind that everybody wears. Black."

Mike put the notebook away. "I think that's about it. Thanks for your help."

Crispin Reid nodded.

In the unmarked again, Mike asked, "What's the location of the other robbery?"

Dalton was eating some red licorice he had bought in the store, and swallowed a wad. "North. Out near Roseville."

Mike studied the initial report. "Says here that they picked up the video from the surveillance camera the night of the robbery. I think that piece of film ought to make for some serious viewing."

Dalton only nodded, starting in on a box of crackers.

They left the second convenience store just after noon, called in a code 7, for lunch break, and headed for the nearest coffee shop.

Dalton hadn't said much since they had talked to Crispin Reid, but Mike understood. There was an undercurrent here that couldn't be denied, something evil hovering close by, just out of reach. And there was no doubt they were dealing with the same guy. Both clerks had reported traces of what looked like black soot on his face, and the theft of petty cash and fruit pies. And then there was the fact that both clerks had had their noses slammed into the counter, not to mention their descriptions of the man's curious gray eyes.

Mike didn't know what they were dealing with here, but he had the gut feeling that the creep was going to strike again. And that the next time, the clerks involved might not be so lucky.

Suddenly, the video from the surveillance cameras seemed more important than ever.

CHAPTER 9

Friday, December 11, 1988: 1200 Hrs.

Tom Runyo and Steve Taylor had favors due from a pretty blue-eyed secretary in Internal Affairs and a smashing, sex-crazed brunette in Records. They had spent the morning collecting.

Now, in the small parking area filled with black-and-whites, Runyo looked over his shoulder at the headquarters building as though it had eyes and could hear every word. He lowered his voice. "Gambling. Would you believe that shit! Neal Jessop was so far over his head, I'm surprised he could function as a cop or a husband."

The shock of their discovery had been twofold, and Taylor shook his head. "I'm having a tough time dealing with the fact that Neal has been under investigation for the last three months. That's heavy stuff."

Runyo looked at his notes. "Maybe that's why he was seeing a city shrink. Maybe he was trying to work out of the mess."

"You think it's possible his wife knew about it?"

Runyo shrugged. "Nothing in the file mentions where this big-time gambling spree took place. Maybe Reno, or Tahoe?"

"Maybe. Or maybe right here in River City," Taylor said. "We've known all along that some of the legal low-ball card rooms are only coverups for the illegal shit in the back room. One of my neighbors got busted a few years ago for dealing in a converted basement. My neighbor. Can you believe that?"

"Right about now, I think I could believe anything," Runyo admitted. He looked at his notes again. "I've got the name and address of the shrink. I think it's time we paid him a visit."

"I wonder if Robert Hollinger knew about the gambling, or the shrink?" Taylor asked thoughtfully, sensing that things were coming up very rotten indeed.

"Well, somebody knew about it, or we wouldn't have the report."

The psychologist's office was located on L Street, in an area where many of the large houses had been chopped up into apartments and businesses. Runyo and Taylor walked into the old converted Victorian and checked the brass nameplate in the foyer.

A receptionist sat behind a circular desk. She looked up and smiled at them, asking, "May I help you?"

Runyo flashed ID. "Detectives Runyo and Taylor, here. We'd like to see Gideon Lester."

The smile downgraded immediately. "Do you have an appointment?"

"We don't need an appointment," Runyo snapped. "This concerns a murder investigation."

She studied them for a moment before punching a button on her expensive white phone. She kept her voice very soft, very low.

Finally, she hung up and said, "Doctor Lester will see you. His office is down the hall, last door on your right."

They found the door open and the fat man on his feet behind

the large, oak desk. He looked uncomfortable, though he seemed hospitable enough.

"Come in," he said, "and have a seat."

Runyo and Taylor walked in, but remained standing.

Runyo spoke first. "I know you're a busy man, so we won't take much of your time."

"You're quite right. I am a busy man. Very busy, so if you'll be brief..."

Runyo compared this whole thing to going through his psych interview again and very quickly decided he didn't like this round, pudgy little fuck. "Yeah, well, we understand that you had some bull sessions with Neal Jessop."

The psychologist sighed. "As professional law enforcement officers, surely you must know that I simply cannot discuss my patients with anyone."

Runyo quickly returned, "And as a professional shrink, as well as one who seems to specialize in problems relating to law enforcement officers, you should be aware of our rights. Neal Jessop, one of your patients, was killed earlier this week."

Gideon Lester scowled. "I heard Detective Jessop had been killed, but it is highly unlikely that I can help you. Wasn't the man killed in the line of duty?"

"Yes, but there seems to be a complication," Runyo said, trying to hold his temper.

"A complication?"

"There is a possibility that Detective Jessop committed professional suicide, and we want to know if he had any problems."

Gideon Lester became very still. "Are you sure?"

"No, we're not sure. That's why we're here. Look, let's lay it all out. The only thing we know is that Neal Jessop was into some form of illegal gambling. The question is, where?"

"I couldn't possibly give you that kind of information, and I wouldn't if I could."

"Why?" Runyo asked. "Are you into the heavy stuff, too?

Are you afraid we're gonna bust the joint and ruin your prime time recreation?"

"Now, see here—"

"No, *you* see here, you miserable fuck!" Runyo shouted. His lip was beginning to twitch, and that was a bad sign. "We're trying to do this the easy way. The safe and sane way, but if you're not going to cooperate, we'll get a court order, and then we'll see who's fucked up."

The psychologist choked out, "Please, close the door!"

Taylor leaned against it, smiling. "No way. Let's let the whole world know what a shithead you are." He winked at Runyo. It was getting better by the minute. He loved it when Runyo got all worked up.

"Have you ever been audited?" Runyo was asking. "I just happen to have a friend at IRS who owes me a big favor."

Red in the face, the fat man asked, "Are you threatening me, Detective?"

Runyo walked around the desk and punched an index finger into the man's chest. "Call it what you like, Lester, but I'm promising you that your life is gonna become shit if you don't come through for us now. Got it?"

With Tom Runyo breathing on him, and because of the determination and rage he could see in his eyes, Gideon Lester finally nodded. "D-Detective Jessop said something about a club on Alhambra run by Louie Cantrall. . . ."

Runyo smoothed the man's lapels and smiled. "Thanks, Doc. Now, you have a good day, ya hear?"

"Louie's, huh?" Taylor said, after they were in the car. "Well, what do you know."

"We should've guessed," Runyo returned, pulling out into a line of traffic.

Louie's Card Room connected to the 400 Club, one of the few strip joints in Sacramento that had managed to stay open after an ordinance a few years back had put a stop to all topless and bottomless clubs within the city limits. Now, the strippers wore G-strings and tassels, when the cops were looking. Runyo had been in the establishment twice, as an observer, and both times he had come away with the gut feeling that there was one hell of a lot more going on below the surface.

"Think we should check with SID before talking to Louie Cantrall?" Taylor asked. "In the event he's already under some kind of investigation?"

Runyo nodded, heading the unmarked up Sixteenth. "The last thing we need are the SID boys after our asses."

SID, the Special Investigations Division, handled vice, card rooms, clubs, bingo parlors, biker gangs, and other related bullshit. Runyo had worked with the department several years before, on loan from patrol, and although the guys had all been decent, the place had been a zoo.

A few minutes later, as Runyo and Taylor stepped into the squad room, Runyo decided that nothing had changed.

A husky, tattooed giant with a full beard and long hair, wearing oily jeans and a black-and-white skull shirt, stood by the copier.

Runyo looked down at the scrub's waist, eyeing the gold shield attached to his belt. He was a "biker" detective, Runyo guessed, and gave the man an awkward grin.

The man grinned back, showing straight, white teeth. "Help you guys with something?" he asked.

Runyo nodded. "I'm Tom Runyo, and this is Steve Taylor. We're with Homicide. Is Jafo Lloyd around?"

The detective nodded. "Yeah. He should be in the back somewhere, maybe at his desk. We've had one hell of a fucked-up morning, so he's probably in a lousy mood."

The detective went back to his copy work, while Runyo and Taylor made their way through the squad room. A few familiar faces nodded greetings, but nobody came over to talk. The whole lot of them were buzzing around like bees on clover, while phones rang and typewriters clacked.

A detective in drag lumbered by, trying to keep his balance on floppy heels, while three hookers ran to keep up with him, screaming their heads off. Up ahead, two undercover cops in black leather were arguing over a report, and a little old lady was screaming at anybody who would listen that her bingo game was legitimate, and wasn't somebody going to do something about it?

"Jesus Christ, what a circus!" Taylor muttered, following along behind Runyo.

They found Jafo Lloyd standing near his desk, scowling, with shirttails out and tie askew. "Hey, Jafo," Runyo said, extending his hand. "What's to it?"

The man's scowl turned into a broad smile as he took Runyo's hand. "Well, well, well. Long time no see, Tommy."

"How's the life of a sleaze?" Runyo asked.

"You know, SSDD." Both detectives translated at the same time. "Same shit, different day."

Runyo grinned. Several years ago, David Lloyd had gone over to the county to fly in a whirly for a few weeks and observe, and then report back to the city, to help the city decide if they wanted to launch a helicopter program. When David resumed his regular job, a new name had been born. Jafo, *Just another fucking observer.*

"You know my partner, Steve Taylor?" Runyo asked.

"Sure, how's it hanging, Steve?"

Steve shook the man's hand and grinned. "You guys sure know how to make a dick glad he's working Homicide."

Jafo laughed. "So what brings you down to our sleazy, but humble, neck of the woods?"

"SID still working card rooms?" Runyo asked.

Jafo sat down at his desk. "Along with all the other bullshit we end up chasing. Why?"

Runyo pulled out a notebook. "How about Louie's Card Room over on Alhambra?"

Jafo smiled. "Old Louie Cantrall. That little sumbitch probably hasn't spent a single legal day in his whole miserable life. Yeah, we're watching him. He's suspected of running several illegal gambling operations right here in town."

Runyo was mentally moving on to the next question. "Is Louie the owner?"

Jafo shook his head. "The business belongs to a company called JSB, Inc., out of La Jolla, California."

"Who's the primary?"

"We don't know. Haven't been able to find out, though we're working on it. New owner, though. Before JSB took over a few months back, it belonged to a businessman in Miami. Why the interest?"

Runyo exchanged glances with Taylor. "Have you heard about Neal Jessop?"

Jafo nodded. "Damn shame. He was a good man."

Runyo cleared his throat. "Well, we've got reason to believe Neal was involved in some big-time illegal gambling, and that the card room is involved."

Jafo dug out the case file, scanning it quickly. "Well, I can tell you this much. We're damned close to putting a search warrant together. You want to be in on it when it comes down?"

"For sure," Taylor spoke up.

"Thought so," Jafo said with a smile. "When we go, we'll give you a call."

"We didn't want to step on any toes," Taylor said, delighted that they were going to get a piece of the action and, hopefully, some answers.

Runyo asked, "You figure Louie is running illegal without the owner knowing?"

Jafo shrugged. "Or they're in it together. Only time will tell." He extended his hand to both detectives. It'll be good working with you again, Tommy."

"Same here, Jafo. We'll be expecting your call."

The detectives made their way through the squad room, trying to keep their laughter in check. The drag queen was sitting at his desk, with his shoes off and his legs up on a chair. Black hair puffed up under the sleek nylons. The old lady was now screaming at an office clerk.

"God deliver us from these animals," Taylor chuckled as they walked out of the room.

CHAPTER

10

Friday, December 11, 1988: 1400 Hrs.

Stu sat at his desk, reading the report Freddy Jenkins had sent over on Mary Attwater. The semen established the killer's blood type as O-positive. Stu's blood type was O-positive. The thought that he shared something in common with the lunatic turned his stomach into knots. And it was stupid. About as stupid as the way he had behaved during the Attwater autopsy. He was definitely going to have to work on gaining some semblance of control. A homicide detective didn't have room for areas of gray. Everything had to be a definite black or white.

He had also located two of Mary Attwater's friends, or associates, and had scheduled the first appointment with one Jenny Marshton at three o'clock. It depended on how it went with her whether or not he'd move on to the next lady this afternoon or wait until tomorrow.

Stu put Freddy's report aside and went over the BOLO, the

Be On The Lookout, bulletin he had written, which had already been sent out to at least a dozen different counties and all law enforcement agencies in the greater Sacramento area.

The BOLO was standard procedure during a homicide investigation, intended to alert all agencies to keep a watchful eye for other cases with a similar modus operandi. It would work especially well when dealing with serial killers, though Stu hoped to God that wasn't what they had. Maybe in Los Angeles, or New York, or Miami. Even San Francisco had gotten in on the act with their infamous Zodiac killer. But not in Sacramento! Stu shook his head, aware that he wasn't being realistic. Though Sacramento didn't have the population of those other cities, it had its share of crime, which was rising all the time. Someday, it could even have a serial killer.

In the bulletin, Stu had included information about the French coin found on Mary Attwater's back, but that information hadn't been given to the news media. So if the fiend struck again using the same MO, the coin could be very important.

Stu cleaned up his desk and stretched, trying to work out the kinks. He was on his way out the door to meet with Jenny Marshton when Lieutenant Stanfield stopped him, arms waving.

"Are those two fucking assholes in here?" Stanfield hollered.

"Sir?"

"They know who they are!" His eyes searched the room. "Well, when you see them, you tell Runyo and Taylor that their worst nightmare just happened! You can tell them that I'm going to chop up their asses and feed the pieces to the stray cats over on Sixteenth Street!"

Stu couldn't help but smile. "Will do, Chief. Should I tell them to pack lightly?"

"Don't fuck with me, Redlam! I'm not in the mood for shit!"

Stu made his escape. There was no need to push the lieutenant into some kind of an explanation. He knew what had happened; Stanfield had found out about the Neal Jessop investigation. He hoped the detectives were ready for a battle. If not, there sure as hell could be a couple of 187s before this day was over.

The town of Fair Oaks, just north of the American River, sprawled out for several miles and was patrolled by the County Sheriff's Department. Fortunately, whenever a homicide investigation was in the works, Stu was free to go where his leads took him without worrying about stepping on jurisdictional toes.

He found Jenny Marshton's house without difficulty, and parked in the driveway behind a white Mazda RX-7. He could tell by the neighborhood, even before he caught sight of the Marshton's house, that he was going to find the trappings of the same opulent lifestyle that he had found in Mary Attwater's condominium.

The house was split-level and had been built on a rolling hill. At least two acres, he thought as he began the long journey to the front door. He hadn't seen the inside of the house yet, but he had the feeling that with the furniture cleared out, you would be able to land a 747 jumbo jet in the living room.

He was thinking about that idiotic thought when the beautiful blonde opened the door. Hair up, sort of soft and wispy, she wore a blue satin robe.

Stu cleared his throat. "Jenny Marshton?"

She smiled. "Detective Redlam?"

Stu coughed. "Sorry I'm late." He couldn't get beyond her face. Smooth skin, high cheekbones, blue, blue eyes.

"No problem," she said huskily. "Please come in."

Stu walked into the living room, all thoughts of the 747 gone. It was rustic, expensive, full of antiques, plants, and exotic stuff he couldn't identify. A huge elk's head stared down at him from above the mantel.

"Pretty place you have here," Stu said, staring back at the elk.

"Thank you," she said, heading for the back of the house.

"Come along, Mr. Detective. We can talk while I catch some sun."

Stu loped along behind her. *Sun? Jesus Christ, lady. It's forty degrees outside, and dropping by the minute!*

They walked into a room full of exercise equipment, where she promptly shed her robe to reveal the skimpiest bathing suit Stu had ever seen. Five threads held it together.

Jenny Marshton turned and looked at Stu, her nipples making an occasional surprise visit when she arched her back just the right way. Stu knew that she knew what was happening, but he didn't care. She was a welcome sight to a man whose life held little in the way of beauty.

Jenny Marshton moved to a table in the corner of the room, put on a pair of sunglasses, and turned on the sun lamp.

Stu decided she didn't know about Mary Attwater's death. She hadn't given any indication of knowing when he had talked to her on the phone, and she certainly wasn't giving any indication of knowing now.

She then proved it by saying, "What can I do for you, Detective?" She sort of pushed it out, cooing through her lips.

"On the phone, you said you were acquainted with Mary Attwater."

"Yes, I know Mary." She began wrestling with her bathing suit. "You're a cop. You don't embarrass easily, do you?"

Stu shook his head.

"Good!" She shrugged out of the top to her bathing suit.

Momentarily stunned, Stu thought, *Jesus, Redlam. You've seen hundreds of tits. Sure,* came the answer, *but not like these!*

She began rubbing her breasts with lotion.

Stu choked out, "How long have you known Mary Attwater?"

"Ten years or so. Why? Is Mary in trouble?"

It occurred to him that she really was an airhead. He had told her he was a homicide detective when he talked to her on the phone. Did it matter? Not in the least.

There was no easy way to say it, so he just blurted out, "Mary Attwater is dead." He watched for a reaction.

Jenny lifted her sunglasses and looked at Stu for a long moment. She then stretched out on the table. "When?"

"Three nights ago." The reaction never came.

Finally, after stripping off the bottom half of her bathing suit and rolling over on her stomach, she said, "Murdered?"

"Yeah. But why would you say that?"

"Mary insisted on running around with creeps."

"And?"

"And, it's a sign of our times. A girl can't be too careful, these days."

Stu studied the smoothness of her rear end and thought about the coldness of her heart.

"Do you know who did it?" Jenny asked, without looking at Stu.

"No. I'm having a difficult time finding out who Mary Attwater was. How about family?"

"Her mother lives back in Delaware."

"Do you have the address or phone number?"

"No. Mary didn't talk about her mother. As far as I know, she left home seven years ago, and that was that."

"You mean, Mary hadn't talked to her mother in seven years?"

"That's right. Mary never talked about her past or her childhood. She always made it sound as though she was born in a cabbage patch."

"Never mentioned a father, or brothers or sisters?"

"No."

"Friends?"

"I have a couple of names I can give you." She turned her head and looked at him. "How 'bout a favor, Mr. Detective Man?"

Stu was having a difficult time focusing his eyes. "What do you have in mind?"

Jenny grinned. "I'd like you to rub lotion on my back."

Stu walked over to the table and picked up the bottle of lotion. He studied every line on her smooth back, while she waited, eyes closed beneath the glasses.

"Wouldn't you be more comfortable without your jacket?" she asked, opening one eye.

Off came the jacket. His Smith and Wesson 645 .45 automatic rested in a shoulder holster under his left arm. Two spare clips and a pair of handcuffs were positioned under his right arm.

Both eyes were on him now as she asked, "Have you ever had to use your gun?"

Stu poured lotion onto his hands and rubbed them together. "Yes, I have," was all he said.

"Did you kill the person you had to use the gun on?"

He caressed her back with a deep massage. "Yes."

"You don't like to talk about it, right?"

"It's not one of my favorite subjects," he said, continuing to rub Jenny Marshton's back. He couldn't figure her out. If Mary Attwater's death was bothering her, she sure as hell wasn't showing it. She was definitely a piece of work.

Stu's hands moved downward.

"I'm sorry. I didn't mean to upset you." She brought her head up and gave him a sly smile. "That feels good."

"You didn't upset me. It's just . . . It's just that the public seems to think that killing a man, like you see on TV or in the movies, is just routine. That afterward, you're supposed to holster your gun, walk away, and forget it. But that's not how it works. It's something you carry around with you for the rest of your life." He didn't know why he was telling her all this, or why he was rubbing her back with oil, for that matter.

But he continued. "It's something a normal person doesn't understand. It's something you've got to experience before you can."

"Cops aren't normal, huh?" She was still smiling, still watching him.

"No, not really. I think you have to be a special kind of stupid to go into this line of work."

Her smile turned sly again. "Well, Detective Redlam, you seem normal enough."

"Ahh, but you don't know me yet."

"Yes, I do. You're Detective Stu Redlam, probably thirty-seven or eight. Terrific gray eyes, brown curly hair touched with gray. You've probably been a cop since your early twenties, and you're a man who believes in your job. You're married . . ." She studied him for a moment. "But I don't think it's a happy marriage."

Stu was impressed.

"No kids. You probably live in the suburbs, and your refrigerator is stocked with beer. I also think you're the kind of man who has more than one woman waiting in the wings to share your bed."

His hands had passed the equator now, and he gave her a silly grin. "You're close, only I'm thirty-six."

"And I might add, you have wonderful hands . . ."

She sort of squirmed under them, and he pulled away. As much as he was enjoying the moment, he had come on business. He wiped his hands on a towel. The fun and games were over, for now. "What do you do for a living, Miss Marshton?"

Jenny Marshton sat up on the table and turned off the lamp. "I'm independently wealthy, though I dabble in art. I'm pretty good at it."

Stu had the feeling that Jenny would be good at whatever she dabbled in. "Rich family or ex-husband?"

"Yeah, both. Would you like to join me in the hot tub?"

"Where did you meet Mary Attwater?"

"You didn't answer my question, Detective."

Stu had his mouth open to tell her that she hadn't answered his question, either, but his pager was beeping, displaying Lieutenant Stanfield's number. Stu sighed. "Do you have a phone I can use?"

"In the hallway, on a little stand."

Stu found the phone and dialed the number. The lieutenant answered on the third ring. "What's up, Lou?" he asked, using the common nickname for lieutenant.

"Roseville PD just called. Got a couple bodies up there. Looks like your killer's MO."

"Swell," Stu said softly.

"What was that?" Stanfield asked.

"Nothing." He didn't want to look at dead bodies; he wanted to join Jenny Marshton in her hot tub.

"Sounds like I interrupted something."

"You could say that."

"Well, put your dick back in your pants, Redlam. Get over to the main office in Roseville and see Detective Franks. He'll fill you in."

Stu finally smiled. "Yeah, but between you and me, I'd rather be doing the filling in."

"Go to work, Redlam, you fucking snake." The line went dead.

Stu walked into the exercise room and gave Jenny an apologetic smile. "Sorry, but I've got to head out. When can I pick up those names you mentioned?"

"I can give them to you now . . ."

Stu shrugged.

"Or, you can pick them up tomorrow, say around eleven? I mean, tomorrow is Saturday . . ."

Stu nodded. "Around eleven would be fine."

The sly smile was back, and her blue, blue eyes twinkled. "Good! We'll have an early lunch."

Stu nodded, put on his jacket, and walked out.

Parked down the street, tucked in under an old oak tree, Walker Moon watched the Blazer pull away from the curb and shook his head. If that fuck-face was the best Jenny Marshton could do, she was in for a real treat tonight . . .

Stu met Detective Franks just after five o'clock. The Homicide office was small and efficient. It was also the main detective bureau for the city of Roseville.

Detective Franks was a short man, probably in his forties, with balding hair and a firm handshake. Stu liked him right off.

The detective briefed Stu on what they had found, adding, "It was a real mess. The man in the front yard had three 9 mm shells in his chest. The woman was in the bathroom, naked and with her throat crushed."

"And you think there's a connection with my one-eighty-seven?"

Detective Franks picked up a plastic bag off his desk and handed it to Stu. "I'd say it coincides with what you had in your BOLO."

The baggie contained a French coin, and a shiver ran down Stu's back.

"How many have trampled the crime scene?" Stu asked, feeling a dull ache at his temples.

"Our department might be small, but we're not stupid," Franks said.

"Sorry. This whole thing has me a little on edge." He read the patrol officer's preliminary report and then studied the coin. There was definitely a connection, but what?

"Where are the bodies?" Stu asked, taking a deep breath.

"Coroner's office in Auburn. Wanna see the stiffs?"

Stu nodded.

"Okay. I'll drive you up. The autopsies are scheduled for tomorrow morning, if you're interested."

Stu quickly shook his head. "Just send me copies of the reports and postmortem stuff."

"Done. Let's get our asses up the hill."

CHAPTER 11

Friday, December 11, 1988: 1700 Hrs.

Robert stood at the ammo bin, holding his Bren 10, 10 mm. He loaded up four clips of the free range silver-tipped ammo and pushed one of the full clips into his gun. He then placed the other three in his back pockets.

The range was empty but for the two range masters standing around central control, and that was the way he had planned it. The range was usually empty this late in the day, so he could concentrate on what he was doing instead of waiting his turn or answering more questions. It had been one hell of a week, and there didn't seem to be a letup in sight.

Robert walked up to the line, turned to the control booth, and said, "Set up the combat range."

"You got it, Rob," the control master said.

The setup would be in a fifty-yard perimeter. Robert would begin walking the timed course, which consisted of a mock street, building fronts, old cars, and alleyways. At random intervals, lifelike targets would pop up in different locations. Some good guys, some bad guys. It was Robert's job to make it through the course without dumping any civilians and to take out all the bad guys with clean, vital hits.

He'd gotten his gun back from the department just this morning, so he figured it was one step in the right direction. And maybe this was the next step, knowing that the range time would be good therapy. He was already beginning to relax, with his mind only on his objective.

He looked back at the control room and nodded.

The course was set up so he could practice barricade shooting or just let go and jump around, running and kicking in doors. He picked the course that had two buildings to be searched and cleared.

The horn sounded, and Robert started his journey into combat.

The first obstacle was a small barn with an old truck out front. He slid the safety off the gun, both hands wrapped around the butt, finger on the trigger. He heard the metal slide sending out the first target and took cover behind a rusted water trough just as he saw the gun in the subject's hand. He fired twice, and both hits were vital.

He was up and moving toward the barn now as another target moved out from behind a tree. The gun was extended, his finger heavy on the trigger.

It was a farm girl, holding a milk pail.

The target slid away, and Robert inched toward the tree. Something moved behind him. He turned, dropped into a crouch, and fired two more shots. Vitals again, head and torso hits.

Robert walked on to the next scene. An old wreck of a car sat to his left, a rundown apartment building to his right. He was just about parallel with the car, his attention on the apartment, when the figure in the car moved. Robert fired two rounds into the car as two targets on his right popped up. One in the doorway, the other on the stairs. He fired one shot at each, dropped the spent clip, and immediately fed in a fresh one, working the slide down.

Another target, over by the corner of the building. Robert used a telephone pole for cover, almost ripped two rounds off, and stopped. It was a little girl holding a bag of candy.

He took a deep breath, heading for an alley. Something moved behind him. He pressed against the wall, turned, and fired. Above him on the balcony! He fired two more times.

He continued up the alley. Five feet in front of him, a target popped. Robert squeezed the trigger, but at the last second, pulled the gun, sending the round into a wooden wall to the right.

It was the target of a patrolman.

Robert was working his way through the final scene now. He had to search and clear a single-story house. He approached the door and found it locked. He was down to his last clip. Sweat beaded his brow; his hands felt clammy.

He took a step back. *They were there at the door in the run-down hotel. Neal stood to his right. But HE was going to kick down the door, not Neal.*

"*It's my door, Neal!*" Robert yelled.

Behind him a body moved. He dropped down, firing on his side. One round ripped through the forehead. He jumped up and in one fluid motion kicked the door. He jumped to the side in a crouch. He turned and saw the body fire once.

He stepped into the room. A mock kitchen was to his right, a small hallway to his left. The kitchen looked clear. He started up the hall as a target popped out from a room, holding a shotgun. *Neal, get down!* Robert fired twice, the slide locked. The gun was empty.

Slowly, he walked toward the kitchen. He knew there was one target left. He pulled his useless gun up to full extension and aimed. The target was a woman holding a frying pan.

The bell sounded, announcing that the course had been completed.

Robert walked out of the house, covered with dirt and sweat

and shaking from head to toe. Neal was dead, but Robert was now convinced that his partner had committed suicide. He didn't know why he did it, but he was going to find out.

When Robert pulled into his driveway, Dana's car was already there. Carrying his gun bag, he walked into the house. He could hear Dana in the kitchen, and something smelled terrific. He was actually hungry, for the first time in days.

This time around, the media had backed off. Possibly because of Neal's death, he didn't know, but it was a far cry from the clusterfuck that time he had killed the black kids. That had been a dog-and-pony show, a three-ring circus, and he had been right in the middle. Well, he was in the middle of this one, too, but it was different. This time a peace officer had gone down, so everybody could hang their heads in sorrow.

He put down his bag. In the kitchen, Dana was hovering over the stove. She wore a pair of gray sweatpants and one of his police sweatshirts. Cute. He pulled a beer out of the frig and kissed her on the lips. "Smells good," he said, twisting the top in the bottle.

"Did you go shooting?" she asked, giving him a warm smile.

"Yeah. No civilians. All enemy targets hit clean and vital."

"I'm impressed."

"What can I say? I'm just this awesome stud who knows how to handle a gun." She heard him laugh lightly as he left the kitchen.

"But don't you forget, you're *my* awesome stud," she yelled after him.

Dana could hear him laugh. God, it sounded good! Slowly, he was coming out of it. She was aware that it could come back at any time, sometimes even worse, but he was strong enough to deal with it. And after last night . . .

Dana checked on the roast as tears filled her eyes. Last night, after making love, he had finally opened up to her. He had talked about Neal, and about his own guilt, and then as she had held him, he had broken down and cried. He let it all go. He had also realized that life had to go on.

In his arms, understanding him, loving him, knowing she would always be by his side, she had made her own silent little vow. Robert Hollinger was the man she was going to marry, and she would not lose him to this godforsaken job.

In the living room, Robert began his nightly ritual. He turned on the stereo but tonight, he skipped his usual look at the evening paper. As the music filled the room, he went to the window. Beyond it, in the darkness of the night, he could see Neal's face.

Robert raised his beer bottle. "Good-by, old buddy," he said softly. "I'll miss the hell out of you. But I know if it was me up there, looking down, I'd want you to keep going. So I won't let you down. Come Monday morning, it's gonna be kick ass and take names. Rest easy, Bro." He stood silently, tears on his cheeks.

Dana walked up behind him, and put her arms around his waist. "You okay, baby?"

"Yeah, I'm okay. I was just saying good-by to an old friend."

Dana turned him around, her bottom lip quivering. "Are you still hungry?"

Robert smiled. "You bet." He leaned down and lightly kissed her. He put his arm around her, and together they went in to eat.

"In my fuckin' office, *NOW!*"

Runyo and Taylor exchanged glances and groaned.

The two detectives went in with their hands stuffed into pockets, their heads down. Taylor headed for a chair.

"Don't bother," Stanfield spit out. "This is gonna be a stand-up ass-chewing!"

He glared at his two detectives. "Thought you were pretty slick, didn't you? You've been out of the office all day, up to your dirty tricks, and you come sneaking back here after hours, figuring I'd be long gone. Well, surprise! This is Friday night, for crissake. I'd be at Toomie's right now if it weren't for you two lumpheads."

The lieutenant took a deep breath. "Okay. Here it is, and I'd better get a straight goddamned answer. Are the two of you working on the Neal Jessop case?"

Runyo spoke up. "Yes, but—"

"Shut up!" Stanfield scowled at the big detective. "And did you threaten one Gideon Lester? The same Gideon Lester who wants to bring the two of you up on psychological evaluation?"

"We really didn't threaten him," Runyo said, looking at Taylor.

Taylor's face broke into a grin. "Tom just sort of told him how it is, sir."

Runyo choked back his own laughter and nodded.

"You fuckheads! You think this is a big joke? I had to talk my goddamned ass off to cool him down, and I still can't promise anything. Where in hell were your brains?"

Runyo began his argument. "Lieutenant, I think if you heard—"

"I've heard enough! If Lester goes through with *his* threats, do you realize what kind of damage that could do to your careers? Two good detectives right down the toilet. No, make that two lame-brain detectives right down the toilet."

Stanfield began to pace while the detectives stood and waited. The lieutenant was a fair man, always had been, always would be. He was known for his quick temper and tirades, but usually when the dust settled, he would listen to reason. And that was what Runyo and Taylor were waiting for now.

It didn't take long. The lieutenant finally sat down at his desk and clasped his hands. "Now suppose you tell me about it," he said, still glaring at them.

Runyo began, "I think if you know all the facts, you might even get into this investigation yourself."

"So stop running around in circles and get to it."

"Well, we've been working on Neal Jessop's apparent suicide, and we came up with a few leads that point toward illegal gambling. Through Gideon Lester, we found out that Neal frequented Louie's Card Room on Alhambra, and through SID, we found out that Louie is under investigation."

"Sir?"

The lieutenant looked at Taylor.

"Something smells pretty rotten here...."

Lieutenant Stanfield lit a cigarette and nodded. "You'll be working with SID?"

Both detectives nodded.

"Okay, go ahead, but if you ever try and fuck me again by breaking general orders, you're both going to be looking for new jobs. And don't let it interfere with our department. Got it?"

Runyo and Taylor both nodded.

"Now get the hell out of here before I lose my temper all over again!"

The detectives had reached the elevator before Taylor said, "I need a drink."

Runyo nodded. "I could use a double, but you're buying."

CHAPTER

12

Friday, December 11, 1988: 2100 Hrs.

After viewing the bodies at the Auburn coroner's office and looking over Leah McVey's lavish house in Roseville, Stu finally headed home. It was nine o'clock, and he was hungry and physically drained. Another beautiful woman had died violently at the hands of the same monster who had killed Mary Attwater. Again, the perpetrator had gone for the throat and, from all indications, had sexually assaulted the victim postmortem. He had also left behind a French coin. Denomination didn't seem to be an issue.

Attwater had been killed at her place of employment; McVey at home, where the killer had also taken out the woman's boyfriend. It had been an ugly, stomach-turning double homicide, giving Stu one more book full of numbers to add to his growing collection. He prayed it would be the last.

As he pulled up in the driveway, Stu was thinking about the weekend ahead, full of dull, boring paperwork, work that would include going over both books. The house was dark. Not a cheery or inviting welcome home. But he was learning to live with it, and with the clutter of unwashed dishes and dirty laundry. Nor was it a comforting thought to realize that if he missed Gail at all, it was for her knack for keeping things neat and clean. He knew that their marriage having gone sour hadn't been her fault alone, that he had had a hand in its disintegration, as had his job, which she so violently detested. And he supposed that some things just weren't meant to be.

Carrying his briefcase and turning on lights as he went, Stu made his way to the bedroom, where he stripped off his jacket and shoulder holster. The answering machine light was blinking, and he rewound the tape. Gail's voice filled the room.

> STU. I KNOW YOU ARE PROBABLY AT WORK, AND I COULD HAVE CALLED YOU THERE, BUT YOU KNOW ME WHEN IT COMES TO IMPORTANT THINGS AND DECISIONS. IT'S EASIER TO WRITE NOTES AND LEAVE MESSAGES. IT'S OVER, STU. I'M NOT COMING BACK. I'LL SEND FOR MY THINGS LATER, AND THE DETAILS CAN BE WORKED OUT BY OUR ATTORNEYS. TAKE CARE.

The machine beeped and Stu turned it off, trying to decide what he felt. The anger was there, hating her for ending eight years of marriage over the phone, but it was typical. Gail had always been good at running when things got tough, and she had always chosen the easy way out. But then he felt a twisting sadness, too, knowing that down deep, in some strange way, he still loved her, and probably always would. The down side of their marriage had always been the front runner, but there had been the good times, too, and these were the things he remembered as he made his way to the kitchen. It wouldn't be a messy divorce. If nothing else, Gail had always been fair.

In the kitchen, Stu poured a double Scotch and smiled slightly, thinking about Jenny Marshton's invitation. It was something to look forward to and, if nothing else, that beautiful lady would be able to take his mind off his problems.

And then there was Julie Clark. He had known all along he was going to call her eventually, but right now, with the Scotch burning his throat and the house he had shared with Gail closing in around him, the thought of her big brown eyes and innocent, almost schoolgirl quality, was more than appealing. A couple of hours with Jenny Marshton would be fun, probably even the experience of a lifetime, but right now, he wanted more. He needed someone he could talk to. Someone who might even understand.

In the bedroom again, Stu opened his briefcase, pulled out his notebook, and dialed Julie's number.

She answered on the third ring, whispering, "Hello?"

"Oh, oh. Bet you were in bed—"

"Who is this?"

"Detective Redlam."

"Oh, hi!" she said, her voice coming through a little stronger. "What can I do for you?"

Not in the mood for idle banter, Stu got right to the point. "I know it's late, but my lieutenant suggested I get better acquainted with Mary Attwater's friends and neighbors. He specifically requested that I get a bit closer to one Julie Clark."

She began to laugh.

"He stated that I should take Miss Julie Clark out for drinks and dinner, so you understand, I'm just trying to follow orders."

"I would love to oblige your lieutenant, Detective Redlam," she replied softly.

Stu breathed a sigh of relief. "Then how about drinks? We can work the rest out later."

"How about drinks, and then we either go to your place or mine for a late supper? I'll cook."

"You've twisted my arm," Stu laughed, feeling better by the minute. "How soon can you be ready?"

"In absolutely no time at all, but considering how late it is, why don't we meet someplace, and we can make the rest of our plans over drinks?"

"And the lady has brains, too," Stu chuckled. "Do you have a place in mind?"

"Well, I don't know where you live, and with me way out here in the canyon . . . Are you familiar with Mastroni's Canyon View Lounge?"

"That rustic place that overlooks the river? Yeah, I know where it is."

"Then I'll meet you there in thirty minutes, Detective Redlam. Don't be late."

Stu already had his shirt off and was on the way to the shower.

Julie was waiting for Stu on Mastroni's sprawling deck with a view that went on forever. But Stu wasn't interested in the view, only in the smiling lady in the short black skirt and blue, hip-length jacket. "Sorry I'm late," he said, giving her an awkward hug. "You should have waited inside."

Julie pulled up her collar, her breath coming out in little puffs against the cold. "It's okay. I've been watching the Christmas lights twinkling across the water. Have you ever gone Christmas shopping in Folsom?"

He couldn't tell her it was difficult to think about the holidays with a crazed killer on the loose, his wife gone, his brother off flying the friendly skies, and his parents clear across the continent. So he just shook his head and walked with her into the lounge.

Typical of anywhere on a Friday night, the place was crowded, but there was one table by the window. Stu steered Julie toward it, but was promptly stopped by a scowling, swarthy-complexioned man. "Sorry, sir, but that seat has been reserved."

Stu turned to the man. "By whom, and for when?" he asked.

"And since when do you, or anybody, take reservations in a bar?"

"In *this* establishment we do," the man said abruptly. "If the need arises. Now, if you'll just wait at the bar...."

Stu turned to Julie. "Wait here," he said. "I'll be right back." He then took the man's arm and escorted him to a secluded corner.

"Sir!" the man exclaimed.

Stu lowered his voice. "Would ten bucks get me the table?"

The man looked thoughtful. "Well—"

"How about twenty?"

The man nodded and took the crisp bill Stu handed him.

After they were seated at the table by the window, Julie asked, "What did you say to him?"

Stu grinned. "I just gave him a few alternatives."

Julie grinned, slipping out of her jacket, and appraising him with her big, brown eyes. She liked what she saw. He had been in a suit that first time, but now in acid-wash jeans, lizard boots, and a tweedy wool sweater, he looked casual and comfortable. She wondered if he was carrying his gun.

After the cocktail waitress had taken their order, Julie said, "That's typical. A cop orders either a Tom Collins or a beer. At least that's always the way it is in the movies."

"It's because we're poor public servants," he said with a smile. "But then you're following your stereotype, too. In the movies, women always order white wine."

"It's the only drink that doesn't put me under the table," Julie confided honestly.

When the cocktail waitress returned with their drinks, Stu brought out his wallet, careful to conceal his badge. Julie watched the process, noting the strength in his hands. And after the girl had gone, said, "Do you usually try and keep your identity a secret?"

"You mean the fact I'm a cop?"

Julie nodded.

"Most of the time. Most of the time, it makes life easier.

They find out you're a cop, and suddenly you're an asshole. You're the guy who beat up a brother or arrested a sister six years back. It doesn't matter that you're out there for their protection."

"It matters to me," Julie said quietly. "How is the Mary Attwater thing going?"

Stu concentrated on the small decorated Christmas tree in the corner of the room and shook his head.

"If that means you don't want to talk about it . . ."

Stu looked at Julie's beautiful face. "It's not that. It's a lot of things, actually. I've got this feeling I'm on the verge of something big, but I can't get a handle on it. Mary Attwater isn't the only one. Two more bodies turned up today."

Julie shuddered. "Connected?"

"We think so. We know it's the same killer." He looked out the window at the darkness. "And that two of the victims had a lot of money."

"And the third?"

Stu looked at her. "A boyfriend who happened to be in the wrong place at the wrong time. Frankly, I think we should change the subject. What else do you do when you're not managing that awesome complex of yours?"

Julie looked into the gray eyes that held so many things. "I sell real estate part time."

Stu finished his drink. "Ever been married?" he asked.

"No. What about you?"

"Getting a divorce."

"Kids?"

He shook his head.

"Let me guess," Julie said in a little voice. "Your wife hated your job and walked out."

Stu tossed some ice in his mouth and prided himself on making the right choice. Julie was not only a good listener, she was also one observant lady. But suddenly he found that he didn't want to talk about his marriage or his job. He just wanted to hold Julie Clark in his arms and forget.

"Your place or mine," he said, noting that Julie had finished her drink.

Julie's eyes twinkled. "Mine. It's closer, and I pulled two New York steaks out of the freezer when you called."

Stu sat across the table from Julie, trying not to gobble. The lady was beautiful, and she could set out a great meal, too! In short order, she had prepared thick steaks, baked potatoes dripping in sour cream, garlic French bread, and a garden salad. A good red wine complemented the meal, and Stu thought for sure, he had died and had gone to heaven.

Feeling much better with food in his stomach, Stu finally sat back and raised his wine glass in a toast. "To one hell of a good cook. That was wonderful."

"It's my aim to please," Julie said, fluttering her eyelashes. "Shall we have coffee in the living room in front of the tree?"

Not interested in the Christmas tree, Stu shook his head and stood up. "I think we should have our coffee in front of the fireplace, but not until I've done the dishes."

"Not necessary," Julie said.

"Necessary," Stu said, gathering up their plates. "Around my house, if you don't do the dishes after each meal, you find yourself forgetting about it until a week or so later, and then you've got a mess not even an ant would tackle. Let's just say it's force of habit, so indulge me."

In the kitchen now, Stu stripped off his sweater and holster and opened the dishwasher.

Julie began to laugh.

Stu looked at her. "What's so funny?"

"It's your T-shirt, Stu. It's great!"

Stu looked down. He was wearing his "Shit Happens" favorite, depicting two patrolmen in a squad car. One officer was holding a shotgun that had just blown a hole in the roof. "You like that, huh?"

"It's really cute." She pushed up her sleeves, put a squirt of soap in the sink, and ran hot water. "Around here, we wash the pots and pans by hand, before we load the dishwasher," she said, blowing a handful of bubbles in his face.

He reciprocated by rubbing soap bubbles into her hair. Next came the little hose used to wash down the sink, and within seconds, they were both soaking wet.

Screaming with laughter, Julie headed down the hallway with Stu in pursuit. Through the bedroom and into the bathroom, Julie grabbed up a can of lady's shaving cream and aimed.

"Oh, no you don't!" Stu exclaimed, putting her into a soft wrist lock.

"That's no fair!" Julie cried. "You're using police stuff on me!"

Stu turned her loose for just a moment, and Julie reached out and tickled his sides. Laughing, they wrestled into the bedroom and landed on the bed.

It seemed like hours, though it was only minutes that they lay there, looking into each others' eyes. And then Stu kissed her, groaning as he slid his tongue into her mouth.

Julie's arms were around him now, and she was making soft, mewing sounds as he worked at the zipper on her skirt. Breathlessly, she helped him, and then helped him out of his jeans and shorts. Finally, with Stu's St. Michael's medallion bouncing between them, they came together. He called her name, she called his, as they matched thrust for thrust, orgasm for orgasm, until they lay together, panting for breath.

Later, they made love again, only this time, it was slower, a time when everything could be forgotten but the discovery of the moment.

Walker Moon pushed open the door of the convenience store and strolled in. It was empty but for the old man behind the counter. He walked over to the long row of glass doors, pulled out a can of beer, and popped the top.

Next, in the pastry section, he grabbed up the usual assortment of pies and made his way to the counter. "Okay, old man, bag 'em and pull all the duckets out of the register. Do anything stupid, and I'll gouge out your eyes and skull-fuck you!"

The old man just stood there, fear gripping his body.

Moon reached up and grabbed the old man by the shirt. "Did you hear me? Start pulling out some of that tender, now!"

While the old man was in Moon's clutches, up against the counter, he slowly reached down and pressed the button. Then, free of the large man's hands, he began fumbling with the register, pulling out all the cash.

Moon was stuffing the money into a bag with the pies when two black kids came through the door. Though they were street-wise punks, they stopped in their tracks when they saw the big man with the gun.

Moon had the Browning Hi-Power up and extended, the first round hitting one kid dead center. He fell back on the entry mat, a gaping hole in his chest. The second kid turned to run, but Moon got him in the back just as he was going through the door, sending him sprawling out on the sidewalk.

Walker Moon turned to the old man, and the gun coughed once, ripping through the man's skull. He was dead before he hit the floor.

Stepping over the kid on the mat, Moon pushed open the door. To his right, he could see a patrol car creeping into the parking lot, headlights out. He brought the gun up and shot four rounds into the front windshield, then ran to his left, jumping the fence that blocked his way.

"Stop, asshole, or I'll shoot!" Moon heard as he pulled himself up, and then he heard the shot and felt the explosive pain in his right arm.

Over the fence now, Walker Moon ran. Down residential streets, through yards, over small fences, until he finally stopped near the river. When his breathing and pulse rate had returned to normal, he began to look for a car. It really irked him that he'd had to leave the Olds Cutless behind in the parking lot. He'd gotten a good car, thanks to Smitovich's connections. Unfortunately, he couldn't ask for another one. If Smitovich found out he'd been chased by the cops and shot in the arm, he would probably rip up the contract. If that happened, then he would have to kill Smitty, and in any event, the fun and games would be over. He smiled slightly, spying a new Buick at the end of the block. He had just put in his order.

As he deftly made his way toward the car, the smile slowly faded from his face. Goddamn fucker cops. His pies were still in the parking lot.

CHAPTER

13

Friday, December 11, 1988: 2300 Hrs.

Dalton had been asleep on the couch for three hours when the phone rang, but because of his years as a cop, he was immediately awake with the first ring. Groggy, he stumbled getting up, tripped over the rug, and kicked the cat's food bowl across the kitchen floor, so by the time he yanked up the receiver, he was yelling, "Who the hell is it!"

"I'm glad to hear your voice, too, dickwad," Mike said. "Our boy just hit again. This time, he decided he'd go for the biggie. Snuffed three."

Dalton shook his head to clear it. "Three?"

"Three."

Awake now, Dalton grabbed a pad and pencil. "Where?"

Mike gave him the address and hung up.

Dalton filled up the cat's bowl with fresh food, grabbed up

his coat, turned off the lights and TV, and ran out of the apartment. The only thing on his mind at that point was just how lucky Crispin Reid really was.

Dalton had to park his Monte Carlo on the street; the parking lot had been sealed off with yellow police tape. He showed his gold shield to the patrolman and went under the tape. He wore an ATF (Bureau of Alcohol, Tobacco, and Firearms) hat, a gift from a buddy who worked for the federal agency, to conceal his head of wild, unruly hair. It wasn't the first time he'd had to take off without a shower or shave, and it probably wouldn't be the last.

Mike was already in the parking lot, where a small neighborhood crowd had gathered behind the police barricade. Red and blue lights bounced off the convenience store and spectators. Dalton squinted against the glare. God, he felt like shit.

Mike appeared to be wide awake; up. He wore a blue jacket with yellow lettering that spelled out POLICE. The constant drizzle had plastered down his hair and dripped off his nose.

"Let me guess," Dalton said. "You were awake when the call came in, working on your plastic models."

"Nope. I was about to give Peggy a long awaited pile driving, that, I might add, we could've both used."

Dalton patted Mike on the back. "So what's the skinny?"

Mike looked around. CSI was out in force on this one, already taking perimeter shots, while three investigators milled around, waiting to talk to Homicide. He sighed. "Well, it looks as though our boy showed up to do his thing, and from what I can see, we've got two very dead, very cold kids." Mike pointed toward the door. "They probably stumbled on the two-eleven in progress, and boom boom. I think he waxed the clerk on GPs."

"Well, for sure, he's one hell of a sicko bastard," Dalton said.

"You get a look at the patrol car over there? The mother blew out the windshield. Got the patrolman in the ear, but in return, he thinks he hit our boy as he went over the fence. We've also got the bastard's car. So far, if you can believe it, it's a rental. We'll have to wait for the rest."

Dalton nodded and headed for the store, deciding it was probably a stolen rental, because good fortune wouldn't give them a name that easily.

On the sidewalk near the door, he looked under the two tarps and winced. "Christ," he muttered to nobody in particular.

Terrance Calhoon, a stocky, black Homicide detective, shook hands with Mike.

"How have you been, Terry?" Mike asked.

"Can't complain, 'cept for being on call when shit like this comes down. Never seems to fail. It's like all the bad guys say, 'Hey, let's fuck with Terrance Calhoon.'"

Mike nodded, understanding. "Got a real mess here."

"Yeah. It's gonna be a real long night." Terrance looked around for his partner. Dutch Morgan was talking to a pretty patrol officer. "Would you look at that? We've got three dead, and Morgan is still interested in T and A." He smiled at Mike. "What's your angle?"

"We've been working a two-eleven for the last couple of days, and we're pretty sure this is our guy."

Calhoon's smile turned sly. "Then you know what that means."

Mike nodded.

"Yeah, this whole clusterfuck is yours."

"I know. You still going to do the preliminaries?"

"I wouldn't leave all this bullshit at your feet."

Mike nodded again. Terrance Calhoon was a good man, and they went way back to their academy days. He watched Terry pull out his can of Copenhagen and take a chew, and grinned. Old Terry was the only black cowboy he'd ever known. Even had horses and his own little museum of Old West stuff.

Terry went to talk to CSI, and Mike joined Dalton in the store. The old man lay on the floor, but he'd left behind part of his brains, splattered all over the Slurpy machine. God, this wasn't a pretty sight at all.

Mike exchanged glances with Dalton; words weren't necessary.

Dalton went back out and headed for Dutch. "Where's the officer who belongs to that?" he asked, pointing toward the disabled patrol car.

"Sitting in the ambulance. Name's Jarwoski. He's pretty shaken up."

Dalton walked over to the ambulance and looked in. "Jarwoski?"

A tall, strapping patrolman stepped out. Not very old, eyes full of emotion. A bandage covered his ear, and his jacket was covered with blood. "I'm Detective Casteel, Robbery," Dalton said. "How's your ear?"

"It was just a nick."

It looked like more than a nick to Dalton, but he let it go. "Did you get a pretty good look at this guy?"

"Sure did," Jarwoski said. "He was a big motherfucker."

"Bigger than you?"

"Without a doubt."

"If you saw him again, would you be able to recognize him?"

"I'll remember that face until the day I die. Lights in the parking lot are as bright as day."

Dalton began writing in his notebook. "Do you feel up to looking at the video in the store?"

"Yeah. If I can help, let's do it."

Mike was already in the store, rewinding the tape to the approximate time of the triple 187s. He looked at the bandage over Jarwoski's ear and shook his head.

"Show time," Dalton said, hitting the play button.

First off, three kids walked into the store, bought some candy and left. Next, they had an old lady, followed by a black man buying a six-pack.

113

A minute went by, two minutes, and then a large man wearing a military jacket pushed through the door.

"That's him!" Jarwoski yelled out.

"Are you sure?" Mike asked.

"I'd stake my reputation on it," the patrolman said. "That's the mother that shot at me."

Dalton smiled at Mike. "It's the same sack of shit we've got on those other tapes, Mikey. And look, the son of a bitch is smiling at the camera."

"We've got our man," Mike whooped, heading for the front of the store. "It's our boy," he said to Terrance, who was watching the coroner load up the bodies. "Goddamn, can you believe it!"

"Good!" Terrance slapped Mike on the back. "Though I don't mind telling you, I would like a piece of this one myself."

Dalton, carrying the video tape that would join the others in the evidence room, came out of the store with Jarwoski.

"Guess what," Mike said to Dalton.

"What?"

"Now we get to play homicide dick."

Dalton looked back at the store, remembering the gore, and the death that had been inflicted here tonight, and took a deep breath.

In his small dingy motel room, Walker Moon pulled off his jacket, grimacing slightly as pain shot up his arm. *Ignore the pain.* Next came the bloody shirt. The bullet had entered the back of his mammoth biceps, lodging against the bone. He could feel it there, rubbing against tissue and muscle.

In the bathroom now, using the mirror to see, he poked his fingers into the wound. *I feel no pain. I am at peace with the Universe.* He opened a medical kit that rested on the back of the toilet and pulled out a small scalpel. The blade felt cold against his skin.

Slowly, he probed the wound, blood flowing down his arm,

off his elbow, and into the sink. He worked the sharp blade around and around, deeper and deeper into shattered flesh. Blood pooled in the sink, and he turned on the faucet. Deeper, deeper . . . And then he heard the scraping sound of the scalpel against the slug. With his fingers, he reached in and pulled it out. It was a silver tip. Very pretty, though it hadn't expanded worth a shit. Next came the rubbing alcohol, poured straight into the wound. He watched it bubble and ooze, applied a field dressing, and left the bathroom.

Seated in a chair now, Walker Moon pulled out the Browning Hi-Power, stripped it down, and began to clean the gun.

On Sunday, Stu woke up in Julie's bed to the winter sun filtering through the window. It was after noon, and the smell of frying bacon filled the room. His stomach grumbled. She was really something, always knowing just what to do to make him happy. He hoped that it was a mutual thing here, because he really wanted her to share this happy, contented feeling.

He hadn't meant to spend the weekend with Julie, but it had happened, and he wasn't sorry. When they hadn't been playing bedroom football, they had talked, about anything and everything. He had told her things he hadn't even told Gail, and she had listened.

He groaned, thinking about all the paperwork he had neglected, but he had the rest of the day. Somehow, he was going to have to break away, go home and face reality. He felt a little twinge of guilt, thinking about Jenny Marshton waiting for him yesterday, but he had the feeling she was the kind of woman who could make substitutions without much difficulty. He made a mental note to call her tomorrow—he still needed those names—but as far as the rest of it, he was no longer interested.

He sat up as Julie walked into the room. "Hello, sleepyhead," she said, smiling at him. "I hope you're hungry."

Stu laughed. "I'm famished, and you're amazing."

She was wearing his "Shit Happens" T-shirt over her sleek body. She leaned over and kissed him. "Are you calling me a party animal?"

"If the shoe fits . . ."

Another kiss, and then she pulled away. "Well, my mama taught me a lot of things, along with being tough with cops." She gave him a sly, provocative look. "Are you sorry you spent the weekend with me?"

Stu grinned. "Not in the least."

"Good! Then let's eat."

At the table across from Julie, Stu ate bacon and eggs, drank cups of rich, black coffee, and scanned both the Saturday and Sunday papers. The piece about the double homicides in Roseville had taken a backseat to the front-page spread about the triple homicide at a convenience store on the east side. Two kids, who had undoubtedly walked into the 211 in progress, and the clerk. The shooter had gotten away on foot, but they had his photo, taken on video.

Stu shook his head. Poor Terrance Calhoon. He was on call this weekend, and wouldn't you know something like this would happen. He always said he was living under a little black cloud, and that if it was raining soup, he'd be caught with a fork.

"Anything interesting?" Julie asked, pouring fresh coffee into their cups.

Stu tossed the paper aside and smiled at her. "Nothing but the same old stuff. It's a zoo out there, and we're the animals."

Julie smiled and blew him a kiss.

By Sunday morning, the "Wanted" bulletin Mike had drafted had been distributed to all patrol officers in the city and county and the news media eager beavers. The massive manhunt was on.

On Monday morning, feeling washed-out and frustrated, Mike sat at his desk, wishing to hell something would happen. He picked up one of the bulletins and stared at the killer's smiling face. Jesus Christ, somebody must have seen this guy!

Dalton was down in Records, looking at mug shots on the off chance the shooter had been booked before, but Mike had the gut feeling he was going to bomb out, just like the rental car had bombed. The car had been rented with a stolen credit card belonging to one Anthony Niddinger, a businessman who lived in Miami, who had reported the card stolen several months ago. It had been the stupid rental agency's fault for not checking the card.

And the car had turned up clean, which was no surprise, with just old smudgy latents here and there, but nothing on the door handles, gear shift, or steering wheel. The shooter had worn gloves, no doubt about it. The vehicle was still impounded, and would be for some time. Mike could picture the guys standing there scratching their heads, trying to decide if they should go over it one last time. Sooner or later, they were going to realize what Mike already knew: It was useless. The guy was a pro.

"Clegg, in my office now!" Lieutenant Cray's voice boomed through the squad room.

Mike groaned. From the moment the lieutenant had found out the shooter was the same piece of scum who had worked over Crispin Reid, the hallowed halls of headquarters had become a dismal place indeed. He stepped into the lieutenant's office and said, "What do you need, sir?"

"Thirty goddamned seconds of your time, Detective," Cray shouted. "I just got off the phone with the chief. Heads are gonna roll if you don't find this maniac, like three weeks from last Wednesday!"

"We're doing all we can, sir," Mike said, keeping his voice under control.

"Not good enough! Take Dalton and get your asses out on the streets. Show the city why you earn your salaries!"

"We do a pretty good job showing the city why we earn our salaries, sir. And wearing out shoe leather isn't going to solve the case."

"So what is? Your good looks?"

The comment was totally uncalled for, and Mike balled his hands into fists. Someday, he was going to show this pompous ass what it meant to be a real cop. "Is that all, sir?" Mike said through clenched teeth.

"For now. Just keep me advised. Understood? Oh, and when Hollinger comes in, tell him I want to see him."

Jesus Christ, Mike thought, heading for his desk.

Dalton was back, shaking his head. "No luck, partner. He ain't there. Maybe in somebody else's mug book, but not ours."

Mike sat down and shook his head. "Asshole is on the warpath," he said, nodding toward the lieutenant's office. "He really grinds my gears."

"You're gonna get an ulcer worrying about that dickless shit in there," Dalton offered.

Mike managed a grin. "Yeah, I guess you're right. Maybe we should wait for him to leave some night, and then just blow his nuts off."

Sergeant Bell walked by then, heard the last of the conversation and said, "Just don't do it without inviting me."

All three men laughed.

Robert pushed through the Robbery Division doors and looked around. It seemed to be BAU, business as usual.

The office was momentarily disrupted while Robert's coworkers shook his hand and welcomed him back, but it was Mike and Dalton who hugged the man with affection and concern.

"You okay?" Dalton asked, noting the dark circles under Robert's eyes.

Robert nodded. "It seems like I've been gone months."

Mike chuckled. "And just think, your first business of the day is with Cray. He wants to see you."

Robert raised a brow. "I suppose it's too much to hope that he's changed in a week?"

"He's worse, if anything," Mike said. "We're in the middle of this puke-spouting case here, and it's really got him on the warpath."

"The triple-decker at the convenience store?"

"Yeah. How'd you find out we're on the case?"

"I put it together in bits and pieces. Figured it was your two-elevens gone haywire."

"Haywire is an understatement," Dalton said with a sigh. "We've got a blood-crazed killer out there, and until we find him, we can consider our asses grass. A clerk in one of the earlier robberies is the son of Captain Reid, Metro. He's putting on the pressure, and so is Cray. They want this guy, as if we don't."

"Apparently the chief is doing his share of yelling, too," Mike said, shuffling through the case files on his desk. "Shit, what a mess. We were already up to our armpits before this. I wonder how long a man can go without sleep before he dies?"

Robert chuckled. Some things never changed.

In the lieutenant's office, Robert waited for Cray to respond to his greeting. The man was writing in a notebook and refused to look up. Robert repeated, "Sir? You wanted to see me?"

Cray was deliberately ignoring the detective. When he finally looked up, he wasn't smiling.

"Sir?" Robert was losing his patience, there was no doubt about it.

"So are you okay?" the lieutenant asked. "No emotional problems or anything like that?"

"I wouldn't be here if I didn't feel up to it," Robert returned.

"Good! I want you working with Casteel and Clegg on this two-eleven murder investigation. I assume they filled you in?"

"I know about it."

"Good! You'll be working with Homicide, so that should be a perk. I don't have to tell you how important this is."

"What about the files on my desk, sir?"

Cray stared at Robert as though the man had just lost his

mind. "I'll tell you what I told Casteel and Clegg. Blow them off on somebody else."

Robert wanted to ask just who he was supposed to blow them off on, but walked out of the office instead. With all of it, the mountains of work, the lieutenant's shitty attitude, and now a case that might just end up bigger than all of it, Robert felt totally alive for the first time in days. It was so damned good to be back!

CHAPTER

14

Monday, December 14, 1988: 1000 Hrs.

Stu sat at his kitchen table wearing gray sweatpants and a white T-shirt, a towel around his neck to catch the perspiration. He had just jogged around the block, and now, with a pot of coffee brewing, he was ready to tackle the paperwork he had been putting off. He had hoped to get home yesterday, but Julie had had other ideas, and that little lady could certainly be persuasive. He grinned, thinking about the weekend, already missing her.

He looked at the clock, noted the time, and got to work, opening Leah McVey's little book, still grimy from the compound used to dust for latents. The short hairs on the back of his neck prickled up as he stared at the familiar sequence of numbers. He picked up Mary Attwater's little black book, compared the two, and closed his eyes. With the exception of the bindings and handwriting, the two books were identical.

And then he found one difference: McVey had listed a few

names and phone numbers in the back of her book. Sweat began to roll down his face, sweat that wasn't the result of his early morning jog.

He got up, poured a cup of coffee, sloshing it all over the counter, and stared out at the dismal, gray morning. The pain he felt was acute, numbing. A grinding thing that spread throughout his gut. Mary Attwater's name and phone number had been listed, as well as Jenny Marshton's. There were other names and numbers, and a few phone numbers without names, but at the moment, they didn't matter.

With his hands shaking, he reached for the phone and dialed Jenny's number. He let it ring twenty times before he hung up and grabbed his jacket and gun.

On the short drive to Jenny Marshton's house, Stu tried to come up with a reasonable story to give the lady that would hopefully explain why he was landing on her doorstep in jogging clothes, disheveled and wild-eyed. He wouldn't let himself think about the fact that she hadn't answered the phone.

He also sorted out the facts. The three women were acquainted, and the two who had been murdered had kept fat little books full of coded numbers. Attwater had managed a fitness center, McVey had been a secretary. Marshton dabbled in art. All three had money that hadn't come from their jobs; Jenny had admitted to being independently wealthy. Was there a connection to the fitness center? Maybe McVey had one, but Jenny had her own state-of-the-art exercise room. And then there was all that kinky stuff in Attwater's closet. Nothing like that had been found in the McVey house, but he had the feeling that with Jenny Marshton, it might be a different story.

Stu pulled onto Jenny's street and realized he had been holding his breath. He suddenly felt lightheaded and exhaled. Her car wasn't in the driveway. Was it parked in the garage? He sincerely hoped it wasn't. He hoped she had decided to go away for the weekend, and just hadn't returned.

Stu parked the Blazer and loped the distance to the door,

his ridiculous story ready and waiting to be told. *I just happened to be out jogging, and just happened to remember that I forgot to pick up those names and telephone numbers.* He shook his head and rang the bell. If she believed him, he would retire tomorrow.

A neighbor's dog barked, and Stu rang the bell again. Finally, he pounded on the door. It gave under the pressure and swung open. The hairs rose on the back of his neck. No woman living alone would leave the front door unlocked.

He opened the door and called out, "Jenny!"

Nothing.

He stepped into the entryway and called out again, "Jenny, it's Stu Redlam. Are you home?"

The house was quiet, lights on. In the living room now, Stu pulled out his .45. A knot was forming in his stomach. Something was very, very wrong. He stared up at the elk's head above the fireplace and moved into the dining room, then the kitchen.

Now Stu was moving down the hallway, checking rooms along the way. Office, art studio, guest room, master bedroom, all empty.

At the end of the hall, the door to the exercise room was closed. Stu just stood there looking at it while his heart thumped in his throat. Moisture beaded his brow and hands as he stepped closer. And then the smell hit him, the sickening sweet smell of death that no cop could ever forget.

With fear grabbing at his throat, he opened the door, bracing himself against the odor, and for what he was going to find inside. She lay naked, face down on the floor, her body already starting to bloat. The sun lamp had been turned on full power, and had sent the temperature in the room incredibly high.

Stu bolted from the room, heaving what little food and liquid he had in his stomach all over Jenny's expensive carpeting. He then staggered out the front door, collapsing on the porch steps, taking in deep breaths of the crisp December air until his stomach began to settle. He still had his gun, clutched in his hand like a security blanket. He stared at it stupidly. Jenny Marshton had known both Mary Attwater and Leah McVey, and now she, too, was dead. He hadn't taken the time to look, but he knew there would be a coin on her back, and probably a little book full of numbers somewhere in the house.

He pulled himself up and headed for the Blazer. Ignition on, he grabbed the microphone. "Ivy two-two-six," he choked out.

"Ivy two-two-six," the female dispatcher returned.

"Could you contact SO and have them nine-forty me at three-four-nine-two Palmdale Drive, ASAP?"

"Ivy two-two-six, ten-four."

Within minutes, a County Sheriff's patrol car came around the corner and parked behind the Blazer.

Stu got out of his vehicle and flashed his ID. "I've got a body in the house," he said, still feeling short of breath.

The deputy looked at the house. "No shit!"

Stu nodded. "I just asked for a patrolman. I didn't want to broadcast the one-eight-seven over the air or the news chasers would've beat you here."

The deputy started for the house, calling over his shoulder, "You coming?"

"Not now," Stu returned. He climbed into his vehicle and closed the door, aware that he suddenly had a case of the chills.

While Stu waited for the deputy to make his initial sweep of the crime scene, he watched the gray morning unfold. More rain was forecast for the week, with temperatures in the low forties. If the storm brewing off the coast of Alaska made it all the way down, snow as low as fifteen hundred feet was also predicted.

Let it snow, Stu thought glumly. Three down, not counting McVey's boyfriend, and how many to go? Sacramento might just have their very own serial killer after all.

He was thinking about Jenny, wondering how long she had

been dead, when the deputy approached the Blazer, shaking his head.

Stu stepped out, shivering again.

"I'd say she's as dead as Julius Caesar," the deputy was saying. "God, it sure ain't pretty in there." He eyed Stu. "I thought you homicide dicks were supposed to be immune to all this bullshit."

Stu forced a smile. "I knew the lady."

"Oops, sorry." The deputy walked over to his patrol car and used the computer. After a few minutes, he joined Stu and said, "I just sent off an automatic message to my lieutenant. He'll have Dispatch contact Homicide, CSI, and the coroner's office. Until then, there's not much we can do but wait." He opened the trunk of his car and pulled out a yellow crime scene tape.

Swell, thought Stu, wondering how he was going to explain to *his* lieutenant why he hadn't gone through the address books until this morning. If he had, Jenny Marshton might still be alive.

"You goddamned idiot!" Jack Smitovich shrieked into the phone. He was no longer afraid of the man he had hired, or worried about offending him. Fear had been replaced by rage. "If I had known you were gonna pull a shithead stunt like this, I would've canceled the contract. You sure as hell wouldn't be sitting there with the file on Gabrielle Messa in your lap. I'd be hiring somebody to take you out, you stupid, frigging—"

"Whoa," Moon interrupted. "You'd better watch your blood pressure, fuck-face, or you're gonna end up croaking before the job is done."

"And you'd better watch out or the cops are gonna have you locked up before the job is done. Jesus, don't I pay you enough money? The papers are calling you the 'Pastry Bandit.' Your picture is on the front page. Christ, fruit pies and petty cash? And did you have to blow all those people away? Oh,

Christ, and then we've got the car. You left it there for God and everybody to find, and then they say you were shot. Oh, shit, fuckin' shit! I knew you were gonna screw this up!"

Walker Moon chuckled. "The car is clean, and the wound is nothing. You told me what I did in my spare time was my business, as long as your business came first. I agreed, and I haven't gone back on my word."

Smitovich thought about that and had to admit that Moon had a point, but he also realized that the man was out of control. Maybe he always had been.

Calmer now, thinking ahead, knowing how close they were to the end, Smitovich said, "Just promise me you'll stop all this bullshit and stick to business."

"Maybe I will, and maybe I won't," Moon replied. "It's really none of your fucking business."

Smitovich gritted his teeth. "What are you doing for wheels?"

"I have my ways."

Smitovich didn't want to know what those ways were, and hung up the phone. Maybe if he offered the lunatic more money, he'd stop the convenience store robberies. *Sure, and maybe I'm gonna be the next president of the United States.*

Smitovich poured a stiff drink and turned on the TV.

Walker Moon turned off the TV and studied the glossy photograph of Gabrielle Messa, then turned to her dossier. This one was dark, with jet black hair and brown Latin eyes. She had pouting lips, too, and he smiled. They were going to have lots of fun.

Moon stretched out, resting his head on the pillow. He hated to admit it, but the gunshot wound had taken a little bit out of him. He needed a day or so before he made his next move. He closed his eyes, concentrating on what it was going to be like to hold the black-haired beauty in his arms.

Sleep finally came to him, as did his turbulent past, creeping like a slithering snake into his dreams.

* * *

Mortar fire had been hitting the ridge for the better part of an hour. Several in the troop lay dead, faceless grunts, cut down in their prime.

Sergeant Barns took cover behind a fallen tree as another barrage sent up a dust of debris. He wasn't alone. Corporal Walker Moon had taken cover, too, and he was grinning from ear to ear.

Barns spoke into his portable radio. "Alpha Company. This is Red Platoon, actual." He waited for a response.

Finally the radio crackled. "Go ahead, Red Platoon."

"We're taking some heavy mortar fire up here, lots of casualties. Where the fuck is our bombing run?"

"Stand by, Red Platoon. We haven't forgotten you. Keep low. The fire mission will be there soon. Alpha Company out."

The sergeant looked at Moon, who was still smiling. "Can you believe that shit?"

"Let me at 'em," Moon said. "I'll stop this fucked-up mortar assault."

Barns thought about the mountainous man who had joined the Army to fight a war, whose drive and ambition went far beyond those of the average soldier. A loner, Moon was feared by the men, but he wasn't afraid of killing or of being killed. "Do it," Barns said then, "but if it falls to shit, you're on your own."

Moon laughed. "Wouldn't have it any other way."

It took Moon fifty minutes to make it behind the NVA mortar line. He was on a small knoll now, looking down at the mortar cannons bombing his platoon and at the base camp a half-click away. He had waited a long time for this and adjusted his M-16 as he got into position. On his stomach, he moved the lever of the M-16 section of the gun to semiautomatic, and with eight quick steady shots, dropped all eight men working the cannons. The mortar fire stopped. He smiled. The troops could rest easy. God had saved the day.

Corporal Moon hoisted his weapon and left the knoll, following a little pathway through the trees. He could smell gook cooking now; he could smell gook itself. He felt the adrenalin start to flow as he moved swiftly through the thick foliage to stand at the perimeter of the village.

No gook soldiers here, just old men, women, and kids. Several women huddled around an open fire. The smell of the food they were cooking turned his stomach. He pumped a grenade into the M-16 and launched it into the group. Body limbs flew in the air.

Further into the village, Moon sent another grenade into a hut, but it was only the beginning. Over a hundred rounds later, the village was quiet.

He stood looking at the massacre and smiled, his breath heavy, eyes glazed. God had spoken.

But God wasn't alone. He could hear breathing, whimpers. A soft female sound. One hut remained standing. He moved quietly, and then he was in the hut with the two young girls. The first one screamed and bolted. He let her go, because his eyes were on the older of the two. She sat huddled in the corner, trembling with fear. He stared at her as she became one with another face. It was an older face of a woman with bright red hair and smoldering eyes. He had walked into her bedroom to ask for his allowance, but she wasn't interested in giving it to him or talking to him. She was in bed with a dark-haired man, their sweaty, naked bodies glistening in the afternoon light. She threw a shoe at him and ordered him out, laughing as he ran down the hallway. He wanted to kill her. He wanted her dead!

In the hut, the girl edged toward the doorway, but Moon had her. He held her at arm's length and laughed as he twisted her neck. The girl lay at his feet now, and now she was his.

An hour later, he walked out of the hut, fastening his trousers. Death had found this place, and death's name was Walker Moon.

He pulled his Gerber out of its sheath and looked around. It was time to start a fresh pile of ears for his collection.

CHAPTER 15

Monday, December 14, 1988: 1200 Hrs.

At Stu's request, Grant Coogan arrived at the Palmdale Drive address a little before noon. It wasn't that the county investigator needed help, just that Grant had been with Stu during the Attwater investigation, and he was a friend. A fact that Stu had found suddenly comforting.

All the windows in the house were open, the air heavy with sprays and cigar smoke. Everything that could be done had been done to cover up the stench of rotting flesh. Stu could actually walk into the house without his stomach heaving.

"It's a goddamned zoo out there," Grant said, shaking Stu's hand. He was referring to the gathering of people at the corner, including yelling, demanding reporters and equally exuberant scanner-runners.

"They're gonna have a field day with this one, that's for sure," Stu said, before giving Grant the details of the McVey and Marshton murders.

Grant listened and shook his head. "So you found two more coins?"

Stu nodded. "And two more books that are filled with coded numbers. What the hell does it all mean, Grant?"

Grant shrugged. "Beats the shit out of me. Speaking of shit, you look like a pile of the stuff sitting out in the noonday sun."

Stu managed a smile. "Now I know why I called you out here. I don't think a murder investigation would be complete without your compliments."

In the house, Grant saw the elk's head and whistled. He snapped a picture of the trophy above the fireplace. "For my scrapbook," he grinned. "Anything taken?"

"I don't think so. Nothing forced, either. It looks as though the guy just walked through the front door, did his thing, and walked out."

Grant shrugged. "Point me in the right direction so I can earn my pay."

They walked down the hallway, stopping short of the exercise room. A young county detective smiled at them. "Any sign of the coroner?"

"He just pulled up," Stu replied.

The detective's smile widened. "He's gonna be late for his own funeral, ha, ha. Has an excuse this morning, though. Had a one-eighty-seven out by the lake. Some kid got shot during a fight."

Stu nodded. "Good way to start the week." He looked up as the deputy coroner made his way down the hallway, pushing a portable gurney. Young and flustered, he muttered, "Two goddamned bodies in two goddamned hours. Is this one ready to go?"

"In a few minutes," the detective said.

The kid muttered something and leaned up against the wall to light a cigarette.

Grant came out of the exercise room a few minutes later and gave Stu a satisfied smile. "We might have a break, Stu. Found some talc on the body, near the groin area. If our boy was wearing surgical gloves filled with talc and happened to take them off, we could have a print, maybe more."

"Is it ready to load?" the coroner asked impatiently.

"She's all yours," Grant said, winking at Stu. He slipped Stu a small plastic bag that contained the coin. It was understood that the less said about it, the better.

"I've got to make a couple of calls," Stu said, stuffing the bag into his jacket pocket. "Okay to use the phone in the kitchen?"

Grant nodded. "Meet you out front."

Stu called Lieutenant Stanfield first, who wasn't in a good mood and ended up in a worse mood after Stu told him what he wanted.

"Jesus Christ, Redlam. We haven't got that kind of manpower! And even if we did . . . Shit, you're talking like a man with a paper asshole. What kind of proof do you have that the rest of the women on your list are gonna get snuffed? I'd sure as hell need more than your say-so to go to the captain with something like that. Now, if those women were to come to me with some kind of proof. . . ."

"You're missing the point," Stu said wearily. "We have a cold-blooded killer walking the streets who just took out number three. All three women are on a list, along with four more. Jesus, Roy, they need some protection."

"My hands are tied," the lieutenant said. "Christ, Stu, you've been with Homicide long enough to know how we operate."

"And as long as I've been in Homicide, we've never had a case like this," Stu muttered, hanging up the phone. It was the same old shit. A person had to be dead before anyone bothered to notice.

Frustrated, Stu called Freddy Jenkins at the coroner's office. "You're gonna get a body in a little while," Stu told him. "Name is Jenny Marshton. She connects with Attwater and a couple of bodies up in Auburn. We might have some prints."

Freddy heard him out and chuckled. "They always end up

making one mistake, don't they? Don't worry, Stu. If there are any prints, I'll make sure the lab boys get 'em."

"Thanks, Freddy. I'll be down first thing in the morning."

Stu thought about calling Julie, but changed his mind. He wouldn't know what to say to her.

Grant was waiting for Stu by the Blazer, glaring up at the news choppers buzzing overhead. Stu climbed into his vehicle. "I'm gonna go home, get something to eat, change my clothes, and start knocking on doors. It's time I visited the rest of the women in McVey's little book. I just hope I'm not too late. If I am, you'll be hearing from me."

"If you are, you'd better call me. And if something turns up on film, or in any other way, I'll let you know." He started to walk away, then turned around. "Oh, Stu, I was just wondering. Did you ever call Julie Clark?"

Stu's wide grin was the only answer Grant needed.

Tom Runyo sat at his desk, looking as bored as he felt. All kinds of shit was coming down around him, what with Stu's big case, which seemed to be getting bigger by the minute, and the manhunt for the convenience store killer in full swing. And all he could do was sit at his desk and wait for Jafo's call. Not that the call wasn't important. It was serious stuff, because all the leads that surrounded Neal Jessop's death seemed to be hidden inside Louie's Card Room. But damn, the waiting was killing him!

He thumbed through some old case files, looked up at Taylor's desk, and said, "Shit!" Things were so bad, he had momentarily forgotten that Taylor was in court, testifying in a year-old case just brought to trial. That was the way it was. You busted them, slapped them behind bars, and three years later, the case might get to trial. *If* they didn't walk first.

Lieutenant Stanfield walked up to Runyo's desk and scowled. "Don't you have something to do besides talk to the air and shuffle papers?"

Runyo looked up at Stanfield. "Just waiting for Jafo to get the warrant. He said he'd call sometime this afternoon."

"Jesus, and the taxpayers pay for this shit. You ought to be ashamed of yourself."

Runyo watched the lieutenant walk into his office, but without his normal reaction to Stanfield's lousy attitude. He was a man with problems. Bodies kept popping up like weeds in the spring, it was eleven days until Christmas, the weather was lousy, the office was understaffed and overworked, and his kid was sick with the flu.

Runyo was thinking about Christmas, wondering if he was going to have any time to shop, when the phone rang.

It was Jafo, and he sounded excited. "Got the warrant, Tommy. We move tonight. The pregame plan will be in our office at eight-thirty."

"Eight-thirty," Runyo repeated, hoping that maybe now they could get some answers.

Stu pulled up in front of Gabrielle Messa's house at a little before two. He hadn't taken the time to call first, but that could work in his favor, with the element of surprise. He hoped he was in time, and wouldn't be walking into another crime scene. And if she wasn't home, he hoped she was at work, out shopping, or had taken off for the holiday. She was the first on his list of the remaining four, and he planned to talk to all of them.

He wasn't surprised to see the beautiful house or the classy neighborhood just off American River Drive. It fit the pattern. He walked up to the solid oak door and rang the bell. While he waited, it occurred to him that he could no longer appreciate the beauty that surrounded these women, because it had been overshadowed by a dark cloud, something very evil.

Stu rang the bell again, and finally, a tall, elegant Latin woman opened the door. She was wearing black tights and top, definitely an exercise outfit, and Stu felt his stomach knot.

"Yes?" she said hesitantly.

Stu pulled out his identification. "Detective Redlam, Homicide. I'd like to ask you a few questions."

A slight frown creased her tapered brows. She was openly appraising him. "Have I done something wrong, Detective?" she asked huskily.

Don't fall for it again, Stu told himself. *Be tough. Get to the bottom of this bullshit!* "No, not at all. I just want to ask you a few questions about a couple of your friends."

"Who?"

"Mary Attwater and Leah McVey." He deliberately kept Jenny's name out of it, planning to use it as his bomb-blaster.

"Are they in trouble?" she asked innocently.

Stu cleared his throat. "Can we talk inside?"

"Of course," she said, showing him in. "Would you like a cup of coffee?"

"That would be nice," Stu said, following her into the large country kitchen, watching her hips undulate as she walked. She was sleek, like a cat, and very cool. Unless the lady didn't read the papers or watch TV, there was no way she didn't know about the murders of Attwater and McVey.

He sat down at the polished oak table, accepted the cup of coffee she placed in front of him, and said, "Your friends have been murdered, Miss Messa, and I'm handling the investigation."

Stu watched for a reaction, but there was none. She just looked at him and shook her head. "That's very sad, but what does that have to do with me?"

"Maybe nothing, maybe everything. How well did you know them?"

She sat down across from Stu and lit a cigarette. "Well enough, I suppose."

"Could you be a little more specific?"

"We were friends."

Stu nodded. "And how about Jenny Marshton?"

Something flickered in her dark eyes. "I know Jenny...."

"Well, Jenny was murdered, too. Just found her body this morning, strangled and bloated up like a dead cow in a dry pasture." *That's the way to go, Stu. Go for the jugular.*

Gabrielle Messa's smooth, creamy face turned ashen as she gripped her throat. "H-how terrible!"

"It was pretty awful all right. It was enough to make a hardened cop puke his guts out."

Gabrielle winced. "But I still don't see what it has to do with me."

"We found the names, addresses, and phone numbers of six women in the back of Leah McVey's address book, Miss Messa, so adding McVey to the list, we have seven. Three have been killed, and you're on the list."

Gabrielle put out her cigarette in a glass ashtray. "But surely you must have found other names. . . . I mean, why should you single us out?"

"We found some other phone numbers without names, and some names without numbers, and we'll check those out, but our real concern lies with you, and the remaining three women, whose names and numbers were complete. And the reason is simple. They are the ones who seem to be getting snuffed."

Gabrielle's dark eyes looked huge in her pale face. "And you think I'm going to be next?"

"I think you're one of the next in line." Stu reached into his coat pocket and pulled out the plastic bag containing the coin. "Ever see this before?"

Gabrielle looked at the coin and shrugged. "It's a French coin." She returned the coin to Stu. "As strange as it may seem, I dabble in coins. A lot of coins like that found their way back to the States after Vietnam. The guys brought them back as souvenirs. The French were there before us, you see, and . . ."

She went on, telling him all about it, but he wasn't listening. The lady was another "dabbler," and he groaned inwardly. "So you can find coins like this one anywhere?"

Gabrielle nodded. "We had the same sort of thing after World War Two. Lots of Japanese coins flooded the market. They aren't worth much, except to maybe a collector."

Stu put the coin in his pocket. So they had a killer who had a thing for French coins, who had either picked them up in Nam—or in the States, or anywhere in the world. They also had a killer who had a thing for seven beautiful, very rich women. He realized he hadn't seen the last three, but they would undoubtedly fit the pattern. But what was the real connection? He had the feeling this Latin lovely knew.

He leaned back in his chair. "How long did you know Attwater, McVey, and Marshton?"

Gabrielle refilled their coffee cups, but this time, her hands were shaking. "We . . . we went to school together."

"Here in Sacramento?"

"Back east . . ."

"Back east. Anywhere near Delaware?"

She just looked at him.

"Jenny Marshton told me that Mary Attwater has a mother in Delaware."

"Y-you talked to her, before . . ."

Stu nodded. "She was going to give me some names and phone numbers, but then I was called away on the McVey killing. By the time I got back to her . . ." He let his voice trail off.

Gabrielle stood by the sink. "Did she say anything else?"

"Like what, Miss Messa?"

"Oh, I don't know."

Stu went in for the kill. "Jenny Marshton had a little address book, too, and oddly enough, depending on how you want to look at it, it was filled with sets of numbers, written in sequence. Would you happen to have a little book like that, too?"

"No, I don't," she said quickly.

"Would you mind if I took a look at your address book?"

Gabrielle Messa turned on Stu, eyes snapping fire. "Not without a court order."

The dancing around was over. "Look," Stu said, "We're gonna find out what those numbers mean, with or without your help. And we're gonna find the killer, with or without your help. But in the meantime, I have the feeling you are living on borrowed time, and my hands are tied unless you level with me. Who in hell would want you and all your friends dead?"

Gabrielle lifted her chin. "I don't know, Detective Redlam. What happened to them, well, it was unfortunate, but it really doesn't concern me.

"Now if you'll excuse me, I have a very busy schedule."

Stu stood up, glaring at her. "You don't get it, do you? The killer could be watching your house right now, waiting to make his move. Give me something, anything, that I can take to my captain, and we'll put a man on your door."

"I don't need a man on my door," Gabrielle returned angrily. "Now please leave, so I can get on with my day."

Stu gave up and stalked out. He was upset and angry, feeling all those things that made a cop's life miserable. She had lied to him. He could feel it in his bones, and he wanted to know why.

Stu jumped into the Blazer and headed for North Sacramento, hoping that the next rich bitch on the list would be more cooperative. And this time, he was going in prepared.

CHAPTER

16

Monday, December 14, 1988: 2030 Hrs.

Runyo and Taylor walked into SID at exactly eight-thirty. The room was crowded with detectives in plainclothes, substantiating that the boys were definitely going in with a minimal amount of bullshit.

"Glad you could make it," Jafo said, shaking their hands. He turned to the detectives sitting around the squad room. "This is Tom Runyo and Steve Taylor from Homicide. They have a stake in this, too, and are going in with us."

Runyo and Taylor acknowledged the detectives they knew and took their seats. Runyo reached down and adjusted his ankle holster, which held a small .38 special. A heavyset detective sitting next to him grinned knowingly.

At the front of the room, Jafo walked up to an easel holding a blown-up section of a *Thomas Map Book*. A large red circle pinpointed the location of Louie's Card Room on Alhambra Boulevard. He whistled through his teeth, waited until he had the attention of everyone in the squad room, and said, "You all know we're hitting Louie's tonight. We have the warrants, we know there is a big illegal gambling operation in the basement, and we have the manpower to blow them high and wide and into fuckin' space. We'll be working on an element of surprise here, so things should go in our favor. Any questions so far?"

Heads shook; a few said, "No."

"Okay," Jafo said, setting up several blown-up photographs of the card room as well as the floor plan. "There are only two ways to get into the basement. One is through the back door, the other is through the club and down a flight of stairs." He pointed to the two locations.

"We'll hit front and back simultaneously. That should eliminate the problem of one level warning the other. Like I said, we're talking about total surprise here. Timing means everything.

"The card room does a good business, so it'll probably be crowded. That's fine, the more the merrier. You all have your assignments, but we'll get to that later. Right now, I want to go through the overall plan.

"We're going in with two teams. Front entry and rear entry. I'll be with the guys in the rear. Tommy and Steve, I want you out front." He pointed to the office on the floor plan. "It'll be your job to take care of the cashier's cage, because it's the only way into the office. Hopefully, that's where you'll find Cantrall." He placed a blown-up picture of Louie Cantrall on the easel. "Take a good look at this, because I don't want that fat little fuck slipping through our fingers.

"The front entry team will take charge immediately, handling the bouncer and the bartender first, because rumor has it that they are probably packing." Jafo looked at Runyo and Taylor. "Same goes for you two in the cashier's cage and office. No telling what kind of weaponry you're gonna run into." His eyes moved around the room as he sighed. "I'm gonna tell you right now, I don't plan on losing any of you.

"Okay. Secure the entrance. Don't let anybody leave, but

keep things calm. You have to remember that the customers in the main card room are probably just innocent people, enjoying a game of low ball. Maybe some of them know about the basement operation, and maybe none of them know. We can sort that out later at the station." Jafo grinned. "Expect a certain amount of bullshit. They're not gonna like having their card games disrupted.

"Any questions?"

Runyo raised his hand. "You want us to keep Cantrall in the office?"

Jafo smiled. "Yeah. Keep him there until we've cleaned out the basement, and then I'll join you. What you do with him in the meantime is your business. Just save a piece of him for me.

"Now, you guys going in with me, we're gonna have to work things a little differently. First of all, there's a padlock on the back door. Anderson and his handy bolt cutters will take care of that."

The detective sitting next to Runyo spoke up. "What about alarms?"

"No alarms. The owner probably thought it was an unnecessary expense. Lucky us.

"From there, we'll move swiftly and quietly. We have no idea how many gamblers we'll find in the basement. If we need extra wheels, we'll call for them then. Speaking of wheels, we'll be taking two vans, along with one unmarked vehicle. The front entry team and the vehicle will park near the entrance. I'll be in the other van, and we'll be parking in the alley in back.

"Now, we're gonna use the next few minutes to go over individual assignments and synchronize our watches. Then, we'll roll. Tonight, we're gonna kick ass!"

When the two large vans reached the card room on Alhambra Boulevard, the van carrying Jafo and eight officers pulled off on a side street and headed for the alley. The second van, carrying seven officers including **Runyo** and **Taylor**, pulled up at the curb. The weapons they held ranged from riot shotguns to Runyo's Sig Sauer .45.

Steve held his Glock 9 mm. His jaw tightened and the muscles in his neck began to cord up as adrenalin flowed. He had always thought of it as "putting on his war face," and it was something he hadn't felt in a long time.

At exactly 2130 hours, the officers jumped out of the double doors at the rear of the van and ran into Louie's. Runyo and Taylor headed for the cashier's cage, ignoring the angry patrons and their protests. Quickly, they ordered the two women working the cage to open the door and step out; then they rushed the office door. It was locked, but instead of taking the time to look for the buzzer, Runyo kicked the door in. Louie Cantrall sat behind his desk, his hand on a button.

"Freeze, motherfucker!" Runyo shouted. "Put both hands on the desk!"

Taylor grabbed his portable radio. "Six-two-five, Ivy two-two-two. Our boy just tipped your second half."

"Ten-four, Ivy two-two-two," came the reply. "We're in."

"What the hell is this!" Louie Cantrall exclaimed.

"Shut up," Steve ground out, his face grim and determined. "We're police officers and this is a raid. Consider yourself fucked."

Jafo and his men had entered the underground gambling room just minutes before the radio transmission from Taylor. Caught completely by surprise, the twenty or so gamblers and the handful of employees just stood there, mouths open, listening to Jafo announce, "This is a raid, ladies and gentlemen; you're all under arrest."

The detectives took charge then, while Jafo looked around at the green felt-covered gaming tables and rows of slot machines that lined one entire wall. He whistled through his teeth. "Holy Christ. We've got ourselves a goddamned miniature casino!"

"We hit the fuckin' jackpot," Anderson laughed.

"You can't do this!" a tall woman with stringy blonde hair screamed at him. "If my husband finds out I'm here . . ."

Ignoring her, Jafo walked around the room. He stopped at a blackjack table, smiled at the dealer, and asked, "How do I get to the card room from here?"

The woman pointed toward an elevator in the corner of the room, adding, "Mr. Cantrall isn't going to be happy about this!"

"No shit. Load 'em up, boys. I'll meet you at the station as soon as I take care of some unfinished business upstairs. Adios, amigos. Job well done."

In the card room, Jafo waved down one of his detectives. "Everything under control here?"

"Without a hitch," the detective replied with a grin.

Jafo shook his head, looking at all the disgruntled patrons. "They should be happy they weren't downstairs. About the only thing they're gonna lose is their money and a little time."

He headed for the office and smiled when he saw the door off its hinges. He walked in and the smile widened. Pale and shaken, Louie Cantrall sat behind his desk while Runyo and Taylor emptied drawers and file cabinets.

"You got some kind of a warrant to back up this shit?" Cantrall asked, looking up at Jafo.

Jafo walked around the desk, pulling papers out of his coat pocket. "This is a search warrant, and this is an arrest warrant," he said, smacking the man across the face with the documents. "Consider yourself properly served.

"Did you read him his rights?" he asked Runyo.

Runyo nodded. "Along with some other stuff."

"Was he clean?"

"Depends on what you mean by clean. He wasn't packing, if that's what you're getting at."

Jafo sat down on the edge of the desk. "Well, fat man, because you've got yourself into a shitload of trouble here, and having your rights in mind, you want to talk to us?"

Louie Cantrall squirmed in his chair. "Fuck you and your goddamned questions. I want my lawyer!"

Taylor pulled his gun. "You're gonna want a doctor if you keep this up!"

"Come on, Louie," Jafo coaxed. "We've got you red-handed. I'll bet there's a couple hundred grand floating around in that basement casino of yours. Make it easy on yourself. Talk to us."

Runyo leaned down until he was level with Cantrall. "We need a name, Louie. Who owns this dump? Tell us, and maybe the DA will cut you a deal."

Cantrall looked off in space.

"You'd better start talking," Taylor said, "or we're all going to take a personal interest in seeing you suffer in the joint. Trust me, Louie. They are gonna love your little round ass out at Folsom Prison."

"I want my lawyer," Cantrall repeated.

Runyo slammed his fist on the desk. "Enough of this bullshit! If you don't tell us what we want to know, like now, we're not only going to nail you with this entire operation, you're going up on murder charges!"

Cantrall's pig eyes grew wide. "Murder?"

"You fuckin' betcha. We'll get you on the murder of a Sacramento police officer without blinking an eye."

"I-I don't understand."

"Your illegal gambling operation was directly responsible for a police officer's death, you creep. Now talk!"

Louie Cantrall slumped back in his chair. "I'm not talking without my lawyer."

Runyo looked at Jafo. "Go get some air, Jafo."

Jafo Lloyd nodded and walked out of the room.

Immediately, Taylor was in Cantrall's face. "All right, you fat scum. You are either gonna tell us what we want to know, or you're leaving here in a body bag." He pulled out his 9 mm, cocked the hammer, and nuzzled the barrel against Cantrall's cheek.

Runyo's gun was aimed at his forehead.

Sweat began to run down Louie's face, and he swallowed hard. "Okay, okay!" He swallowed again. "Please put the guns away."

"We're waiting," Taylor said, easing his gun into his holster.

"His name is Jack Smitovich."

"Jack Smitovich."

"Yeah. He—"

"He what, Louie?" Taylor asked.

"You won't believe me."

Runyo laughed. "Does it make a difference?"

Louie sighed. "I've never met the man. I've talked to him on the phone, but . . ."

Runyo opened the door and called to Jafo. "He gave us a name, but Louie claims he's never met the man."

Jafo walked in and closed the door. "The name, Louie?"

"Jack Smitovich. He calls to see how things are going, and that's it."

"Who picks up the money?" Jafo asked.

"Some tall skinny dude comes around every week. I give the receipts to him, less my cut and enough to cover salaries."

"Bookkeeper?" Runyo asked.

"Same dude."

"Ever heard of LSB Inc.?" Jafo asked.

Cantrall shook his head.

"So you don't know where this Jack Smitovich lives?"

"No, but I think it's a local call. Sounds like it, anyway."

Jafo got Louie Cantrall to his feet and slapped on the cuffs. "Not much information," he said glumly to Runyo and Taylor.

Runyo nodded. "But we've got a name, and that's a start."

From his hiding place in the hall closet, through a small crack in the door, Walker Moon could see Gabrielle Messa in the bedroom, changing her clothes. It had been a long wait. He felt cramped and hungry, but it wouldn't be long now.

Earlier, when she had gone out for a few hours, he had

entered through the back door. Her absence had also given him the opportunity to go through her things. And then later, after she had come home, he had listened while she talked softly on the phone and then prepared a meal. He had almost taken her then, but he liked the idea of the closet and the long anticipation.

Now, she was going out again. He watched her take off her clothing in the flickering light from the television set, and slip into a slinky dress. He knew that his wait had been rewarded.

He watched her walk into the bathroom. The time had come to make his move.

Silently, he crept across the hallway and into the bedroom. He heard water running in the sink and moved up to the door. And then he was behind her, his large hand around her mouth, muffling her screams.

In the mirror, Gabrielle could see the monster behind her and immediately drove the three-inch spike heel of her shoe into the arch of his foot. It took him by surprise, and that was long enough for her to catch him in the eye with her elbow. He made a sound and relaxed his grip. This time, she caught him in the throat with the side of her hand, breaking away as he gagged and choked.

He was coming at her again, but she was ready, screaming at him as she plunged the hot curling iron into his face.

He reeled backward, clutching his face, while Gabrielle ran for the door. She was in the bedroom now, on the way to the hallway, when he caught her, tackling her from behind. She squirmed out of his grip and heard the material of her dress rip.

On her back now, Gabrielle caught him in the groin with her foot. She struggled up and raced into the dark living room.

With a roar, Moon followed her, but stopped in the middle of the room. He couldn't see her, but he could hear her breath coming in short, ragged gasps. He smiled and turned, but was met with a flying object that connected with his head.

Down on all fours, Moon shook his head to clear it. But before he could get up, a heavy object smashed across his shoulders and neck. He reached out for her ankle, but she was gone. He could hear her in the kitchen, screaming over the phone. "Please help me! He's trying to kill me!"

Moon got to his feet and made his way to the kitchen.

She was still screaming. "I'm not going to fucking calm down! The bastard is trying to kill me!"

Moon was behind her now, smiling, head bleeding, gun extended.

Gabrielle turned and screamed again. "No, please!"

The 911 emergency operator heard the shot, and then the line went dead.

CHAPTER

17

Monday, December 14, 1988: 2100 Hrs.

After attempting to contact the three remaining women in Leah McVey's little book several times without success, Stu had spent the afternoon at his desk, cleaning up paperwork, but with one eye on the clock. It appeared that all three women worked, but when he had tried to contact Gabrielle Messa to confirm that fact and possibly get their work numbers, he had gotten her answering machine. He hadn't left a message.

Finally, at six o'clock, Stu left for home, where he showered, changed his clothes, ate a frozen dinner, and called Julie. She seemed happy to hear from him, but not so happy when he told her he might have to spend the next couple of nights working. When she asked him if it had anything to do with the case he had been working on, he said that it did, but didn't elaborate. "Well, take care," she said softly, and hung up.

Stu replaced the receiver in its cradle and felt a lump form in his throat. What he really wanted to do was screw the case and spend the next two months in Julie's arms.

After packing a thermos of coffee, packages of sunflower seeds, two bananas, and a hard-boiled egg in a sack, Stu climbed into the Blazer and headed for Rachel Harrison's house, choosing it over the others because it was the closest.

As Stu drove through the winding streets that led to the Arden Estates area of Sacramento, the thought occurred to him that all three women could already be dead, and that that was why they weren't answering their doors or phones. For that reason, he had already made up his mind that he wasn't going to sit around forever. He would give it a reasonable amount of time and then go in, and to hell with police procedure and protocol.

Stu pulled onto Rio Linda Way and drove by the dark house three times before pulling up to the curb. Another rich house, another rich neighborhood, another goddamned day closer to Christmas. Cards had started coming in from his family, who knew nothing of the split with Gail. He made a mental note to call everybody on Christmas Day, and poured a cup of coffee.

Stu was just starting on a sack of sunflower seeds when headlights approached from the rear, stopping behind the Blazer. He watched the man approach, realized he was a security patrol officer, and rolled down his window.

Flashlight on, the security guard looked around inside the vehicle. He then aimed the light in Stu's eyes. "I've got a lot of complaints on you, buddy. State your business."

He was just a kid doing his job, and Stu reached for his badge.

"Keep your hands where I can see them," the guard ordered.

Stu looked at the kid. "I was just reaching for my—"

The Mace hit him in the face before he could finish the sentence. Although he saw it coming and ducked, he was not fast enough to avoid a good shot of the stuff; it was like sticking your head in a bucket of battery acid.

"Son of a bitch!" Stu roared, gagging and choking while he

seriously considered killing the kid. "I'm a cop, you stupid little fuck!"

"Prove it," the guard said, backing away from the vehicle.

Eyes blurred and watering, and still choking, Stu fished in his pocket for his badge and held it up. "Jesus Christ! Get me some water!"

"Oh, shit," the kid said, staring at the badge. "Oh, holy shit! God, I'm sorry...."

Stu rolled out of the car. "I said get me some water!"

The guard ran to his patrol car and lugged back a water jug. "Geez, officer, I didn't know. We've had a lot of robberies in the area, and some cars have been stolen...."

Stu flushed out his eyes with the water, but when he tried to drink some, he choked, spitting it into the gutter. "Keeeerist, that's nasty stuff!"

"It should be pretty fresh," the guard said. "I filled it myself just a couple of hours ago."

Stu groaned. "I'm talking about the Mace, you shithead." Stu leaned against the Blazer. His vision was beginning to clear, but his throat still burned like the devil. He took in deep breaths, deciding right then that every woman should carry a can of the stuff in her purse.

"Is there anything I can do?" the kid was asking.

Stu resisted the urge to tell the kid what he could do and asked, "The lady that lives in that green house. Have you seen her today?"

The kid nodded quickly, like maybe he could make up for his blunder. "I didn't come on until five, but I saw her about an hour ago. She took off in her car."

Stu heaved a sigh of relief.

"Is she in some kind of trouble?" the guard asked.

"You could say that," Stu said, climbing into the Blazer. "Go back to work, kid. No hard feelings."

The kid was still standing there when the car phone rang. "Go back to work," Stu repeated, picking up the phone.

"Redlam here," Stu managed to get out.

"Stu, this is Grant."

"Yeah, Grant, what's up?"

"Christ, Stu, what's the matter with your voice? You sound terrible."

"You wouldn't believe it if I told you."

"Well, you're not gonna believe this, either. We've got another body."

"Where?"

"Over on Joplin, off American River Drive."

Stu suddenly felt ill. "Son of a bitch! Gabrielle Messa, right?"

"Gabrielle Messa. Don't tell me. You talked to her earlier today."

"I told her I thought she was on the killer's list, Grant, but she wasn't about to cooperate. She admitted knowing Attwater, McVey, and Marshton, but that was it."

"Well, this is a fresh one, and things look a bit different. Also, the victim called nine-one-one before she was killed. That's why we got the call. So far, we've managed to keep it quiet."

Eyes watering again, Stu looked at his watch. "I'll be there in ten," he said, and hung up.

The kid was still parked behind him when Stu punched the accelerator, burning rubber as he pulled away from the curb. As soon as he was out of the residential area, he mounted the red ball and flipped on the siren.

On his code three run to Gabrielle Messa's house, something very rotten was growing in his gut. He had talked to the last two victims just before their deaths, and the thought of it wasn't making him a very happy man. Was the killer following him around? The only thing he knew for sure was that now maybe he could get the three remaining women the protection they needed and possibly catch the killer in the process.

Terrance Calhoon was waiting for Stu when he pulled up in front of Gabrielle Messa's house. "Jesus, Stu, what happened to you?" he said, getting a look at Stu's face in the light from the porch.

"An eager security guard Maced me while I was waiting for one of the women on my list."

Terrance tried to stifle a laugh. "Christ, Stu, all in the line of duty, huh? And I suppose the lady never came home?"

"Not while I was there. Where's Grant?"

"Inside taking pictures and doing the usual CSI stuff. He happened to be on patrol tonight when the nine-one-one came in, and I happened to be in the neighborhood. He seemed happy to be in on it. Said he's been working on the case with you. Said that tonight, he gets to wear two different hats.

"Looks like she put up one hell of a battle before he finally got her."

They walked into the living room, and Stu shook his head as he looked around at the overturned furniture, broken vase, and bloody smears all over the beige carpeting.

"We think she hit him with the poker, too," Terrance said, "and then ran to the kitchen where she called nine-one-one. That's where he shot her."

Stu's head snapped up. "He shot her?"

Terrance held up a single 9 mm shell casing in a small plastic bag.

Stu walked into the kitchen and nodded at Grant. Gabrielle Messa sat slumped under the mounted phone, her back against the wall. Blood soaked the front of her torn dress. He looked at her beautiful, vacant face and whispered, "I tried to warn you."

Grant cleared his throat. "It looks as though the struggle started in the bathroom, Stu. Found a hot curling iron with bits of flesh sticking to it on the floor. I think she burned the son of a bitch."

They started down the hallway. Grant pointed to the piece of material on the floor. "That's off her dress. She probably broke away from him in the bathroom and he caught up with her here. She broke away from him again, and he followed her into the living room. She was one spunky lady."

In the bathroom, Stu surveyed the scene but kept his hands in his pockets. "Anybody call the coroner?"

"After I called you." Grant pulled a plastic bag out of his pocket. "Thought you might want this."

Stu looked at the bloody French coin, struggling with the rage he felt. "I'm gonna get this cocksucker," he said, gritting his teeth, "or I'm turning in my badge." He took a deep breath. "You find a book, too?"

"Yep. In a dresser drawer. I'll pack it up after it's been dusted."

"Same coded numbers?"

"Same coded numbers."

"Okay if I use the phone in the bedroom?"

Grant nodded.

Stu wearily sat on the edge of the bed and dialed Lieutenant Stanfield's home number.

Stanfield answered on the fourth ring, barking out, "This sure as hell better be good."

"This is Redlam, Lieutenant. We've got another body. This one almost made it. She called nine-one-one before he snuffed her.

"Now this is the story, short form. There were seven women on my list, and now I have three. As far as I know, the killer has already taken them out, too. If we're lucky, and he hasn't, then we might have a chance to catch him *before* he strikes again.

"I know about the lack of manpower and the goddamned budget, but in case you haven't noticed, we've got a friggin' maniac on the loose."

There was a long pause before the lieutenant said, "You really think we can get him if we set this up?"

"If we can save the last three, it's worth a try."

"Well, I'll see what I can do. Check with me first thing in the morning."

Stu also had a meeting with Freddy Jenkins in the morning. He closed his eyes. "If tomorrow morning isn't too late," he muttered, hanging up the phone.

Experiencing a gut-wrenching kind of frustration, Stu then dialed the remaining telephone numbers on his list, beginning with Rachel Harrison. He let the phone ring twenty times at each location and finally gave up.

In the living room now, Stu walked over to Terrance and asked, "What have you got for me?"

Terrance peeled back a layer of paperwork. "I did the casualty face sheet, the one-eighty-seven form, but when Grant told me this was your case, I stopped."

"I appreciate the help," Stu said, taking the reports from the detective. "What about the nine-one-one operator?"

"His name is David Russo. He's going down in the morning to make a statement."

Stu looked down at Grant, who was on his hands and knees, bringing up samples of blood from the carpeting. "How much longer do you think you'll be?"

"At least another couple of hours." He looked up, studying his friend. "You look like shit, Stu. Why don't you go home and get some sleep, and I'll talk to you in the morning."

Stu didn't want to leave, feeling as though it were a cop-out. But the Macing had taken something out of him, or maybe it was the case. Whatever it was, he felt like shit and nodded his head, mumbling, "Talk to you in the morning."

Stu woke up to the sound of a garbage truck lumbering up the street. It was eight-thirty, and wouldn't you know. On the day when everything seemed to be coming down, he had overslept.

He staggered to the shower, finished dressing fifteen minutes later, and made his way into the kitchen. His head pounded, his throat ached, and his stomach felt as though it was being trampled by twenty thousand elves. He opened the refrigerator and stared at the grungy array of leftovers, feeling his stomach churn. Next came the cupboard, but he was out of coffee. No tea, either, so he reached for the bottle of Johnny Walker Red Label. One mouthful; he gagged on the liquor running down his throat. In anger, he threw the bottle against the refrigerator door, and then stared down at the mess. Jesus

Christ, what is this shit! he wondered, sitting down at the table. It wasn't like him to go off the deep end. He was always the smooth, cool detective in control.

He ran a hand through his hair and knew it was the case that was doing it. The goddamned case was going to turn him into a raving lunatic before it was over.

Come on, Redlam, he told himself, getting to his feet. *Crap like this doesn't solve cases, it hinders them!*

Grabbing his jacket and topcoat, Stu headed for the Blazer. Today, he was going to get some answers!

Stu went straight to the coroner's office, and caught up with Freddy Jenkins sitting at his desk.

Stu looked at the dark circles under Freddy's eyes and shook his head. "Tough night?"

"I was still here when they brought in Gabrielle Messa, so I went ahead with the autopsy. Figured you'd want the report ASAP."

"Jesus, Freddy."

Freddy grinned. "Don't give me any bullshit, Stu. When Grant Coogan called and told me that the Messa woman was a part of this case you're on, well...."

"I owe you one," Stu said, reaching across the table to shake Freddy's hand.

Freddy's grin widened. "A couple of beers should do it.

"Now, first of all, I got a couple of good prints off Marshton." He pulled out a plastic bag containing the print card and handed it to Stu.

Stu looked at the prints. "I'll send it to DOJ today. What about Messa?"

Freddy shook his head. "Bet you all thought she died of the gunshot wound, huh?"

Stu felt a sinking sensation in his stomach. "She didn't?"

"Nope. He shot her okay, but that wasn't the cause of death. She was suffocated. You guys find a plastic bag?"

"No."

"Well, my guess is, he shot her to get her attention, and then went in for the kill. Nice guy."

"Was she sexually assaulted?"

"Not like the others. I found traces of semen around her mouth. Matches all the other semen samples we have. I think Buster Brown didn't have much time. He knew she had called nine-one-one, and about the computer printout, linking all incoming calls directly to the caller."

"Makes sense," Stu said, standing up. "And this time, our boy very nearly got the crap beat out of him. Gabrielle Messa was a hellcat, and literally fought for her life. She was on the phone with nine-one-one when he shot her. The nine-one-one operator heard the shot over the phone."

Jenkins nodded. "The fucker almost got caught this time."

Stu started for the door. "Yeah, but you know, I don't think he cares. I don't think anything bothers this perverted animal." He opened the door. "Thanks for everything, Freddy."

"Yeah," Freddy said. "Let's hope it stops here."

Stu hoped so, too, but he knew better. It would only stop when the maniac was dead.

CHAPTER 18

Tuesday, December 15, 1988: 1000 Hrs.

Word had come down that Neal Jessop's funeral was finally going to be held on Friday afternoon. It had been delayed because of an ill relative who lived out of state, and now that it was official, it only added to the gloom hovering over Homicide and Robbery divisions. It was something that no one was looking forward to.

Steve Taylor sat at his desk waiting for Runyo, wondering how Robert and Cindy were going to hold up. Robert had Dana, but Cindy . . . He shook his head and opened the file on Louie Cantrall. It had been one hell of a good bust, and they could thank Jafo and his detectives for the plan and execution. Damned good department.

He looked at his watch and tapped his foot impatiently. Runyo was down in Records, trying to dig up some information on the man who called himself Jack Smitovich, but Taylor had the feeling it was a wasted effort. If the man had managed to keep his identity from Louie Cantrall, he was a man who knew how to cover his tracks.

Keep positive thoughts, Taylor told himself, and took out a fresh sheet of paper, printing JACK SMITOVICH across the top. He had just underlined the name in red pencil when Runyo walked in, grinning from ear to ear.

"You're not gonna believe it," Runyo said, sitting down across from Taylor. "I didn't find anything on Smitovich in Records, but I found him in the phone book."

"The phone book. You mean like in the *phone book?*"

Runyo nodded. "No home phone or address, but I found him listed as a planning consultant. Has an office over on J Street."

"Jesus, Tom, are you sure it's the same Smitovich?"

Runyo stood up. "There's only one way to find out."

Taylor took the time to write PLANNING CONSULTANT under Smitovich's name and then followed Runyo out the door.

Jack Smitovich's office was on the eighth floor in one of the older office buildings in town. The detectives rode the clanky elevator up. They looked at each other, and Runyo crossed his fingers.

In the reception area, a pretty blonde smiled at them. "May I help you?"

"Detectives Runyo and Taylor to see Jack Smitovich," Runyo said, pulling out his ID.

Her eyes narrowed. "Please have a seat."

They watched her walk through a heavy oak door, and Taylor whistled through his teeth. "Nice ass."

"Cold eyes," Runyo said. "I sure as hell hope this is our man."

A few minutes later, the receptionist returned. "Mr. Smitovich will see you now."

Taylor followed Runyo into the office, where a dumpy, deeply tanned man sat behind a large desk. Pig eyes watched the two detectives intently.

"What can I do for two of Sacramento's finest?" he asked, smiling slightly.

Nice kiss-ass attitude, Runyo thought.

Taylor spoke up. "Mr. Smitovich, do you own a club called Louie's Card Room?"

Smitovich tapped his fingers on the desk and laughed. "Why, yes."

Taylor continued. "And you also do business as JSB, Inc.?"

"I do."

"Are you aware that Louie's Card Room was raided last night?"

The shock on Smitovich's face was genuine. "What!" he exclaimed, jumping up. "Raided for what?"

"Illegal gambling operations."

"B-But that's crazy," Smitovich sputtered. "Louie's is a legitimate low-ball establishment."

"Are you telling us that you have no knowledge of the illegal end of the operation?" Runyo asked.

"That's exactly what I'm saying. I run a very honest and very legitimate investment corporation. My small businesses are for tax purposes only."

"Your shingle says 'Planning Consultant,'" Taylor said.

"I plan investments for people, Detective."

"Including some of your own, and one of them is Louie's Card Room, right?"

Smitovich nodded. "I've just admitted to owning Louie's. I own several small businesses. Is that a crime?"

Runyo looked straight at the fat man. "Well, Mr. Smitovich, the business at Louie's Card Room was anything but small. We're talking about several hundred grand a night."

Smitovich whistled. "I really am shocked. Was Louie there?"

Runyo nodded. "And now he's in jail."

Smitovich clucked his tongue. "That little worm. I never really trusted him." Pig eyes looked at both detectives. "Is this going to implicate me?"

"Not at the moment, but I would suggest you stick around town, in the event we need you for further questioning." Taylor handed him a card. "And if you come up with anything that might help, either you or us, give us a call."

"I'll most certainly do that."

As Runyo and Taylor made their way to the door, Runyo looked back. "By the way, that's a pretty impressive tan you've got there, Mr. Smitovich, considering we haven't had that much sun the last couple of months."

Smitovich's smile was brilliant. "I just got back from a vacation in Florida. You boys really should try it. There is nothing like a week in the sun."

Runyo nodded. "One more thing. We'd like to have your home address and home phone number, just in case we have to contact you after business hours."

Jack Smitovich was no longer smiling. "My receptionist can take care of that for you. Good day, gentlemen."

On the way down in the elevator, Taylor spoke first. "Do you buy that shit?"

"Not on your life. He's as guilty as Louie, but proving it might be a problem."

"I think we should run him through Records in Florida," Taylor suggested. "Never can tell what we might turn up."

Stu was at his desk by ten-thirty, and after reading the statement from the 911 emergency operator, he carried it into Lieutenant Stanfield's office and tossed it on his desk. "Read that, sir, and you can't help but feel the urgency surrounding this case. That lady was pleading for her life."

Stanfield read it over and nodded. "I know the urgency, Redlam. The captain says you can have a man on each house. He's working on it now. Just get him the addresses." Stanfield sighed. "He's getting a ration of bullshit, too. Everybody wants answers. Do we have a serial killer on our hands, or a hit man?"

Stu ran a hand through his hair. "His MO tells me he's a

raving, psychopathic killer, but the list of names tells me he's getting paid to do a job."

"Unless he's a psychopathic killer with his own list of names," Stanfield said thoughtfully. "Do you have a theory on why this madman might be snuffing out a group of rich women, who are all friends to boot?"

"No, but I might get some answers this morning. Hopefully, this time, I'll find one of them at home."

It was noon before Stu pulled up in front of Rachel Harrison's house. A new Ford LTD was parked in the circular driveway, and Stu found himself grinning. It was about time things started going his way.

He wasted no time getting to the door and ringing the bell.

A solid blond surfer-type opened the door with a scowl on his pretty-boy face. "Yeah?"

Stu held a file in one hand and his badge in the other. "I'm Detective Redlam. Is Rachel Harrison at home?"

"What the hell is this all about?"

"I'll tell Rachel when I see her."

The surfer stared at Stu for a long moment and then slammed the door.

This wasn't going well, and Stu was beginning to lose his patience. He was about to bang the door down when it was opened again, but this time by a petite brunette with big blue eyes. She wore faded blue jeans and a pink, fuzzy sweater.

"Yes?" she said softly.

Pretty voice, thought Stu. Pretty girl. It wasn't a surprise. "Rachel Harrison?"

"Yes?"

"I'm Detective Stu Redlam, and it's important that I talk to you."

She blinked her bright blue eyes. "Well, I guess so, if it's important...."

"It's important."

"Then come in."

Stu followed her into the house filled with Christmas. Red garlands, green garlands, holly, poinsettias, and the pièce de résistance, a giant decorated tree at one end of the living room.

"What's this all about?" she asked, motioning toward a chair.

Stu continued to stand. "I think it would be best if we talked in private, Miss Harrison," he said, looking at the surfer, who was standing near the sliding glass doors to the patio.

"Whatever you want to say to Rachel, you can say to me," the surfer said, taking a few steps toward Stu.

Stu glowered at the kid. "I don't think you understand. I don't want you here."

"Hey, listen, cop, I don't give a fuck who you are. Nobody talks to me that way!"

"I just did." Stu was tired of playing nice guy. He had talked to Jenny Marshton and Gabrielle Messa like a big huggy-bear uncle who was only interested in their safety and well-being. Well, now they were dead, and this one was going to listen. He turned to Rachel Harrison. "I suggest you get rid of your boyfriend, now."

The surfer was across the room in three strides, poking Stu in the chest with a finger. "I think it's time you went on your way, cop."

Before the surfer could react, Stu had him in a thumb lock, quickly turned it into a wrist lock, and had him on tiptoes. "Now we're going out the front door, fuckhead," Stu growled out. "Just like in the movies."

By the time they had reached the door, the kid had stopped protesting. "Open the door," Stu ordered.

The kid opened the door. Stu took him down the driveway and to the street. "Now take a ride, Clyde. And don't come back until after I'm gone."

In the house again, Stu found Rachel where he had left her. Her face, dark and angry.

Stu picked up the folder and sat down. "Now we can get to business," he said, smiling at her.

Rachel sat down in a chair and clasped her hands. "Please

get to the point. I'm not accustomed to having rude men in my house."

"I'll get to the point. Do the names Mary Attwater, Leah McVey, Jenny Marshton, and Gabrielle Messa mean anything to you?"

Her blue eyes became very dark, and her chin trembled slightly. "Yes . . . Yes, I know them."

"So if you've read the papers or watched any TV, you also know they're all dead."

The pain was beginning to show through. "I-I read something about it, but what do their deaths have to do with me?"

Stu opened the file. "Well, I'll tell you, little lady. I talked to Gabrielle Messa yesterday, much the way I'm now talking to you, but she wouldn't listen to me when I told her she was in danger. Now she's dead." He waited a few moments before going on. "We either have a madman who wants your little group of friends dead, or we have somebody who hired a madman to take you all out. Either way, you and your two friends who are still alive are in big shit trouble.

"I got the feeling yesterday that Miss Messa knew more than she was telling me. I get that same feeling now."

Tears filled Rachel's eyes. "I-I don't know what you're talking about, Detective Redlam."

"Do you own an address book?" he asked.

"Yes . . . No . . ."

"Well, which is it?"

Beginning to tremble now, Rachel asked, "Why do you ask?"

"Because each of your deceased friends had a little book full of coded numbers. But in Leah McVey's book, I found a list of seven names, addresses, and phone numbers, too, so let's just take it from the top. Mary Attwater, Leah McVey, Jenny Marshton, Gabrielle Messa, Rachel Harrison, Irene Pennington, and Phoebe Baker. Four are dead, three to go."

Rachel sat rocking on the couch. "I-I have a gun, and that's why Jed is here. He used to be a bouncer and can handle himself."

Stu's heart gave a little lurch. "So, you admit you're worried that you might be next. Why? Who would want to do something like this to you?"

Tears rolled down her cheeks. "I can't tell you."

"Goddammit, woman! I don't give a rat's ass what happened in the past. I just want to catch the person or persons responsible and try to keep the rest of you alive!"

She shook her head.

"Okay, if that's the way you want it." He took a stack of photographs out of the file and walked over to the coffee table. "Come here, Rachel. I think you should see these."

Rachel slowly walked over and sat on the sofa.

Stu threw down the first picture and said, "That's your friend, Mary Attwater, during her autopsy. And this one is Leah McVey. See those bruises on her neck? He strangled her and then he raped her, just like all of them.

"How about this one, Rachel. Recognize her?"

Rachel was weeping openly.

"That's Jenny Marshton. Sorry she's so bloated, but the killer left the heat lamp turned on high, and we didn't find her for a couple of days.

"How about this one? Believe it or not, Gabrielle tried to fight him off, but she still ended up like all the others."

Almost hysterical now, Rachel sobbed, "We did it to avenge Suzy!"

Stu ran a hand through his hair. "What did you do, and who is Suzy?"

Rachel curled up on the sofa. "Suzy was my best friend in New York."

Stu pulled out a note pad and sat down beside her. "Okay, Rachel. Start from the beginning, and take it slow."

Rachel wiped at her tears and murmured, "Five years ago, I was in New York City with those girls you just showed me."

"What about Irene and Phoebe?"

Rachel nodded. "And Holly Anderson."

"Christ," Stu said, sucking in his breath. "You mean there are eight of you?"

"No. Holly lives in Oregon. We never hear from her."

"Okay. Five years ago, you were in New York City."

"We . . . We worked as escorts."

"Hookers," Stu said, writing.

"Call girls. Very expensive call girls. A grand a trick."

Stu whistled through his teeth.

"Our manager was a guy named Jack Smitovich."

Stu smiled. "So that's what you called him, huh? Your manager?"

"When you're talking about that much money, yes. There were nine of us. We were good friends, and did everything together."

"The ninth one was Suzy?"

Tears fell again, and Stu was really beginning to feel sorry for her. "You want a drink of water or something?" he asked.

She shook her head. "I just want to get this over with. One day, Jack came to us and told us he had a business opportunity for one of us. He said a big-time porn producer was looking for a model for one of his productions, and whoever decided to take the job could make some serious bucks."

"And Suzy took the job."

"We drew straws."

"And what happened?"

"She left one day to start filming and never came back. Jack tried to sweep it under the rug, so to speak, but we knew something had happened to her. Bunny . . . I mean Jenny, had some street connections, and we found out the truth. Jack had made this outrageous deal with the director, and Suzy was killed in a snuff film. We never let Jack know we were on to him or that we knew what had happened to Suzy."

Stu was on his third page of notes. "So what did you do to him?"

"Well, at first we decided to kill him. But with all the big-time friends he had, we thought that would be too risky. So Marty . . . Gabrielle, the one with all the brains, decided to get close to Jack's accountant. In no time, she had him wrapped around her finger and agreeing to help us clean Jack out."

Stu shook his head. "Embezzlement?"

"Sort of. Actually, it was more like a straight rip-off. It only took a couple of months. Sanchez worked it so Jack wouldn't find out until it was too late. Lots of fancy paperwork. He was a real pro."

"How much?"

Rachel started to answer, but stopped.

"Look, I don't really care about this," Stu assured her. "I don't care about your criminal fling in New York City. How much?"

"A little over three million."

"Jesus! I guess maybe that would do it."

"We left New York and changed our names."

"Why Sacramento? I mean, this isn't exactly New York City."

"Buffy . . . Irene's mother lives here."

"Well, the money certainly explains your lifestyles. What about this Smitovich character? Do you think he's here in Sacramento? Do you think he could've found out your new names?"

"God, I don't know. If it's him, he's not actually doing it. He'd hire somebody."

"What about Sanchez?"

"He went to Florida with his share."

"Did he get an even share?"

Rachel smiled slightly. "No, we took him, too. But he ended up with enough."

"What about the address books?"

Rachel sighed. "We each had one. It's in code and tells everything that happened. All the names, too. I figured if Smitovich ever caught up with us and tried to get us for embezzlement, we'd get him for accessory to murder."

Stu stuck his note pad in the folder. "What about coins, Rachel? This Smitovich collect coins?"

Rachel shook her head. "Gabrielle dabbled in coins...."

Stu grimaced. "I know about that.

"Okay. Well, I can tell you now," he went on, "we've got a man on all three houses. Here, and at Irene's and Phoebe's. But I don't think it's going to be enough. I think the three of you should be placed in a safe house, at least until after we've caught the killer."

"Phoebe went away for the holidays, but I talked to Irene this morning. She was leaving with her boyfriend for Tahoe for a few days. We've been so damned scared. I thought about leaving, too, but now..."

"But now we'll get you to a safe house, and you can rest easy. Pack a few things, and I'll make a few calls and arrange for transportation."

"What about Jed?" Rachel asked. "Can I leave him a note?"

"Is he important to you?"

"No."

"Then just lock the door when you leave, and let him worry about figuring it out."

CHAPTER

19

Tuesday, December 15, 1988: 2200 Hrs.

Walker Moon left his motel room and started up Stockton Boulevard, squinting his eyes against the constant cold drizzle. A few hookers, braving the weather, walked the strip or sat at bus stops, shivering and miserable.

Moon thought the cold air felt good, especially on the part of his face that was still tender from the burn he had received the night before.

He was sorry he couldn't kill a person twice, because he would have surely killed the bitch again for what she had done to him. He hadn't controlled the scene, she had. And he had been forced to use his gun, ruining her beautiful body. She was no longer the perfect image in his mind.

But the next one would be different, he reminded himself, stuffing his big hands into the pockets of his military jacket, feeling the smoothness of the coins that rested there. It would be fast and furious, giving her no time to resist.

Moon's stomach grumbled; he hadn't taken the time to eat. There was a convenience store two blocks up, but not even the thought of all those gooey fruit pies could make him go anywhere near the place. He had decided after the last incident, which had almost cost him his life, that the fruit pies were going to have to wait. Later, after he had finished the last job for Smitty and had blown this town, he would go on a mission that would award him all the fruit pies he could eat. And he wouldn't be taking prisoners.

Moon was so intent on his thoughts, he didn't see the passing patrol car making a U-turn in the middle of the block.

The cruiser drove by the large man in the military jacket again, and Officer Willy Brown felt his heart thump in his chest. "Jesus Christ, it's gotta be him!" He grabbed the microphone. "Charles twenty-one."

A female voice answered, "Charles twenty-one."

"I think I've got our two-eleven/one-eighty-seven suspect from the convenience store robbery at the corner of Twenty-third Avenue and Stockton Boulevard."

"Charles twenty-one, ten-four. Units to start for Twenty-third Avenue and Stockton Boulevard."

Three voices came over the radio almost simultaneously, all advising that they would head in that direction.

Willy pulled the cruiser into the fast lane and then used the suicide lane to make a second U-turn. He was now heading toward the suspect, who was walking north, the same direction he was traveling.

The southbound lanes were void of traffic, and Willy decided to make his move. "Charles twenty-one, I'm going to attempt contact."

"Charles twenty-one, ten-four. All units, keep the air clear."

"I'm right behind you, Willy."

Willy looked into the rearview mirror as another patrol car driven by Ray Haley moved into position.

A string of cars were now approaching in the southbound lanes, headlights reflecting off the wet street.

Walker Moon heard an engine accelerate and chanced a

glance over his shoulder. The patrol cars were right behind him.

Move!

He broke into a sprint across Stockton Boulevard as several cars skidded to avoid hitting him.

"Suspect is running east across Stockton Boulevard," Willy spoke into the microphone.

"Charles twenty-one, ten-four."

Willy flipped the control switch for the lights and siren and punched the accelerator again, sending the patrol car sliding sideways across the street, narrowly missing several oncoming cars.

Walker Moon was running north again, but on the opposite side of the street. Willy kept the patrol car at pace, traveling against the traffic, lights and siren on.

Moon saw the alley just ahead and pinpointed it as his destination. He reached it as the patrol car accelerated again, the large engine sounding like a locomotive.

Now!

The patrol car skidded, up and over the curb, slamming into the corner of a liquor store, coming to rest across the entrance to the alley.

"Charles twenty-one, I've nine-oh-oned. Suspect is now eastbound up an alley at Twenty-second and Stockton."

"Charles twenty-one, ten-four. Charles twenty-five, Charles twenty-six, Baker twenty, Alpha twenty-seven. I also need you to start."

With the driver's door crushed against the building, Willy scrambled over the seat, exiting the passenger side. Ray had pulled his unit in close and had taken off on foot. Willy brought up the rear.

At the end of the alley, Walker Moon saw the fence and quickly made his decision. He could hear the leather and wood batons clack as the cops gained on him.

Expecting bullets to come whizzing by at any moment, Moon hit the fence and was over, dropping into a small garbage-filled field. Up ahead, he could see an old apartment building and began to run, once again pinpointing it as his destination.

Ray hit the fence first, followed by Willy.

Once over, Willy grabbed for his radio. Out of breath, he gasped, "Suspect is still eastbound, crossing a field behind Caldwell Liquors. He's headed for the old Green Point Apartments."

"Charles twenty-one, ten-four. Do you have a description on the suspect?"

Willy keyed the microphone. "White, dark hair. Six three or four. Wearing blue jeans and a green military jacket."

"Charles twenty-one, ten-four."

Willy and Ray raced across the field. In the long straightaway, they were slowly gaining ground. The suspect had reached the rear of the complex now, stopped momentarily by a chain-link fence. And then he was over it, running into the rear of the complex.

Willy keyed the microphone. "Charles twenty-one. Suspect has entered the Green Point Apartment complex."

The radio squawked to life. "Charles twenty-six, I'm at the front of the apartment complex, Willy."

Willy choked out, "He's northeast of your location, Lester."

"Charles twenty-five. I'm here, too."

Dispatch acknowledged with a "Main copy."

As Willy hit the fence, he felt as though his ears and chest were about to explode. He gasped for breath as he watched the suspect turn north and then east.

On the microphone again, Willy shouted, "He's running right at you, Brian!"

Walker Moon had lost sight of the two persistent cops for the moment and used the time to catch his breath. Neighborhood dogs barked, and loud music could be heard from inside several apartments. But the complex courtyard was dark enough, allowing him to slip along through the shadows.

Suddenly alert, Moon stopped, sniffing the wind. Danger lurked ahead, but he was ready.

The quick blow to the back of Moon's head stunned him and momentarily put him on his knees. His arms were being driven back; he could hear the sound of cuffs....

Lester and Brian struggled with the suspect as Lester tried to cuff him, but a sudden rage brought the man up swinging, sending Lester through the air, where he landed on a small patch of juniper bushes.

Brian reached for him again, but Moon's fist caught him in the face.

Walker Moon was free, and moving.

Lester yelled out, "Suspect is running east on Centennial!"

Willy and Ray cut through to Centennial, but it was Ray who reached Moon first. "Freeze, motherfucker!" he bellowed.

Moon turned and charged the officer, oblivious to the gun in his hand. His big arms hoisted the heavyset officer as though he were a sack of feathers and slammed him against a parked vehicle, smashing out a window.

But Willy was there, his Sig Sauer pushed into the big man's back. "One fucking move," Willy said calmly, "and you're dead."

Walker Moon was not a stupid man. He knew certain death. He could smell it in the air. He slowly raised his arms, a smile starting at the corners of his mouth.

Out of the corner of his eye, Willy saw a black-and-white pulling up and two officers approaching. In that split second, Moon turned, knocking the gun out of Willy's hand with such force it sent Willy spinning.

The two officers were joined by two officers from another unit, and the four of them finally wrestled Moon to the ground.

Willy watched as flashlights and batons connected with the man's head, a thick chopping sound as wood and metal connected with skull bone. He felt his stomach turn.

After several seconds, the suspect was cuffed and face down on the sidewalk.

Willy took a deep breath and keyed the radio. "Charles twenty-one, resume. Suspect in custody."

The smooth voice said, "Ten-four, units resume. Charles twenty-one, do you still need units to respond?"

Willy had no idea what had happened to Lester and Brian, but Ray looked in pretty bad shape, still down beside the car. "Roll two units and a couple code two ambulances. Also, we'll need CSI."

"Charles twenty-one, ten four."

The four officers were now standing over the suspect, shaking their heads. "Strong bastard," one of them said.

"Guess we missed the fun," Lester said, limping up. He held his right arm and grimaced with every move.

Brian followed, his face covered with blood. "I think the son of a bitch broke my nose . . . Shithouse mouse, what happened to Ray?"

"Godzilla tossed him against the car like so many potato skins," Willy muttered, wanting to go to his unconscious friend but knowing better than to touch him.

Within minutes, Centennial Way looked like the scene of a massive freeway accident with squad cars, the fire department, the rescue squad, ambulances, and unmarked vehicles, all with bright, rotating lights.

Grant Coogan pulled up and sighed. The neighborhood was going to get an eyeful tonight.

He climbed out of his vehicle and walked over to Willy. "What the hell happened here?" he asked.

Willy looked around, dazed. "Beats me. All I know, it started over on Stockton Boulevard and ended up here with all hell breaking loose. The guy has the strength of eight men. Took four to bring him down."

"You think he's the two-eleven/one-eighty-seven?"

"Take a look for yourself. He matches the wanted bulletin, that's for sure."

Grant looked over his shoulder. Two officers were now stuffing the giant into the back of Brian's patrol car. "What's his name?"

"Walker Moon."

"You serious?"

Willy handed Grant the Florida driver's license. "Take a look."

Grant looked at it and chuckled. "Well, at least it's original."

The patrol sergeant walked up to them then, shaking his head. "This is one hell of an incident, ain't it?"

Grant nodded, adjusting his camera.

"You gonna take some pictures of my injured officers?"

"Sure thing," he said, heading toward Lester and Brian, who were already grinning at the camera.

"Any word on Ray?" Willy asked the sergeant.

"They think it's a concussion. He was lucky he didn't get a broken neck."

"Where are the suspect's personal belongings?" the sergeant asked.

"In my patrol car," Brian said, walking up. "All bagged and ready for Booking."

"Then I suggest you get him out of here before the media arrive, and believe me, it's only gonna be a matter of minutes before they do."

Brian smiled at the camera while Grant snapped off a couple of shots, and then got into his patrol car, keeping one eye on the very still, very quiet suspect in the back seat. The paramedics had patched the man up some, but his face and head were still a bloody mess. Tough! Brian's nose felt like shit. If the creep wasn't such a big ox, he'd take him to the station by way of the nearest alley and beat the holy snot out of him.

Brian strapped on his shoulder harness and started the vehicle, all the time feeling the man's strange eyes watching him.

Grant was finishing up some shots of the black officer and the ambulance attendants were getting ready to transport when the media arrived. It amused Grant because they were actually a little late. Most of the excitement was over.

Not wanting to be a part of it or answer questions, Grant walked up the street several hundred feet and leaned against a patrol car where two officers were talking about the bust. He had seen the officers around, but he didn't know them.

"Don't mean to be bothering you, here," he said, "but I'm trying to dodge the news crews."

The officers nodded, continuing their conversation.

Grant listened, forming his own opinions, and then one of the officers said, "Did you get a load of that handful of foreign coins they found in the guy's pocket?"

"Sure did," the other officer replied. "At first I thought they were Spanish, but then I realized they were French. Now why in hell would he be carrying around a pocketful of French coins? He sure as hell couldn't use 'em to buy anything with."

Grant shut his eyes, his heart up in his throat. "Don't mean to be eavesdropping," he said numbly, "but what about the coins?"

"Nothing much. Just like I said. Why would he be carrying around all those French coins?"

Grant hurried to his patrol car and grabbed the microphone. "Charles twenty-five, eight-two-six."

"Go ahead, eight-two-six."

"Try channel two."

"Ten-four."

On channel two now, Grant said, "Brian, are you there?"

"Yeah, Grant."

"Is what I'm hearing true? Did you guys find a bunch of French coins in Moon's pocket?"

"Yeah, why?"

"I think you might have a one-eighty-seven suspect."

Brian chuckled. "I've already got a one-eighty-seven suspect. The two-eleven/one-eighty-seven, remember?"

"No, this is a different one-eighty-seven, Brian."

Brian looked in the mirror again and met the cold stare of Walker Moon.

"Trust me on this," Grant was going on. "When you get to Booking, contact Stu Redlam in Homicide. He'll want to be there."

Brian was still looking in the mirror. "Sure, all right, I'll..."

Moon's face began to shake, turn red. His eyes began to puff out, and then a piercing scream filled the patrol car as the handcuffs snapped. Moon's hands were free.

"Jesus Christ!" Brian cried. "My subject has just broken the cuffs. Roll me some cover. I'm heading west on Florin Road, near the mall!"

Brian slammed on the brakes just as Walker Moon kicked the back door of the patrol car off its hinges. He rolled out, landing in the middle of Florin Road.

Car brakes screeched in all directions as Brian grabbed his shotgun and jumped out of the car. Moon was on his side, eyes closed. Brian was racking a round into the shotgun when Moon reached out and grabbed his ankle, pulling Brian off his feet. In a split second, Moon had the gun, had turned it around, and used it like a baseball bat, exploding the stock against Brian's head.

Cars stopped, horns honked, and people yelled and screamed. Moon straightened his body, glared at them, and bolted across the street into a car dealership.

Grant had relayed Brian's frantic message and had taken off immediately, arriving at the scene just as several county patrol cars pulled up.

A citizen kneeling beside Brian looked up at Grant helplessly. Grant looked down at the wounded officer and felt his stomach knot. The top of his head had been crushed.

"Somebody already called an ambulance," the civilian said, standing up. "And I think you guys should know, he went that way."

The man was pointing toward the Toyota dealership on the south side of Florin Road.

Grant ran to his vehicle. "Eight-two-six, resume. Officer down. Ambulance is already en route. Break." He looked off toward the dealership. "Suspect fled south across Florin Road, near Toyota dealer."

"Eight-two-six. Ten-four. Units to check the area."

The ambulance arrived within minutes, but it was too late. Brian Young was already dead. Grant watched the attendants place the young officer in the vehicle and felt tears in his eyes. He knew now that Stu had walked into something incredibly evil, and he had the feeling this wasn't the end of the killings. Death had a name, and it was Walker Moon.

CHAPTER

20

Wednesday, December 16, 1988: 0035 Hrs.

Julie lay on the deep pile carpeting in front of the fireplace, her head on a stack of pillows. She wore only a pair of pink bikini underpants, which complemented the glow of her skin. Stu sat beside her, naked but for a pair of socks. He traced patterns on her breasts with a finger, reveling in what they had just shared and in the warmth from the fire.

He had come to her straight from work, with a need so overpowering he had taken her in his arms the minute she opened the door. No words had been spoken. She had clung to him, feeling his desperation. And they had made love, stopping eventually to eat hot dogs and potato chips, and then they had made love again.

Now Julie watched him with a sweet smile on her face. "Do you feel better?" she asked.

He leaned over and kissed her. "A lot better. I needed to

see your pretty face. I needed to touch you, and make love to you, and try and forget all that stuff out there."

He was pointing toward the front door, and Julie nodded knowingly. "You can talk about it if you want."

"And ruin our evening? No way."

"Are you hungry?" she asked. "We had those hot dogs nearly four hours ago."

"I'm starved," he said with a wink.

She laughed, getting to her feet, putting out her hands to him. "How does a mushroom omelet sound?"

Stu got up and took her hands. "Sounds great, if you add some cheese."

"Lots of cheese," she said softly. It was so good to see him smile.

The omelet was in the pan when Stu's pager went off. With a groan, he hurried into the living room, searching for it under the pile of clothing. He found it near the bottom and looked at the digital readout. It was the number for Homicide.

Glumly, Stu walked back to the kitchen. "Gotta call the office," he said, unable to look at Julie. He couldn't believe the rotten timing.

He dialed the number and waited.

Grant answered on the second ring.

"What the hell are you doing at Homicide at this hour of the night?" Stu asked, hoping there was no cause for the wariness he felt.

"We got your boy tonight, Stu."

"Oh, Christ! Where? When?"

"Don't get your nuts in an uproar. We had him, but he got away. He Nazi-stomped several patrolmen and killed Brian Young." Grant paused for a moment. "I thought you'd want to know. Everything is in one big clusterfuck."

Stu looked at Julie, who was watching him intently. "I'll be right down."

He hung up the phone and sighed. "They had the guy tonight, but he got away."

Julie's concern was genuine. "I'm sorry."

"I'm the one who's sorry, and not only because he got away. I was looking forward to that omelet and . . ."

She went to him and put her arms around him. "Don't be sorry. Don't ever be sorry. The man I met last week is a cop. I wouldn't want you any other way."

Stu gave her a hug and a kiss. "Where have you been all my life, Julie Clark?"

She looked up into his eyes. "Waiting for somebody like you. Call me?"

Stu nodded, and went to get dressed.

For a change, the main lobby of the police station was quiet, almost eerie at one-thirty in the morning, with only a skeleton crew working and not much happening on the streets. Stu took the elevator up to Homicide, where Lieutenant Stanfield, Grant Coogan, and two detectives he recognized from Robbery were waiting for him.

Stanfield paced the floor; he didn't look up or miss a step as he said, "It's about time, Redlam. Hope we didn't disturb you."

The lieutenant didn't like being called away from home in the middle of the night either. He wanted everyone to share his misery.

Grant sat on the edge of a vacant desk, swinging a leg. He looked pale and drawn. Without a word, he handed Stu one of the coins.

Stu stared at it. "Where did you get it?" he asked finally.

"In the suspect's pocket, along with these." Grant handed Stu the small bag of coins. "An alert patrolman spotted him on Stockton Boulevard, recognized him as the suspect wanted in the convenience store robberies and killings, and the pursuit was on. He is one strong son of a bitch and ended up breaking the cuffs, kicking out the back door of the patrol car, and killing Brian Young with the butt of his own shotgun, right in the middle of Florin Road.

"I put it all together when I found out about the coins. Your one-eighty-seven suspect and the two-eleven/one-eighty-seven convenience store suspect seem to be one in the same."

"Jesus Christ!" Stu said, taking a deep breath.

Lieutenant Stanfield stopped pacing. "This is Mike Clegg and Dalton Casteel with Robbery, Stu. They've been working on the convenience store case with Robert Hollinger."

"The detective involved in the Neal Jessop shooting?" Stu asked, shaking hands with Mike and Dalton.

Mike nodded. "Robert should be here any minute."

"So it looks as though we've been working on the same case," Dalton said, handing Stu a file. "Maybe you'd better look at this."

Stu sat down at his desk and read the file. The dates corresponded, and each convenience store was only a short distance away from the murdered women's houses. And then there were the coins. He looked up at Dalton. "Did your suspect leave one of these at the scene when he took out the clerk and those two kids?"

"Grant just filled us in, Stu, and told us about the coins, but we didn't find any at the scene. I have the feeling the bastard saved those coins for special occasions, like when he snuffed the women."

Mike added, "What about the time? How does that compare?"

"It tells us he killed the women first and then hit the convenience stores," Stu said, thinking about the section in the robbery reports that mentioned black camouflage make-up. He looked at Grant. "Any black make-up on the curling iron we found at the Messa house?"

Grant nodded.

"So we can assume he was wearing the camouflage shit while he was murdering and raping the women."

"We can assume that," the lieutenant said, looking up as Robert walked through the door.

Robert looked disheveled and glum, but managed a smile as he shook hands with the detectives.

"Do we have a name?" Stu asked while the lieutenant gave Robert a brief rundown on what had happened.

"Walker Moon," Grant said.

"ID?"

"Florida driver's license."

"Personal belongings?"

Lieutenant Stanfield spoke up. "Just the stuff over there on the desk. One Browning Hi-Power 9 mm, his wallet, two hundred-dollar bills, the coins, and two keys. One key looks like a locker key of some kind, the other, a motel key. He was first sighted on Stockton Boulevard, so we can assume the motel is in that vicinity. Find it, search it, and shake down the area. Somebody must have seen this goddamned giant. He knows we have the key, so I don't think he'll go back to his room, and that's gonna make things tougher.

"Then hit the bus depot and airport. Anyplace that might have lockers.

"Questions?"

The detectives shook their heads silently.

"Okay. Anybody have any objections to working all night?"

Again heads shook.

"Good! I talked to the chief earlier, and he wants Homicide and Robbery to join forces. Officially. Specifically, the four of you. He agrees that we've got one sick asshole on the loose, who we all know has already killed eight people. Let's keep him from making it nine."

Stu searched through the Robbery file. "I don't see a report for a convenience store robbery after the night of December eleventh, when he took out those two kids and the clerk."

"Because that was the last robbery," Dalton said, "but then that was also the night Patrolman Jarwoski took a shot at him. Maybe he realized the heat was really on and decided to lay low. Who knows what goes on in the mind of a sicko like that."

"But the killings didn't stop with the two kids and the clerk," Stu said, looking down at the grinning face on the wanted bulletin. "Sometime Monday night, he killed Gabrielle Messa, and it wasn't pretty. Now we've got a cop with his brains bashed out all over Florin Road.

"I've got three names left on the hit list. One of them, Rachel Harrison, is in a safe house in El Dorado Hills. The other two are out of town. Let's get this bastard before they come home and become two more statistics."

Stu glanced at Grant's forlorn expression and understood how he felt. Though he had been in on the case from the beginning, for now his job was over. Stu managed a smile. "I'll keep in touch, Grant, and if we find the motel or Moon, you'll be one of the first to know. That's a promise."

Grant nodded and watched the detectives walk out of the room.

The motels all looked alike, and Stu's stomach was beginning to cramp up with nausea as he walked into the office of the Red Lantern, the fourth on the list of six sleazy motels in the area. The detectives had agreed that they wouldn't split up, but would take turns going into the offices. It was Stu's turn, and this sorry establishment was without a doubt the worst of the lot. It was a real armpit, used by local hookers and hypes. If they had come to bust the joint, they would probably end up with several pounds of crank and narcotics, felony arrests, and drunken bums. The place wasn't fit for rats.

Stu rang the buzzer and waited until a sleepy-eyed woman came through a door behind the counter. Stu guessed her age to be around fifty, but she looked a lot older, with dark, puffy circles under her eyes and wild, red hair.

"Whatdayawant?" she grumbled, running the words together.

"I'm a police officer," Stu said, holding up his badge. "Is this one of your keys?"

She squinted at the key and nodded. "So what?"

"So call the room and see what you get."

"Jesus, cop, do ya realize what time it is?"

Stu was quickly losing his patience. "I wear a watch. Just make the call."

"What if somebody answers?"

"Then hang up and tell me. Do the same if nobody answers."

The woman punched in 105 and waited, yawning and scratching. She finally hung up and shrugged. "Nobody there, I guess."

"Thank you," Stu said, walking out of the office.

"Pay dirt," Stu said to the waiting detectives.

Room 105 was on the ground floor, in the rear, near a cement staircase. No light could be seen through the drapes at the window, but that didn't mean that the suspect wasn't there. He might have refused the manager's call deliberately.

Guns drawn, the detectives rushed the door, with Stu making contact first, splintering it off its hinges. The motel room was dark and empty.

With the lights on, Stu headed for the bathroom and then stood there, staring down at the sink splatterd with dried blood and the 9 mm silver-tipped slug sitting by the soap dish.

"Jarwoski got him," Stu called out. "Looks like he cut the slug out with a knife."

"Or he used his fingers," Mike said, looking in the sink.

Dalton chuckled. "Or maybe he used his teeth. I'm impressed."

"Found another gun," Robert announced, using a white T-shirt to lift it out of a dresser drawer. "This one is a Colt .45 auto."

Stu ran his hands through his hair. "The question is, is there a third gun, and does he have it? Grant's report said he headed south from Florin Road after he escaped, but he could've doubled back. Could've gotten another key from the manager."

"Did she say anything about seeing him?" Robert asked, still poking around in the dresser.

"No, and I could probably break both arms and legs, and she still wouldn't talk. These people are like that. They protect their own."

Dalton whistled through his teeth. "Would you look at this! More coins, and a shitload of cash." He was going through an old tattered suitcase he had found stuffed under the bed.

"How much?" Stu asked, finding it difficult to look at the coins.

"Maybe forty grand."

"The fuck was paid to kill those women, Stu," Robert said quietly. "And this proves it." He handed Stu a fat file he had found in the bottom dresser drawer. It was all there. All the necessary information, along with large glossy photos of all four women. Gabrielle Messa's picture was on top.

Stu sorted them out on the bed while the detectives looked on. "He had their addresses, places of employment, banks, and every physical description possible, including their dress sizes. This is one hell of a professional hit list, compadres, and I put my money on Smitovich. He has the motive."

"What's a Smitovich?" Robert asked.

Stu explained, and Robert whistled. "I'd say that's a pretty good motive. You think he's sitting in New York, pulling the strings?"

"Or he's here in Sacramento. I found one Smitovich in the telephone book listed as a planning consultant with an office on J Street. I'll check him out tomorrow, but I doubt that he's our man. First of all, I don't think he would advertise like that, and he probably hasn't been in town long enough to be listed in the phone book."

"The new phone books just came out," Mike reminded him. "And then, and it's just a thought, maybe he's been here the whole time, just waiting to make his move."

"Or waiting to find the right hit man," Robert said, looking at the photo of Gabrielle Messa. "She was beautiful."

"They all were," Stu said, picking up the phone. He dialed nine for an outside line, and then the number for Homicide. When Stanfield answered, Stu said, "We found the motel room, a Colt forty-five, more coins, about forty grand in big bills, and a hit file, Lieutenant. Found the sink full of dried blood and Jarwoski's slug. We think he cut it out with a knife. Is Grant still around?"

"He's here."

"Send him over to print the room, and send over a unit to stake out the motel in case Moon decides to come back. We're going to shake down the neighborhood and then start looking for lockers that this key might fit. We'll try the bus depot first."

While Stu gave the lieutenant the address of the motel, the detectives began packing out the evidence.

A few minutes later, Dalton popped a lemon drop in his mouth and suggested, "Why don't you and Robert head for the bus depot? We'll wait for the unit and advise, and then hit the street." He grinned. "We don't mind. Might even see somebody we know."

Stu looked at Robert. "Okay with you?"

Robert nodded, already heading for the Blazer.

Dalton watched Stu pull out onto the boulevard and put up his collar. It was drizzling again, and cold. He was sure he saw a snowflake; maybe they'd have a white Christmas after all.

When the patrol car pulled up and the officer had been briefed, the two detectives hit the 'Stroll', a large section of Stockton Boulevard frequented by hookers, street people, drunks, pimps, hypes, drug dealers, and assorted other crazies. It was also a part of town that never slept.

"You take the blonde and I'll take the brunette," Dalton said, nodding toward two hookers, standing under the eaves of a building.

Dalton headed for the blonde, but before he could clear his badge from its case, she was snapping, "Whatcha want, cop?"

Dalton had decided a long time ago that these ladies of the night could smell a cop at three hundred paces. "I'm looking for a man who is staying at the Red Lantern Motel. He's about—"

"You're talking to the wrong girl. I don't work that place."

"Then who does?" Sensing her reluctance, he said, "Right now, I don't care what you're doing or who you're doing it to. I'm just trying to find a guy."

The blonde pointed down the street. "Go talk to Toy. She's on the next corner."

"These fuckin' people wouldn't admit to seeing a nuclear blast if they saw it level the block," Mike said, pumping his short legs to keep up with Dalton.

Dalton said, "We might have something up ahead."

"I still think we're pissing in the wind," Mike grumbled.

On the corner, three girls stood in the light rain. One black, two blondes, one tall, one short, their hair matted from the rain. Anything for a trick, Dalton thought, walking up to the black hooker. "Are you Toy?"

"I'm Toy," the tall, leggy blonde said.

"I'd like to ask you a couple of questions."

She smiled up at him. "Well, you might be a cop, but you're awful cute."

Dalton found himself blushing. "Yeah, well, will you talk to me for a minute?"

Mike was looking extremely bored.

"Sure. What's it worth?"

Dalton looked at Mike. "Have you got a twenty?"

Mike reached into his front pants pocket and pulled out a crumpled twenty. "You owe me, Skippy," he said, handing it to Toy.

Toy stepped back a few feet and lowered her voice. "What do you wanna know?"

"We're looking for a man who is staying at the Red Lantern up the street. He's a very sick, very dangerous man, Toy, and it's important that we find him."

"So what's he look like?"

"About six four, maybe two-forty. He wears a green military jacket."

"And does he have weird gray eyes?"

Dalton look at Mike. "Yeah, weird gray eyes."

"I've seen him around."

"Have you seen him tonight?"

Toy shook her head. "Not tonight."

"Then you wouldn't have any idea where he might be?"

"Sorry." She smiled up at Dalton. "You know, you have the cutest dimples."

Mike thought, oh, brother!

Dalton blushed again. "I'm going to give you my card and my pager number. If you see him again, call me. Will you do that for me?"

"I'd do anything for those smiling eyes." She took the card.

"Thanks," he said, and turned around. Mike was already heading down the street.

Stu pulled off the freeway onto J Street. The downtown section of Sacramento at three o'clock in the morning was virtually empty of cars and pedestrians. They had discussed the case on the drive from Stockton Boulevard, and Stu was impressed by Robert's intelligence and attitude.

Stu knew about the young detective's previous shootings, and if nothing else, they had proved his ability to keep moving on after a crisis. Stu hoped he could handle this one. Coming back after losing a partner was no easy feat.

Stu hadn't brought up the shooting, and he wasn't going to. Robert Hollinger had enough crosses to bear and demons to face.

Stu parked the Blazer in a red zone in front of the bus depot and placed a plaque in the front window that read, CITY OF SACRAMENTO POLICE DEPARTMENT. It was placed there to keep a bored patrolman from writing a useless parking ticket.

The detectives walked into the quiet depot, nearly empty now but for a few street people using benches as beds. Stu felt a twinge of pity for them, aware of how miserable it must be for them in the dead of winter. His own shoulder was talking to him, telling him that it was getting colder. A lot colder.

He dug the locker key out of his pants pocket. "Two seventeen, and keep your fingers crossed," he said to Robert. They were in the section of lockers with lower numbers, and kept walking.

They found a locker numbered 217 to the right of the coffee shop. Stu inserted the key, gave it a turn, and the door popped open. "Bingo!" he said, giving Robert a grin.

Stu pulled out a manila folder and a standard-size business envelope. He handed the envelope to Robert, knowing what he would find in the folder before he opened it up. He stared down at the glossy print of Rachel Harrison. The pertinent information had been attached to the back.

Stu looked at Robert. "Rachel Harrison, the lady stashed in El Dorado Hills. What have you got?"

"I'd say we've got somewhere around ten grand here," Robert said, thumbing through the cash.

"This is the drop point, Robert, and somebody sure as hell is making the drops."

Robert sighed. "Back to Smitovich."

"Yeah. But it all means shit unless we find him."

"We'd better get a stake-out on the depot."

Stu nodded. "First thing in the morning. Moon is hiding out, doesn't have the key anyway, and I don't think Smitovich, or whoever in hell is responsible, will show until he can blend in with a crowd."

"Let's go back to the office. I'm going to run a records check on Moon in Florida. That should be interesting."

Stu looked at his watch as they walked back to the Blazer. It was three-thirty. No doubt about it; it was going to be a long night.

CHAPTER 21

Wednesday, December 16th, 1988: 0345 Hrs.

Dalton and Mike were watching an old rerun on TV in the squad room when Stu and Robert pushed through the doors.

Dalton swung his feet off the desk. "Looks like you had more luck than we did."

Stu handed Dalton the manila folder and envelope stuffed with money. "We found the locker at the bus depot, and the girl in the glossy is Rachel Harrison."

Dalton looked down at Rachel's smiling face. "Well, at least this one is safe. Must be a recent drop, or Moon would have it."

"And this must be the payoff," Mike said, thumbing through the currency in the envelope. "If Moon gets this much for each hit, we're talking about some serious bucks."

"We're also talking about somebody out there who has to have a pretty serious motive to dish out this kind of cash," Robert said.

"Smitovich," Mike muttered, and everybody nodded.

Stu sat down at his desk. "We'll have the hit file, along with this one, dusted for latents, and we'll put somebody on the bus depot in case our man makes another drop. When he sees the empty locker, he'll assume Moon has the folder, and it'll be business as usual."

"Unless he connects with Moon in the meantime," Robert said thoughtfully. "Then he'll know we're on to him and that we have the file on Rachel Harrison."

"It's a chance we'll have to take," Stu said, looking around the squad room. "Did the lieutenant go home?"

"Yeah," Mike said. "Just to check on his wife, who is now down with the flu, and then to get his kid ready for school."

Stu shook his head. "Jesus, this is a shitty job, and getting shittier by the minute. What about you guys? I assume you bombed out on your friendly neighborhood stroll?"

Mike chuckled. "You might say that, though Dalton found a new girlfriend."

Dalton scowled at Mike. "I found a hooker who recognized Moon from the description I gave her. Said she's seen him around, but not recently."

"Are you sure she was actually identifying Moon?" Stu asked.

"Yeah. She mentioned his 'weird gray eyes.'"

Stu took a deep breath, sorting through the files and papers on his desk. He pushed the mess to one side, uncovering a large manila envelope. It was from Rich Morton at the Department of Justice and contained Mary Attwater's fat little book and a stack of papers that had been stapled together.

Stu scanned the papers quickly and grunted with satisfaction. "Morton at DOJ decoded the Attwater book, and it's just like Rachel Harrison said. It's a blow-by-blow account of how they got the money from Jack Smitovich, and tells the sad story of their friend, Suzy. Lists names and dates, the whole enchilada. I can see why the girls wanted to keep the books around as insurance."

While the detectives in the office went over the report, Stu closed his eyes. He had reached a point beyond tired, the point when the body finally begins to protest.

Stu felt a hand on his arm and opened his eyes. Robert stood above him, handing out a cup of coffee.

"How long was I asleep?"

"Just a little over an hour."

Stu took the coffee and looked around. "Where's Dalton and Mike?"

"Crashed in the lounge."

Stu looked at his watch. It was almost five. He stood up, stretched, and rubbed his eyes. "Christ, I need more than coffee."

"Take a look outside," Robert said. "Maybe it'll make you feel better."

Stu walked to the window and gazed out at winter white in the early morning. "God, would you look at that!"

"It's been snowing for the last half-hour," Robert said. "I don't think it'll stick, but it's kinda nice. For once, the weather people knew what they were talking about."

Stu watched the gentle flakes for a long moment and thought about Julie, wondering if he might be falling in love with her. Did she like snow? Or did she prefer the dry, hot days of summer? Did she like dogs and cats, and picnics at the lake?

He finally went back to his desk. Though the snow was nice and made him feel a little better, there was work to be done; they had a killer to catch. He corrected himself. They had two killers to catch. Smitovich, or whoever was responsible for hiring Moon, was just as guilty.

Stu pulled out Walker Moon's driver's license and dialed Records.

A sleepy female voice answered, "Records."

"This is Redlam in Homicide. I need ten-twenty-eights and

twenty-nines on one subject, last name, Moon, M-Mary, o, o, n-Nora. First name, Walker, middle, Tristan. DOB four-twelve-fifty."

The voice repeated the vitals, then said, "Stand by." Stu was put on hold.

He looked up at Robert, who was stacking his lip with *Skoal* chewing tobacco. Stu made a motion with his hand.

"You chew?" Robert asked, tossing the can at Stu.

"Not for years, but right now, it sounds damned good. Before this case is solved, I might start smoking, too, and beating my cat." Stu pulled out a small pinch of tobacco, placing it between his cheek and gum, then pulled out his wastepaper basket, spitting the loose grains and quick-forming liquid into the can. He hadn't forgotten how it worked.

The voice on the phone said, "Hello?"

"Yeah," Stu answered.

"Twenty-eights and twenty-nines are negative. I show Moon living in Florida. I'll need a reference number before I can access the Florida record."

Stu thought for a second. "I don't have the reference number, so forget it. I'll call Florida myself. Thanks." He looked at Robert. "No wants or warrants."

Robert shrugged. "Now what?"

"I'm calling the DOJ office in Miami." Stu looked through his Interstate Department phone book, found the number, and dialed. After several rings, a recorder kicked on, reciting the office hours and the number to call in case of an emergency.

With a three-hour time difference, it was eight o'clock in Miami. "Lazy bastards don't open until nine," Stu grumbled. He looked at Robert and sighed. "So we've got an hour. I could sure go for a good cup of coffee and a stack of pancakes. Shall we hit Denny's?"

"Sure. What about Dalton and Mike?"

"Let them sleep. They've put in a long day."

* * *

It was six straight up when Stu and Robert returned to the office, rosy-cheeked from the cold and brushing snow off their jackets. The break had done a lot for their spirits, and they both smiled at Dalton, who was sitting behind Stu's desk, going over the case file.

"Mike still asleep?" Robert asked.

"Last time I saw him, he was in the john. Can you believe this shit?" he said, referring to the weather. "Commute traffic should be a lot of fun this morning."

Stu smiled. "Why don't you find Mike and get something to eat. An hour from now, you might not have time."

Dalton nodded and headed for the door.

Behind his desk, Stu dialed the Miami DOJ number again. This time, a woman answered.

"This is Detective Redlam, Sacramento California Police Department. Would you connect me with Records?"

The voice said, "And your name again?"

"Detective Stu Redlam."

"Hold please." Stu could hear the buzzing of the long distance connection.

Finally, a soft voice said, "Detective Redlam? This is Shelly Jacobs, records officer. How can I help you?"

"I'm investigating a series of murders, and a possible suspect has a Florida driver's license. I want you to check on wants, warrants, and priors."

"And the name?"

"Last name Moon. First, Walker. Middle Tristan. DOB four-twelve-fifty." He gave her Moon's driver's license number.

"This won't take long," she said. "Please hold."

Stu listened to the sound of computer keys, and then, "Here you go, Detective Redlam. Walker Tristan Moon. Six-four, two hundred and forty-six pounds. Brown hair, gray eyes."

"That's him." Stu pulled out a blank piece of paper. "Go ahead."

"He shows no warrants, but I do have a fingerprint number, eight-eight seven-six-six-eight. Last arrest was in February, nineteen eighty-eight, on suspicion of murder. Released same month."

Stu was writing it all down. "Does it give any information about military involvement?"

"Yes. All arrest reports state that kind of information."

"When?"

"Late sixties."

"Vietnam?"

"I would assume so."

"Does it show anything about stateside orders or anything?"

"No . . . Wait a minute. I just ran into a classified section."

"Under orders from the Army?"

"I think so. This is really strange. I've never seen anything like this before. Sorry, but that's it."

"Well, thanks. You've been a big help."

"He was in Nam?" Robert asked after Stu had hung up.

Stu nodded. "That could be why he's got all those French coins. But after Nam, the file was sealed, labeled 'classified.'"

"So how do you break through that?"

"I have no idea," Stu said, getting up to get a drink from the water cooler. He then walked to the window. The snow had let up.

Robert saw the pensive expression on the detective's face, and understood. He also realized he really liked Stu Redlam. He was a good cop, and working with him was a pleasure. He also liked working in Homicide.

"I'll make a fresh pot of coffee," Robert said.

"Sounds good," Stu said. "Meanwhile, I just might have an ace in the hole after all." He flipped through his Rolodex and took down the local FBI number.

Robert walked back to the desk and looked down at the slip of paper. "The FBI?"

Stu explained. "I have a friend who works for the Bureau, and who used to work Army Criminal Investigation. Maybe he can help." He pulled up another number, wrote it down, and added "Smitovich." "And I'll call the Smitovich I found listed on J Street, too. Maybe this will be our lucky day."

At eight o'clock, Tom Runyo and Steve Taylor walked into Homicide, fresh from a full-night sleep and bitching about the weather. They looked at the four detectives hunkered around Stu's desk and shook their heads.

"What the hell is this?" Runyo asked. "Are we slumming now, bringing in cheap help from Robbery?" Runyo laughed, slapping Dalton on the back. He shook Robert's hand. "Glad to have you back, Robert."

"It's good to be back," Robert said, smiling.

"It seems we've been working on the same case and didn't know it," Stu said to Runyo and Taylor. "It's been one hell of a night."

"Then you've been here all night?" Runyo asked, sitting down at his desk.

"In and out and around," Stu said. "I'll fill you in after I make this call." He dialed the number for the FBI, was told that Agent Baskin hadn't come in yet, and hung up, muttering, "Shit, doesn't anybody work before nine?"

Taylor, in the middle of his own conversation with his partner, asked Runyo, "Did anything come in from Florida on Smitovich?"

Runyo shook his head. "For two cents, I'd go over to his office and drag him out in a back alley."

The office suddenly became very quiet, as all eyes turned toward Runyo and Taylor.

"What?" Taylor said, looking at the detectives' stunned faces. "Hey, if somebody farted, it wasn't me."

"Did you just say 'Smitovich'?" Stu asked, feeling his legs grow weak.

"Yeah, why?"

"Jack Smitovich?"

Runyo nodded, very much aware that something serious was happening.

"And he's in town?"

Now Taylor nodded. "We just talked to him yesterday."

Stu could feel the relief spread through his body.

"Jesus H. Christ, now that's what I call a break!" Dalton whooped.

"Would somebody care to tell us what the hell is happening here?" Runyo asked.

Stu began to pace between the window and his desk. "He's one of our suspects, and it's one hell of a long story."

Runyo looked at Taylor. "No shit. Well, we think we've got him in connection with Neal Jessop's death...." Runyo stopped and looked at Robert, grimacing at the sight of his face. "Sorry."

"It's okay," Robert said, taking a deep breath.

Taylor got up. "Let's take a walk, Robert."

Without a word, Robert followed Taylor out of the office.

Runyo shook his head. "Christ, what a mess. Neal was way over his head in gambling debts, bled dry in a place called Louie's Card Room. Smitovich owns the establishment, along with a lot of other small businesses around town, and professes to be a legitimate businessman. Claims he didn't know a thing about the illegal end of it and put the blame on his manager, a little fuck by the name of Louie Cantrall."

"What does Cantrall say?"

"Not much. I think he's more afraid of what Smitovich might do to him than of what we are for sure going to do to him. But we're working on it."

"Do you have any idea how long Smitovich has been in town?"

"We've been working with SDI on this, and Jafo's records show him, or his dummy company, taking over a couple of months ago.

"This is just a wild guess, but I'd say he used to live in Florida. Has a hell of a tan, though he says he just got back from a vacation."

The adrenalin was beginning to flow through Stu now, all weariness gone.

He was on the phone with Agent Baskin when Robert and Taylor returned to the office. The detectives waited quietly while Stu listened and made notes.

Stu hung up and looked at Robert. "You okay?"

"I'm okay, but we've gotta nail this fuck, Stu."

"We'll get him, and we'll get Moon. You can count on it. Now, this is what we've got.

"Baskin at the Bureau knows a captain in Records at the Presidio. He's giving him a call right now. If Moon was in the military, classified or not, he'll break into the files as a personal favor."

"Which only proves it pays to pick your friends," Mike said then. "Shit, it's really beginning to come together."

Stu gave Runyo and Taylor a quick rundown on the Smitovich connection to Walker Moon while they waited for the call, and then repeated it when Stanfield arrived.

"Well, we'd better get some answers damned soon," the lieutenant muttered, chomping on an unlit cigar. "The turkey vultures are hovering around every corner. One caught me on the way in, demanding that I tell him what we're doing to catch the crazed killers roaming our streets. If they find out one man is responsible for all of it, our asses are gonna be grass."

Stu was thinking, tapping his fingers on the desk. "Okay, I think this is the way it should go down. Runyo and Taylor know what Smitovich looks like, and Dalton and Mike are pretty familiar with Moon. Runyo and Dalton stake out the bus depot. We could go over to his office and bring him in, but I want to catch him at the locker.

"In the event he doesn't make a drop today, Taylor and Mike can stake out his business and house. Do we have a home address?"

Runyo nodded.

"So just follow the scum and see where it leads. Meanwhile, Robert and I will wait here for the call. If the captain at the

Presidio has anything for us, we'll make a quick trip to San Francisco."

After the detectives had gone, Stu gave Robert a wan smile. "Now we wait."

The call came in at a little after nine. Stu picked up the phone, acknowledged the call, and held his breath.

"I'd like to talk to Detective Redlam," the deep voice said.

Stu exhaled. "This is Stu Redlam."

"Detective Redlam, this is Captain Douglas, Army CID. I was told by a mutual friend that you need access to a certain classified file."

Stu's heart pounded. "Yes, if it's possible."

"We do have proper channels that might be able to help. Of course it would take time...."

"We don't have the time, Captain. This man has killed eight people, including a police officer. It's a desperate situation."

"I understand. Give me his name."

"Walker Tristan Moon. DOB, four-twelve-fifty."

"If you'll hang on, I'll check."

Stu looked at Robert with hope in his eyes.

After what seemed like endless hours, though it was only a few minutes, the captain came on the line. "Detective Redlam?"

"Yes."

"We have your man. I was told you'd pick up the file?"

"That's correct. My partner and I should be there before noon."

"That will be fine."

Stu hung up and smiled at Robert. "Now, we move!"

CHAPTER

22

Wednesday, December 16, 1988: 1000 Hrs.

Jack Smitovich pushed through the doors and walked into the crowded bus depot, wondering what had happened to sunny California. His shoes squished from all the slush on the streets, and not even his topcoat could keep out the cold. It didn't matter that the snow had turned to rain. The forecasters predicted more snow tonight, and with the temperatures hovering in the twenties, the streets would become solid sheets of ice.

He made his way to the locker, concentrating on white sandy beaches and bikini-clad beauties.

The locker was empty, and Smitovich sighed with relief. He hadn't heard from Moon in days, and he had deliberately stopped reading newspapers and watching the news on television, because he didn't want to know what the fuck was up to. It was a scary thought knowing the maniac was walking the streets. That was one reason why he had given Moon part of the bonus in advance. Ten grand a pop strained the budget, but with only three to go, he could handle it. He'd hoped with the extra money up front, Moon might settle down and forget about all that robbery shit. And maybe he was spitting in the wind, too. Maybe Moon didn't care about the money.

Smitovich stuffed the folder and envelope in the locker and closed the door. It was almost over. One thing he knew for sure: if and when his private dick located the eighth hooker, he was going to hire somebody else to take her out.

He started for the door, experiencing a sudden chill, and it wasn't because he was cold. He stopped, quickly glanced around, and hurried off.

From his vantage point near the terminal entrance to the buses, Walker Moon watched Smitovich's every move with cold, gray eyes. It would be so easy to walk over and snap the fool's neck.

Moon hadn't called him in the last few days because he hadn't wanted another lecture on what he should or shouldn't be doing with his spare time. Nor did he want the fat shit to know the cops had his locker key and his motel key. A silent rage had been building because of it, fueled by the fact that the cops had his belongings, too, and had put an unmarked unit on the motel.

He wore sunglasses, a black stocking hat, and a dark blue parka. It wasn't the best disguise in the world, but it had worked, thanks to a street bum he'd left naked in an alley. He was out walking the streets, and nobody had looked at him twice.

His big hand went to his pocket, searching for his coins, and then he remembered, feeling the rage within him build. The cops had his coins....

His mother had his coins—mostly dimes and pennies—and called him a thief because he had taken them out of her purse. She held him against the wall, shoving the coins down his throat, one at a time. He choked and gagged, but finally swallowed them.

The next day, after he had passed them, she made him scoop

the turds out of the toilet and find the coins with his fingers. She had then locked him in the backyard shed with the filth on his hands, where he had stayed for five days, existing only on bread and water. When she had finally yanked him out, she screamed at him that if he ever took anything out of her purse again, she would lock him in the shed for a year. And he believed her....

Moon felt the blood vessels in his head expand, his eyes puff up behind the dark glasses. Through the doors to the street, he watched two men stop Smitovich on the sidewalk. Cops. What the hell had the fat fuck done to stir up the cops? A tall, red-headed cop had Smitovich by the arm, prodding him away from the door.

Moon walked up to the locker, grabbed the handle, and ripped the metal door off its hinges, while the people around him gasped in shock.

He took out the file and smiled. He was in control again. This one would be good, a message to the cops: don't fuck with Walker Moon. Smitovich would get his message later.

Out on the street, unaware of the uproar inside or of the man who had run out the terminal doors and around the waiting buses to a side street, Runyo had Smitovich up against the wall. "Got any guns, knives, or hand grenades?" he said, patting him down.

Smitovich was shaking. "I-I don't understand. What the hell is this all about?"

Runyo smiled at him, showing lots of teeth. "Well, Smitty, you're under arrest for conspiracy to commit murder. What do you have to say about that?"

"I'd say you're crazy. I thought you were crazy that day you were in my office, trying to implicate me in that illegal gambling operation. Is that what this is about? If so, what the hell does murder have to do with it?" He was trying to act tough, but his insides felt like mush.

Runyo located the locker key in a front pocket, outlined between slacks and body. "Remove the key," Runyo ordered.

"What key?"

"*That* key," Runyo said, giving him a poke on the spot.

"You know, there are laws protecting decent law-abiding citizens," Smitovich protested.

"And there are laws protecting decent law-abiding citizens from slimeballs like you," Dalton returned. "You were asked to remove the key."

Smitovich removed his gloves and pulled out the key.

"You right-handed?" Runyo asked.

Smitovich nodded.

Runyo slapped one handcuff on Smitovich's left wrist and snapped the other onto Dalton's right wrist. "Now, we're going inside. Keep the key where I can see it. One stupid move, and you're history."

A large group of people had gathered around the lockers, talking among themselves and to a security guard. The metal door to locker 217 lay on the floor.

"What the shit happened?" Runyo demanded.

The security guard shook his head. "Apparently some big dude just walked up to the locker and pulled the door off its hinges. Hell's bells, can you imagine somebody being that strong?"

Runyo looked at Smitovich. "Was there a file in the locker?"

Smitovich refused to answer, but his mind raced. *Why in hell hadn't the maniac used his key?*

Runyo looked at the mangled locker and then at Dalton before he said, "Mr. Jack Smitovich, you have the right to remain silent. If you give up that right, anything you say can and will be used against you in a court of law."

Stu and Robert sat in leather chairs in front of a large mahogany desk.

Captain Douglas sat across from them and said, "Before you read this, I might suggest that you also contact Dr. Alvin Market, the psychiatrist on the Walker Moon case while he was a patient in the Florida State Hospital. I know Dr. Market personally, and he's a good man. It's possible he might be able to give you some details that aren't in the file.

"Feel free to use my office and my phone. If you need me for anything, I'll be in the office next door."

Stu thanked the captain and turned to the file.

The cover page listed personal data.

> WALKER TRISTAN MOON   D.O.B. 4-12-50
>
> S.S.# 171-00-9107   PLACE OF BIRTH: ATLANTA, GEORGIA
>
> HT. 6' 4"   WT. 230   EYES: GRAY   HAIR: BROWN
>
> ENLISTMENT DATE: 8-23-67
> BASIC TRAINING: FT. LEWIS, WASHINGTON.
>
> PLACED WITH 377TH INFANTRY DIVISION, 11-4-67, SAIGON.
> HONORABLE DISCHARGE: NONE.
>
> SECTION 8, SEE ATTACHED PAGES.

Stu flipped to the next page and continued to read:

> THE UNITED STATES ARMY, SAIGON: COLONEL PRESTON HATCHER FILED CHARGES OF NUMEROUS UNAUTHORIZED KILLINGS OF VIETNAMESE REGULARS. COLONEL HATCHER SIGNED WARRANT FOR THE ARREST OF CORPORAL WALKER TRISTAN MOON, 12-12-68.
>
> CORPORAL MOON ARRESTED ON 12-20-68. ESCAPED ENROUTE TO THE CITY OF SAIGON. RECAPTURED 12-28-68. NEW CHARGES FILED FOR TREASON AND UNAUTHORIZED KILLINGS OF VIETNAMESE REGULARS.
>
> COURT MARTIAL DATE: 1-15-69.
>
> ON 5-22-69, CORPORAL WALKER MOON WAS

> FOUND NOT GUILTY BY REASON OF INSANITY FOR THE CRIMES BROUGHT AGAINST HIM.
>
> COLONEL JOHN FOREST COMMITTED CORPORAL MOON TO THE FLORIDA STATE HOSPITAL, AND ON 6-5-69, HE WAS PLACED IN THE NAMED MENTAL FACILITY, (BOCA RATON).
>
> PSYCHIATRIC TREATMENT CONDUCTED BY DR. ALVIN MARKET. (SEE ATTACHED NOTES BY DR. MARKET.)

Stu flipped through the pages until he found the doctor's notes. He looked up at Robert and read aloud:

> SUBJECT: WALKER TRISTAN MOON.
>
> TESTS FOR MULTIPLE PERSONALITIES OR SCHIZOPHRENIA CAME BACK NEGATIVE. IT IS MY OPINION THAT WALKER MOON BELIEVES HE IS A COMBINATION OF GOD AND THE DEVIL, AND AFTER EXTENSIVE TESTING, IT IS ALSO MY OPINION THAT THE PATIENT IS SUFFERING FROM PSYCHOPATHIC PSYCHOSIS AND IS DANGEROUS.
>
> SHOCK TREATMENTS AND THERAPY FAILED TO PRODUCE RESULTS. CERTAIN DRUGS HELPED, BUT ONLY TO CONTROL HIM.
>
> IT IS MY PROFESSIONAL OPINION THAT WALKER TRISTAN MOON WILL NEVER BE WELL ENOUGH TO REENTER SOCIETY.

Back in the bulk of the file now, Stu read:

> ON 6-10-72, WALKER TRISTAN MOON ESCAPED FROM THE FLORIDA STATE HOSPITAL, KILLING A NURSE AND TWO ORDERLIES. SEE INVESTIGATORS' FILE.

> ON 6-10-72, I, SPECIAL AGENT TANG, AND SPECIAL AGENT MOOREHOUSE, WITH THE CRIMINAL INVESTIGATION DETACHMENT, FORT GORDON, GEORGIA, WERE DISPATCHED TO BOCA RATON TO SEARCH FOR AND CAPTURE ESCAPED MENTAL PATIENT, WALKER TRISTAN MOON.

Stu closed his tired eyes and handed the file to Robert. "Take over, Rob. What we have here is a pile of shit. We already know he's crazy."

Robert read along for a few minutes and closed the file. "I think this was a wasted trip, Stu. The CID agents almost had him a couple of times, but Moon managed to slip through their fingers. Sound familiar?

"After two years, they closed the case and handed it over to the FBI, apparently never to be reopened again."

Stu sighed. "I'll give Dr. Market a call in Florida, and then we're going home. At least there, we have a half-ass chance of getting our hands on him."

Stu got the number for the Florida State Hospital from information. It took five minutes of waiting and transferred calls, but the doctor was finally on the line.

"This is Detective Stu Redlam, with the Sacramento California Police Department, Doctor Market. I'm in Captain Douglas's office at the Presidio, and it was his suggestion I call you."

"Yes, Detective. How can I help you?" the doctor replied.

"Back in the late sixties and early seventies, you treated a man named Walker Tristan Moon for what you believed was psychopathic psychosis. Do you remember the patient?"

There was a long silence, and then, finally, "Yes, I remember him."

Stu waited for the doctor to go on, but he didn't. "Okay, so this is what we have. Walker Moon is in Sacramento, and he's killed at least eight people. We're looking for something, anything, that might help us capture him. I guess you could say we need to understand what makes a man like that tick. I understand he escaped from your facility in nineteen seventy-two."

The doctor's laugh was pronounced, forced. "He escaped all right, out of a maximum security facility. I can tell you right now, Detective, that I've prayed to God that I would never hear his name again."

"You called him a psychopath, Doctor, or words to that effect. What does that mean, exactly?"

"You must understand, Detective, that labeling somebody a psychotic or a psychopath can easily have a dozen different meanings. In Moon's case, I believe he built his life around delusions of persecution and false beliefs, twisting the facts around to suit himself. He was a man filled with hate. I might add, his mental disorder is one of the most difficult to cure, if it's possible at all. That was why I put in my report that I didn't believe the man could ever reenter society."

"Any idea what could have caused his condition?" Stu asked.

The doctor chuckled. "If I could answer that one, the whole world would be in a lot better shape. Though I will say, usually this kind of condition goes back to childhood. You've heard about the kid who burns up neighborhood cats and puts Super Glue on the perches in bird cages. I have no doubt that Moon was one of those kids.

"Out of all the sessions I had with him, only one thing became absolutely clear."

"And what was that?"

"Walker Moon was a very sick and very dangerous man. I'm sure he hasn't changed. Might even be worse. I truly pity the man assigned to bring him to justice."

Stu swallowed with difficulty. "About those sessions, Doctor. Did anything else come of them?"

"Not really. He knew how to play the game."

"What about this God-devil thing?"

"That's simple, really. If you think you're God, then nothing is going to harm you. If you think you're the devil, then you are in control and inflict the harm. It's not a good combination. I know you might be thinking this is all so much bullshit, and maybe it is, but I think you need to be forewarned. Take the man seriously."

"We intend to, Doctor Market. Now back to his childhood. What about his family?"

Alvin Market paused. "This wasn't in my report, Detective Redlam, but I suppose I should tell you. When Moon was twelve, they found his mother's mutilated body in a field near the family house. Nothing ever came of it, with the local authorities looking for the killer in all the wrong places, but his family has always believed that Moon killed her. So do I."

"What about his father?"

"As I understand it, he was a drifter who wandered in and out of town. Moon was an only child, and after his mother's death, he went to live with an aunt."

"Is the man capable of committing suicide, in your opinion?"

"I wouldn't call it suicide, but I think he could self-destruct. But I also believe that a great many people would suffer the agonies of hell before that happened."

Stu thanked the doctor and hung up. He looked at Robert and shook his head wearily. "Let's get the hell out of here. I'll fill you in on the way."

Robert nodded, sharing Stu's urgency.

CHAPTER 23

Wednesday, December 16, 1988: 1600 Hrs.

Steve Taylor sat across the table from Jack Smitovich in the interrogation room and watched sweat bead up on the fat man's brow.

"Okay, Jack, let's try this again," Taylor said. "We know you're in this mess up to your ass, so why not make it easy on yourself and talk to us."

More frightened than angry, but determined to keep up a front, Smitovich muttered, "I have the right to remain silent, and I have a right to have my attorney present. Isn't that the way it goes?"

"The way it goes is our way, tough man, so cut out the bullshit. You're going down on a conspiracy to commit murder charge, and we're going to put you away for a long time. You're not that young, Smitty, so a long time could mean forever to you."

Smitovich looked up at Taylor, hating the bastard cop. "Go

pound sand, you four-hundred-dollar-a-week flatfoot. You miserable pukes have nothing on me!"

It was the most emotion Taylor had seen in the last hour, and that was good. It was hard to break them down when they kept calm and refused to talk.

Taylor leaned across the table, hand raised to strike.

Furious, Smitovich ducked. "Go ahead, hit me!" he cried. "Let me own your badge!"

Taylor walked out of the room, taking in huge amounts of air. He hadn't wanted to slap him. He'd wanted to remove his head from his body.

Taylor walked into an adjacent room where Runyo, Dalton, and Mike had been watching through a one-way mirror and listening through a speaker.

"That little fuck is as dirty as my socks," Mike said adamantly.

"And it's gonna be a bitch to prove," Dalton muttered.

"All we have on him is the fuckin' locker key," Taylor said, sitting down and rubbing the back of his neck. "And it's not enough. I can see any good defense laughing us out of court. Duplicate keys can be made; somebody was using the locker without Smitovich's knowledge. Christ, they'll come up with a dozen good explanations. We needed to catch him at the locker with the file in his hand. Now Moon has the file and we've got Smitovich. Big shit deal."

Runyo shook his head dejectedly. "His hotshot Miami lawyer should be here tomorrow. We've gotta break him down before then."

Mike sighed. "And Moon has the file. Thank God we've got that much covered. Doesn't matter if it's Irene Pennington or Phoebe Baker. Both women are out of town and we've got a unit on each house."

Taylor stood up, nodding toward Smitovich. "The little fuck is pacing. I'm gonna try this one more time."

Smitovich scowled at Taylor when he walked into the interrogation room, but kept pacing.

"Sit down," Taylor ordered.

Smitovich sat down.

Taylor walked over to the wooden chair and kicked it out from under him. Smitovich went down with a thud.

"That's it, cop!" Smitovich yelled, scrambling up. "I'll have your—"

Taylor grabbed Smitovich by the shirt. "What's your connection with Walker Moon, you little fuck!"

Smitovich spat on the floor. "You gonna beat me now?"

"Something better. You're going into cold storage."

"When am I gonna be arraigned?"

"When I feel like taking you to court."

"You can't do that!" Smitovich protested. "That's against my rights!"

"You don't have any rights because I own your ass," Taylor announced, pushing Smitovich out the door.

The three detectives met them in the hallway. Mike stayed to help Taylor; Runyo and Dalton gave Taylor the "thumbs up" sign and headed for Homicide.

Smitovich glared at Taylor and Mike. "You cops just dug your own graves. My lawyer is gonna eat you alive."

"Not before you have your share of justice," Mike announced.

"Justice? That's a laugh. You limp dicks couldn't find justice with a flashlight and a net!"

"Shut up, shit," Taylor said, prodding the fat man toward the elevator.

In the booking area, Mike told Taylor to wait while he pulled in a favor. He then walked up to the booking counter, whispered something to a deputy, and waited, smiling at Taylor.

Within minutes, a short Asian deputy wearing sergeant stripes walked through a metal sliding door, shook hands with Mike, and talked with him in a secluded corner.

After a few minutes, they shook hands again, and Mike walked over to Taylor and Smitovich. "Let's get him booked," he said, nonchalantly.

Taylor handed the booking officer the arrest forms and

again metal doors opened. A deputy then escorted Smitovich into the fingerprint room, the doors closing behind them.

It wasn't until Taylor and Mike were on their way to Homicide that Taylor asked, "Would you mind telling me what the hell that was all about?"

"I asked the sergeant to lose the paperwork on Smitovich," Mike said with a grin.

Taylor chuckled and slapped Mike on the back. "That'll help."

In the squad room, Runyo listened to Rachel Harrison's nearly hysterical voice on the phone and felt a growing uneasiness. "Take a deep breath and start over, Miss Harrison," he said gently. "Just go slow so I can get it all down."

Rachel Harrison struggled for composure and repeated, "I got permission to call Irene's mother, Detective Runyo. I didn't want her to worry about me. It's nearly Christmas, and I knew she would be calling me. We've all been really close to her, like family, and I knew if she tried to call me and—"

"Okay. So you called Irene Pennington's mother because you didn't want her to worry about you. And?"

"She told me that Irene and Phoebe are back in town! Irene had a fight with her boyfriend in Tahoe, and left him there. Phoebe apparently had an argument with her family in Denver and hopped the first plane to Sacramento. She talked to them this morning."

"And they were home at that time? I mean, here in Sacramento?"

"Y-yes . . . Well, I guess so. . . ." Her voice broke again. "I-I tried to call them, Detective Runyo, but both answering machines were on. I left messages, and then Officer Halen called Detective Redlam, and he wasn't at his desk, and. . . ."

Runyo could tell she was losing it again, and said, "Detective Redlam went to San Francisco for the day, Miss Harrison, but not to worry. We have a unit on both houses. As soon as we can reach Miss Pennington and Miss Baker, we'll have them transported to the safe house."

"But—"

"Put Officer Halen on the phone, ma'am."

"Yes, sir?" Halen said.

"Are you going to be able to handle things up there? The lady seems pretty upset."

"She is, but she'll be okay," the officer said.

"Well, if you need help, let us know. Oh, and Halen, as soon as we locate the other two women, we'll be transporting them up to you. Hang tough."

Runyo hung up and looked at Dalton. "You get the gist of that? Pennington and Baker are back in town, but Rachel hasn't been able to reach them.

"Have we heard anything from the units covering the houses?"

Dalton shrugged. "I'll find out."

Runyo looked up when Taylor and Mike walked in, noting the grins on their faces. God, he hoped it was good news. "Did you get the fat fuck booked?" he asked.

Taylor nodded and filled Runyo in. "Heard anything from Stu or Robert?"

Runyo shook his head. He told the two detectives about Rachel Harrison's call, and concluded, "With the two women back in town, we'd better turn this into a full-fledged stake-out. We can't be too careful. It would be one hell of a lot easier if we knew which file Moon has, but we don't so we'll just have to treat them both with equal caution."

Dalton joined the detectives, dragging over a chair. "The last contact with the covering units was about a half hour ago. No sign of anyone at the Baker house, and the house is dark, so Phoebe Baker obviously didn't go straight home. Irene arrived home an hour ago. The lights are on and the officer can see her moving around. So far so good."

Runyo walked over to Stu's desk and thumbed through the case file until he found the hit list. He dialed Phoebe Baker's number first and left a message on the machine. He repeated the procedure with Irene Pennington. He looked up at Dalton and sighed. "Now all we can do is beef up security, and wait."

On the drive home from San Francisco, during the conversations about the case and Walker Moon, it occurred to Robert that Stu Redlam really was a standup kind of guy, a cop's cop. He was a professional all the way, somebody a fellow officer could look up to. He also had the feeling that Stu would always be there for his partner, somebody to count on no matter what the situation.

They were on the outskirts of Sacramento, just west of the Yolo Causeway on Highway 80, when Stu looked over at Robert and said, "Why don't you call the office and report in. Maybe they have Smitovich and Moon in custody by now, and we can relax and go to dinner."

"I've always liked believing in fairy tales." Robert grinned, picking up the cellular phone.

Runyo answered on the first ring, and hearing Robert's voice, said, "Well, it's about time! We figured you two lamebrains fell into a snow bank."

"Sorry to disappoint you," Robert answered, "but it's not snowing in the City by the Bay. Just damp and drizzly. What's up? Anything?"

"Besides my dick on a Saturday night? How much time do you have?"

"We're in West Sacramento."

"That should do it. We got Smitovich after he dropped off the file."

"You got Smitovich *after* he dropped off the file." Robert looked at Stu's face in the light from the dashboard. Eyes straight ahead, mouth tight. "So you got the latest hit file, and Smitovich, but separately?"

"Something like that, but it's a lot more complicated. We caught up with Smitovich outside the bus depot, after he dropped off the file, but he had the key. Unfortunately, by the time we got him inside, Moon had ripped the locker door off its hinges and gotten away with the file."

"Jesus Christ!" Robert exclaimed, quickly relaying the information to Stu.

"Yeah, Jesus Christ, and long live the king," Runyo grumbled. "The fucker was probably there the whole time, and we just didn't see him."

"So you've got Smitovich, and Moon is running around town with the file. Any idea which one?"

Runyo grunted out, "No, and this is where things start to get serious. Rachel Harrison called. She apparently talked her watchdog into letting her make a call to Irene's mother, and through that conversation found out that Irene and Phoebe are back in town. She called both numbers and left messages on their answering machines. I called them and left messages on their answering machines. Dalton contacted the units patrolling the houses. Irene is home. The officer reported activity, and the lights are on. No sign of trouble.

"The officer at the Baker house said he hasn't seen anybody around, and the house is dark, so we can assume Phoebe Baker didn't go home at all.

"We were about to step up security at the Baker house and send someone out to talk to Irene Pennington when you called."

"I think you'd better talk to Stu," Robert said, handing over the phone.

Runyo repeated the information to Stu, adding, "I don't think we can do one hell of a lot more. Wait a minute...."

"This is really one goddamned sorry mess," Stu said to Robert while he waited for Runyo.

And then Runyo was back on the line, and Stu's attention was focused on the detective's words.

"Dispatch can't seem to reach Officer Clayborne at the Pennington house, Stu. No contact in about fifteen minutes, and he's not responding to his call."

Stu's mind was racing. "Take Mike and Taylor and head

for the Baker house in Fair Oaks. Check it out and then sit tight until you hear from me. Pennington lives in Elk Grove. We're coming up on the loop now, and we can be there in five. Give me the address, and tell Dalton to meet us there."

Runyo quickly complied.

"Put up the light and hang on," Stu said to Robert, moving over into the fast lane as he punched the accelerator.

CHAPTER

24

Wednesday, December 16, 1988: 1800 Hrs.

Stu parked the Blazer around the corner from the Pennington house and turned off the lights. From where they were parked, they could just make out the patrol car across the street from the house and down the road, partially hidden by a wild overhang of trees and bushes. It was a good position. Just subtle enough to keep the neighborhood calm, but bold enough to catch attention. Bold enough, he hoped, to have kept Walker Moon at bay.

The Pennington house was further out in the country than the others had been, and could even be considered modest, if you ignored the candy-apple red Porsche 911 parked in the driveway.

Stu made an attempt to contact the patrolman one last time. "Metro ten, this is Ivy two-two-six. Do you copy?" Stu repeated the call and shook his head. "I don't know about you, but this whole thing really smells."

"I was thinking of something a little more explicit," Robert said, opening the door.

Across the street now, guns drawn, Stu and Robert quietly moved in and out of the shrubbery until they reached the patrol car. Out of the silence, Robert muttered, "Shit!" as Stu shone his flashlight on the open door of the vehicle, illuminating the officer slumped over the wheel.

Stu reached in to feel for a pulse, and the officer groaned. The large lump on the back of his neck was already turning an ugly shade of purple.

Stu reached for the microphone. "Ivy two-two-six. Roll ambulance, and back-up, code two at five-four-six-three Falcon Park Drive, Elk Grove."

The response was immediate. "Ivy two-two-six, ten-four."

Robert moved in closer. "Doesn't look like Moon's handiwork, Stu."

"I agree, but with a man like Moon, who knows? Poor guy is going to have one hell of a headache tomorrow."

Out of the corner of his eye, Stu caught a movement at the corner, stiffened, and then realized it was Dalton, running in and out of the shrubbery, just as he and Robert had done.

Coming up on the scene, Dalton peered in the patrol car and shook his head.

"Yeah, I know," Stu muttered. "This doesn't look like something Moon would do, but we can't leave anything to chance. Ready? We're going in."

The three detectives approached the porch quietly and professionally. Through the filmy living room curtains, they could see a dark-haired woman cringing on the couch while a monster of a man loomed over her. Instantly, they moved into action. Robert took the point, kicking the door off its hinges. Robert immediately dropped down, as Stu broadjumped over him, slamming to a halt in the middle of the living room, yelling, "Police officers, freeze! Down on your knees, sucker!"

Robert and Dalton moved in, guns cocked and extended.

The man on his knees looked up at the detectives, swaying

slightly, trying to keep his balance and focus his bloodshot eyes. "More goddamned cops!"

The son of a bitch was drunk, and Stu suddenly had the feeling they had made one hell of a mistake.

"Who are you!" the woman cried, anger sparking in her eyes.

"Are you Irene Pennington?" Stu asked.

"Yes, I'm Irene Pennington, and this is my house, and this is my boyfriend. My God, what do you want? You can't come barging in here like this!"

The detectives holstered their weapons, and Stu slapped on the cuffs, jerking the boyfriend to his feet. "We didn't come here to bust your boyfriend, Miss Pennington. We're here for an entirely different reason, but a cop has to do what a cop has to do. Are you aware that bozo here, in all probability, beat the snot out of an officer who was trying to protect you?"

Irene Pennington's anger switched to her boyfriend. "Oh, Brad, you didn't!"

The man swayed again and grumbled, "Figured you'd called the cops on me, sweetie...."

Now the anger had turned to rage. "Sweetie? Don't you *dare* call me sweetie! Jesus, Brad, why do you think I walked out on you in Tahoe? You were drunk, surly, and stupid. Stupid, stupid, stupid! Oh, God, I hate you!"

The ambulance and patrol car had arrived, the revolving lights filtering in through the curtains.

"I'll take care of it," Dalton said. "What do you want me to do with 'Bozo'?"

"Take him out, read him his rights, and turn him over to the patrolman. I've got more important things on my mind than worrying about a hot-tempered, drunken fuckhead."

After Dalton had shoved the boyfriend out the door, Stu turned to Irene. "I'm Detective Redlam, and this is Detective Hollinger. That cop your boyfriend slam-dunked was put out front for your protection."

Irene Pennington looked very confused. "I-I don't understand...."

"I had a long talk with Rachel Harrison, Irene, and I know the whole story. Your friends Mary Attwater, Leah McVey, Jenny Marshton, and Gabrielle Messa are dead. That leaves three out of the seven on the hit list. You, Phoebe Baker and Rachel Harrison. We have Rachel stashed away in a safe house, so that leaves—"

"I told Rachel he was after us," Irene choked out. "When I read about the first two . . ." She buried her head in her hands and sobbed.

"Are you talking about Jack Smitovich?"

Irene nodded.

Stu walked over to the phone on a side table and dialed. When he had Rachel on the line, he carried the phone to Irene. "Here," he said. "Somebody wants to talk to you."

Stu and Robert could hardly hear Irene's mumbled end of the conversation, but it didn't matter. Rachel would set her straight.

Irene hung up and looked at Stu. "I want to be with Rachel," was all she said.

Stu took a deep breath, nodded, and made the call. After he had hung up, he managed a smile. "We'll have a patrol car here in a few minutes, Irene. The two officers will take you to Rachel. Better pack a few things."

Irene stood up. "Is . . . Is Jack doing these terrible things?"

Stu shook his head. "Smitovich hired a hit man," Stu said, but didn't elaborate.

"What about Brad? What's going to happen to him?"

"Do you care?"

Irene nodded.

"Well, I can't promise anything. A lot stems on the condition of the officer, but let's just say his problems aren't as serious as yours."

Within ten minutes, they had cleared at 5463 Falcon Park Drive. In the Blazer on the way across town, Stu said to Robert, "One left, partner. If you know how to pray, it wouldn't be a bad idea to do it now."

*   *   *

The house and neighborhood were dark. Taylor killed the lights on the Monte Carlo and parked by the street-side mailbox.

Mike looked around from the backseat of the unmarked, and said, "I don't like this. I've never liked neighborhoods without lights. Christ, you would think the taxpayers pay enough so they'd install goddamned street lights!"

In the front seat, Runyo sat thumping his flashlight against his leg, trying to get it to work. "I don't like it either. Not even a Christmas tree in a window."

"Maybe everybody in the neighborhood is Jewish," Taylor said, peering up the street. "Either one of you see a patrol car?"

"Shit, no," Mike muttered. "I saw a movie once where a whole neighborhood was zapped up into space by aliens."

Taylor shook his head. "That's really funny, Mike. Just put a cork in it while I try to zap the cop back from Venus. Ivy two-two-two to Metro eleven. Do you copy?" Taylor repeated the call three times and gave up.

The front yard was large, with a knee-high, split-rail fence surrounding the perimeter. The long driveway to their right ended with a three-car garage. This was the section of Fair Oaks that had a horse in every backyard instead of a Mercedes in every driveway. You were more apt to find horse trailers, vans, and station wagons.

The detectives climbed out of the car, bracing themselves against the bitter cold. Mike hopped the fence, while Runyo and Taylor took the driveway. Somewhere behind the house, a horse blew its nose.

"This is fuckin' spooky," Taylor whispered, hitting the porch with his flashlight.

Guns were immediately drawn, almost as though Taylor's words had been a cue.

"I'm going around back," Mike said, heading toward the garage.

Runyo and Taylor were on the porch now, staring at the open front door.

"Uh oh," Taylor muttered as Runyo aimed his flashlight through the door.

They stepped into the foyer and then into the living room. "Clear," Taylor whispered.

In the backyard, Mike tripped over a garden hose, slipped on an icy spot on the walkway, and almost took his head off with a tree branch, so by the time he discovered the horse with its head sticking out of the small stall, he glided right by without even saying hello.

Finally, up on the redwood deck, Mike found the back door and turned the handle. When the door swung open, he waited a few moments and then stepped inside. He stood in the middle of the laundry room; he could smell freshly washed clothes. He opened an inside door and moved into the kitchen, watching a flashlight beam heading his way. "The back is clear," he whispered to the two detectives as they joined him in the kitchen.

"All clear in front," Runyo said, thankful Mike and Taylor couldn't see his sweating palms.

Taylor's hands were clammy, too, as they made their way toward the back of the house. They found all the doors off the hallway open and clear, until they reached the closed door at the end.

Taylor swallowed hard and looked back at Runyo and Mike. "I don't want to do this," he said as he turned the doorknob. With the door open, flashlights scanned the room, settling, finally, on a large pool of blood on the pink bedspread.

Taylor stepped into the room and stopped. A trail of blood led into the bathroom.

"Somebody's gotta do this," Mike mumbled, walking across the room.

Runyo and Taylor followed, guns and flashlights ready.

Mike flipped on the light switch, and stared at Phoebe Baker. She sat naked on the vanity, hands tied to the light fixture. Vacant eyes stared into space above a throat that had been slashed from ear to ear, the sink catching the life blood that had drained from her body.

Mike made a whimpering sound. "Holy Mother of God!"

Runyo couldn't move. His legs seemed to be frozen in time. He finally whispered, "Jesus Christ, Stu, what kind of a monster are we chasing?"

Taylor turned and hurried through the house, out to the Monte Carlo, which he fired up. Grabbing the microphone, he choked out huskily, "Ivy two-two-six, this is Ivy two-two-two." He waited for a response, then repeated, "Ivy two-two-six, this is Ivy two-two-two."

"Ivy two-two-six."

"Channel four, two-two-six." Taylor felt winded, unable to catch his breath.

"Ivy two-two-six on four."

"Stu, we've got a one-eight-seven."

The radio was quiet.

"Stu, he ripped her to pieces."

"We'll be there in ten," came Stu's shaky reply.

Taylor turned the car off and walked back to the house. Runyo was using a flashlight to turn on all the light switches. And the bright light brought the death scene even closer.

Feeling sick, Taylor looked at the once-beautiful woman and turned away. In all his years with Homicide, he had never seen anything like this. The savagery of it was overwhelming. For the first time in his life, he knew total fear.

Two patrolmen were sealing off the perimeter of the house when Stu and Robert pulled up.

"It makes you think that maybe death isn't enough punishment for a monster like Moon," Robert said, climbing out of the Blazer.

Anger was building in Stu to such great proportions he could hardly answer. When he did, he said, "I can't think of a punishment strong enough to fit the crime."

Taylor met them at the door, pale and shaken. "It's a real mess. Back bedroom and bath . . ."

Stu and Robert walked down the hall, through the bedroom, and into the bathroom. Neither detective could speak as they stared at Walker Moon's latest victim.

"Did the other women end up like this?" Taylor asked woodenly.

Stu felt a sudden pounding in his temples. "No, not quite."

"If Smitovich is behind this, he's gonna pay," Taylor muttered. "Just like the maniac is gonna pay."

Out in the living room now, Stu nodded at Grant as he walked through the door.

"Moon?" Grant asked.

"Has to be, only this time, he didn't leave his calling card, because he's fresh out of coins."

"Bet that frosted his ass," Grant said, heading for the bedroom.

Stu looked around at the milling patrolmen. "Any of you know anything about the officer who was supposed to be on duty here?"

A tall, skinny patrolman stepped forward, head down. "I was on duty, Detective. I-I . . . Well, the house was dark, so I figured nobody was home. I went out on Fair Oaks Boulevard to . . . Well, I had to go to the john, and . . ."

Stu waved him off and walked outside, breathing in the cold night air. It didn't matter. Four patrol cars out front wouldn't have mattered. The pieces were beginning to fall into place. Frightened because she knew that her friends were dropping like flies, Phoebe Baker had to have known she was on the list. Had she been home the whole time, afraid to move, afraid to breathe, living in a silent house by day and a dark, silent house by night? Probably, and Moon had somehow figured it out.

Stu shook his head. Ten patrol cars wouldn't have mattered.

* * *

It was three A.M. on Thursday morning when Steve Taylor and Mike Clegg arrived at the jail. It was time to call in another favor, and this one was a big one.

After talking to the sergeant on duty, they waited in the quiet, dimly lit garage where the transport buses were kept and mentally prepared themselves for their meeting with Jack Smitovich. It wasn't difficult. Had they seen Phoebe Baker's mutilated body and the bloody *Friday the 13th*–style crime before Smitovich's interrogation, things might have gone differently. They might have gotten some answers.

Within minutes, they heard Smitovich's whining voice as he walked through the door. "What the hell is my lawyer doing down here at this hour of the morning?"

Jack Smitovich saw the waiting detectives and stopped. "Now wait just a damned minute! My lawyer isn't here. What the hell ... Take me back to my cell!" He turned around, trying to push between the two deputies, but the deputies closed rank, shoving him along toward the buses.

"What the hell is this bullshit!" Smitovich cried, beginning to struggle. "You can't do this!"

Mike grabbed the front of Smitovich's orange jumpsuit and slammed him into the side of a bus.

Taylor nodded at the deputies and they moved off, smiling slightly.

Taylor approached Smitovich. "Well, Mister Tough Guy. I hope you still have that silver tongue of yours working. You're going to need it to stay alive."

"You can't do this!" Smitovich choked out, gawking at Taylor in disbelief. "Now, I'm really gonna own your badge!"

Taylor unholstered his 9 mm.

Smitovich stared at the gun, shaking his head. "Jesus, you fucked-up mother. You're crazy!"

Taylor jerked Smitovich to his knees, placing a boot on the back of his neck. "I don't think you understand, Smitty. We need some answers here, and we're gonna get 'em. The first time I don't get an answer to one of my questions, I'm going to blow your head off." He cocked the hammer. "Now I've asked you this before, and I'm gonna ask you again. What is your connection with Walker Moon?"

Smitovich spat on the cement. "I'm not talking, you bastard cop!"

"Oh, I think you'll talk to us, Smitty, because I have a little story I want you to hear. We just came from Phoebe Baker's nice house, where we found her tied to a light fixture in the bathroom, nearly decapitated. Her nude body was covered with blood, as was the sink where her blood was draining. And she had been sexually assaulted, like all the others, *after* she had taken her last breath. Moon is a rabid animal, and rabid animals must be put out of their misery.

"Again, Smitty. What's your connection with Walker Moon?"

Sitting up now, with his back against a bus tire, Smitovich shook his head. "I ain't saying shit."

With the hammer cocked, Taylor placed the end of the barrel against the fat man's forehead. "Have you ever seen what a 9 mm auto can do to a man's head, Smitty?"

"You can't shoot me. I'm in jail!"

Taylor laughed. "I can read the story now, Smitty. Smitovich shot while trying to escape."

"Jesus Christ, Steve, just shoot the son of a bitch and get it over with!" Mike exclaimed. "If you don't, I will! Nobody will miss the fuck, we'll probably get medals, and I can go home and go to bed."

Taylor's finger eased over the trigger. Smitovich watched, his face pale beneath his tan. He started to tremble, false teeth clacking in his mouth. "Jesus, okay! I'll tell you. Just take that cannon out of my face!"

Taylor didn't move the gun. "Walker Moon."

Smitovich groaned, seeing his life suddenly over no matter what direction he took. "I-I hired him."

"For what?"

"To kill . . ."

"Who?"

He stumbled over his words, spit flying out of his mouth. "M-Mary Attwater, Leah McVey, Jenny Marshton..."

"And?"

Smitovich closed his eyes, shaking uncontrollably. "Gabrielle Messa, Rachel Harrison, Irene Pennington, and Phoebe Baker."

Taylor winked at Mike. "And how did Moon get the information on the women?"

"The bus depot, in a locker."

"Number?"

"Ah . . . It was two-seventeen."

"Did you ever have personal contact with Walker Moon?"

"Yeah, but only when I hired him. The rest of it was over the phone."

"And where did you hire him?"

"In . . . In Florida."

Taylor took a deep breath. "What was your connection with Neal Jessop?"

Smitovich opened his eyes. "W-who?"

"The dead cop who got involved with your sleazy illegal gambling operation and owed you over a hundred grand."

"We bought him off."

"Explain."

"He was in the hole for a lot of money and had no way to pay off the debt. So we used him to get information."

Mike took a deep breath. "And he kept gambling and you kept using him. I'll bet the debt got bigger instead of smaller. Jesus Christ, you fucking hunk of slime!"

"Take a walk, Mike," Taylor ordered. "I'll finish this."

Mike walked a short distance away and squatted down, his back to Taylor and Smitovich.

Taylor turned back to the fat man. "Where is Walker Moon?"

Smitovich shook his head. "I-I don't know. I haven't heard from him in the last couple of days."

"One last question. Did you put the files on the four murdered women in locker two-seventeen at the bus depot?"

Smitovich nodded, weakly.

"I didn't hear you."

"Yeah, I put the files in the locker."

Taylor pulled the trigger, the click sounding very loud in the quiet building.

Smitovich slumped over, crying like a baby.

Taylor whistled for the deputies to take Smitovich away and then joined Mike. "Are you okay?" he asked.

Mike stood up and looked at Taylor with anguished eyes. "You should've killed the bastard, Steve. You should've blown his head off his shoulders."

CHAPTER

25

Thursday, December 17, 1988: 1200 Hrs.

It was almost noon before Stu finally walked into Homicide, shaking water from his hair and grumbling about the weather. It had started to rain around four A.M., just after he had gotten home from the crime scene, and the torrential downpour wasn't helping his mood.

He looked at no one and spoke to no one as he made his way to his desk, concentrating instead on the capture of Walker Moon; the monster had to be stopped.

He shuffled papers around on his desk and considered the fact that Moon had no idea that Rachel Harrison and Irene Pennington were at a safe house in El Dorado Hills. And with Smitovich in jail, what would Moon do now? Would he be smart enough to figure it out? Would he self-destruct, as Dr. Market had suggested? Would he move on to some other unsuspecting city or hamlet? Or would he go off on an even bigger killing rampage, because the plans he had had with Smitovich had been thwarted?

Stu rubbed his eyes, trying to push all thoughts of that kind of blood bath out of his mind.

"Stu?"

Stu looked up at Steve Taylor. The hours he had spent in and around Phoebe Baker's house hadn't been easy on him, either. His eyes were red-rimmed, and his shoulders drooped. "What's up, Steve?"

Taylor hated to bother Stu. The detective had dark circles under his eyes, clear evidence that he hadn't gotten any sleep, that the case was really beginning to get to him. But that was the overall problem; it was beginning to get to all of them, one way or another. "Can we go for a walk?" Taylor finally asked.

Stu had a strange feeling in the pit of his stomach, but nodded, following Taylor into the empty lounge. "Has something happened that I should know about?" Stu asked, getting a root beer out of the machine.

Taylor walked to the window and looked out at the rain. "I got a confession out of Smitovich, Stu . . ."

Stu groaned. "Let me guess. You took him someplace, like an empty closet or office . . ."

"I pulled in a favor and had him taken to the bus barn."

Stu sat down in a plastic chair. "Is he still alive?"

"Hasn't got a mark on him. I got it on tape, too."

"The tape isn't worth shit, Steve. He's gonna tell his hotshot Miami lawyer, and the next thing you know, IA will bring you up on charges, and the fat fuck will walk."

Taylor rested his forehead against the windowpane. "That fat fuck bought off Neal Jessop. He owned Neal's ass for heavy gambling debts."

"Did Smitovich confess to that, too?"

"He did. I've got the tape in my desk if you want to hear it."

Stu shook his head. "Just give me the high points."

Stu was on his second root beer by the time Taylor had given him the details, and the liquid hadn't settled well in his stomach. Or maybe it was the fact that Taylor had walked into this mess without thinking about the consequences. They didn't have enough on Smitovich as it was, and now what little bit they did have was going to go right down the toilet. Taylor had acted unprofessionally, irrationally. And they were all going to suffer for it.

"We've got to tell the lieutenant about this, Steve. Before he hears about it from the boys upstairs."

"I know. He's been on the warpath all morning over the Baker killing, so I've been putting it off. I wanted to talk to you first anyway."

Stu headed for the door. "Well, I don't think we can put it off any longer. The time is right now."

Mike had been at his desk when Stu and Taylor had walked out of the office. Now he watched them go into the lieutenant's office. It could only mean one thing: Steve was going to tell Stanfield about the incident with Smitovich in the bus barn, and he planned to keep him out of it.

Mike hurried into the lieutenant's office and closed the door behind him.

Stanfield scowled at Mike. "This isn't a family gathering, Clegg. If you want to talk to me, you'll have to wait your turn."

Taylor spoke up. "Stay out of it, Mike."

Mike straightened his shoulders. "No way. If you're gonna fall on your ass, I'm falling with you."

Stu looked at Mike and shook his head. "I don't think I want to hear this."

Stanfield looked puzzled. "Hear what? Would somebody like to tell me what the hell is going on?"

"I got a confession out of Smitovich last night," Taylor said.

The lieutenant closed his eyes. "Oh, shit." He opened his eyes and looked at Mike. "You, too?"

Mike nodded.

"Mike didn't do a damned thing but stand there and give me moral support," Taylor said. "It was my game all the way."

Lieutenant Stanfield sat down behind his desk, aging before their eyes. "I don't want to hear about how you got him out of jail, where you took him, or what you did to him. Just give me the fucking bottom line."

"There isn't one," Stu said. "At least not yet. Smitovich confessed to hiring Moon to make all the hits, confessed to putting the files in the locker at the bus depot, but said he hasn't heard from Moon in a couple of days. And there's more...."

The lieutenant groaned.

"Smitovich told me that he had Neal Jessop in his pocket over some bad debts," Taylor added. "I got the whole thing on tape."

Stanfield began to doodle on a note pad. "The DA called this morning, and said he'd received the reports and booking slip on Smitovich. Said he had the beginning of a case, but needed more."

"So I went out and got more," Taylor said glumly.

Stanfield drew big circles and little circles. "Smitovich's attorney is supposed to be here today, isn't he?"

Stu cleared his throat. "He is."

Stanfield tossed the pencil on the desk and looked at the three detectives. "So we wait it out. Maybe the ax will drop, and maybe it won't. Smitovich knows by now he hired more than a hit man. He hired a raving maniac who is out there somewhere with blood on his mind. If Smitovich is really the weasel you've all made him out to be, maybe he'd rather be in jail than out there walking the streets. Nobody knows what Moon is going to do now.

"Go back to your desks and keep busy. Keep this conversation under wraps, and we'll play it the way it comes in."

The detectives did as they were told, but it was a long time before Stu could concentrate on any work. Taylor had made a bad mistake, but then the whole case had been a simmering potboiler from the start. Personal feelings had entered into it, and that was always a bad sign.

And then there was the one thought Stu kept trying to avoid. If Smitovich walked with Moon still on the loose, then God help them all.

Deputy District Attorney Sam Boyes walked into Homicide at exactly four-thirty and headed straight for Lieutenant Stanfield's office, looking neither to the left nor the right. The detectives involved, and even some who were not, exchanged glances around the room. Boyes was a big, blond German with fair skin, and his face had been the color of a Washington State red apple, giving them all a very good indication that the ax was about to fall.

A few minutes later, the lieutenant called the detectives on the Moon-Smitovich case into his office, waited until they had filed in, and then shut the door.

Boyes stood at the window with his back to them. Water dripped off his raincoat, making puddles on the floor. Without turning around, he said, "I had an interesting visit with Smitovich's attorney today. He claims Detective Taylor threatened his client into giving a false confession."

"It wasn't false," Taylor blurted out. "The little slime is one-hundred-percent guilty."

The DA turned around and scowled. "You know that, and I know that, but a lot of good it's going to do us now." He looked around at the detectives. "I'm holding each and every one of you responsible for this. Off the record, I'd like to crunch Smitovich's skull, too, but there are ways of going about it without getting a tit caught in a wringer.

"I want Smitovich as badly as you do, and I was trying to build a case. Now, because one member of your team went off half-cocked, I've got a complaint thirty miles long, and police brutality is at the top of the list."

Finally, Stu spoke up. "Steve had just come away from a

crime scene, sir. The kind of a blood bath that would turn the stomach of a twenty-year veteran. I'm not condoning what he did, but to be honest, this case has us all a little crazy."

"Steve shouldn't have to take the heat alone," Mike spoke up. "I was there with him."

The district attorney shook his head. "I told you I'm holding you all responsible. Smitovich's arraignment is tomorrow morning, and because of this horseshit, he's going to walk, and there isn't one goddamned thing I can do about it."

"You want the tape I got of Smitovich's confession?" Taylor asked the DA.

The DA stuffed his hands in his pockets and nodded. "Under the circumstances, it's inadmissible evidence, but what the hell. It'll give me something to listen to on those lonely nights when I feel like sticking needles in my eyes."

"I didn't touch him," Taylor spoke up. "I never laid a hand on him."

Boyes looked up, interest flickering in his eyes. But just as quickly, the light was gone. "Not good enough. Smitovich's attorney is the best dirty money can buy.

"If anybody is interested in watching a three-ring circus, the arraignment is at nine A.M."

After the district attorney had gone, Stu was the first to speak, and his words were directed at Taylor. "We'll get them both, Steve. Sooner or later, we'll get the break we need. That's all it'll take, and it'll even the score."

Feeling shit-stinking miserable, Taylor nodded his head. Maybe they would and maybe they wouldn't, but one fact remained: he had singlehandedly, stupidly, fucked up the investigation.

Twenty minutes later, with the detectives at their desks trying to come up with ways to make Taylor feel better while fighting with their own ideas on the subject of truth and justice, Dalton's pager went off. He didn't recognize the number on the display, but picked up the phone and dialed.

On the first ring, a female said, "Hello?"

Dalton immediately decided the call was from a phone

booth, because of the vehicle noise in the background. "This is Detective Casteel."

"It's me, Toy. I talked to you the other night over on Stockton Boulevard. Remember?"

Breathing suddenly became difficult. "Sure, I remember."

"Well, you know that guy you were looking for? You know, the one with the funny gray eyes?"

Dalton waved an arm for attention, bringing detectives' heads up. "Yes, the big guy with the funny gray eyes."

"I know where he is."

"You know where he is."

The detectives gathered around Dalton's desk.

"Yeah. Well, I know where he's staying. I got a girlfriend who works J Street, see. Down there by the old Franciscan Hotel. You know where that is?"

"I know. What about the guy?"

"Well, it was my friend's night off, and it was my night off, so we went and had some dinner—"

"And?" Dalton said, interrupting.

"And after we had dinner, we were standing around out front of the hotel talking, when this big guy comes out of the door, bumping right into us."

"And that's it?" Dalton asked.

"No, 'cause when I looked up at him to yell at him for being such a clutz, I recognized him as the gray-eyed creep from Stockton Boulevard.

"He looked really mad, so I backed off. There's something else, too. Maybe it doesn't matter, but something was wrong with his face. I figured it out after he'd stalked off. He had a long burn mark across his cheek, sort of purple from the cold."

Dalton's heart raced. "It matters. You say he came out of the Franciscan Hotel on J Street. How long ago was this, Toy?"

"Maybe three minutes ago. I'm in a phone booth right outside the hotel." She paused. "Did I do okay?"

"You're a sweetheart, Toy. You deserve ten dozen roses.

Now do me another favor? Take your girlfriend and get out of the area."

Toy giggled. "Geez, are we gonna have the Fourth of July in December?"

"Something like that. Just do it, honey, and I'll make sure you get those roses."

"Anything for you, Detective," Toy giggled again.

Dalton hung up and looked at the detectives. "You heard?"

"Jesus," Robert said. "He's right under our noses!"

The lieutenant walked out of his office, asking, "Now what the hell is going on? I haven't seen this much activity in weeks!"

Shirts were coming off and padded vests were going on. Even Taylor was smiling. "A tip just came in," he told Stanfield.

"Moon was spotted at the Franciscan Hotel on J Street," Runyo added. "Son of a bitch! We're gonna do him!"

Stu looked at the phone, experiencing a sudden chill. He reached for the phone and dialed Julie's number. When she answered, he said, "Julie, it's Stu."

"Well, hi, stranger," she said, sounding really happy to hear his voice.

Stu took a deep breath. "Hi, yourself. I just called to tell you that I've fallen in love with you. I-I just wanted you to know, and . . ."

Julie's voice cracked. "Stu, what is it? Is something wrong?"

"Just remember what I said, Julie. It's important."

"Sure I'll remember. I've fallen in love with you, too." She paused. "You found him, didn't you?"

"I gotta go, Julie. Take care."

Stu hung up and reached for his vest.

Robert was on the phone with Dana; it was a night when two very special ladies would wait up, praying for the men they loved.

* * *

The Franciscan Hotel was located between Fifteenth and Sixteenth on J Street, flanked to the west by an old abandoned apartment complex and to the east by three Victorian-style homes. An alley running through to I Street separated the apartment complex and the hotel.

Stu had parked the Blazer around the corner on Fifteenth Street, but in full view of the hotel entrance. Dalton and Mike were positioned a half-block west on J Street, with Runyo and Taylor parked near the alley on I Street to cover the rear entrances to the hotel.

Stu looked at his watch and then at Robert, who sat beside him with his eyes closed. "You okay?" Stu asked.

Robert opened his eyes and nodded. "I was just thinking about Neal's funeral tomorrow afternoon, wondering how Cindy is holding up."

"I saw you on the phone before we left the office. Were you talking to Dana?"

"Yeah. I didn't have to tell her it was coming down. She knew it by the sound of my voice. If I . . . If I get through this tonight, I'm gonna ask her to marry me."

The radio squawked to life then, with Dalton's excited voice. "He just turned the corner on Sixteenth, heading for the hotel."

Stu could see Moon now, and grabbed the microphone. "We give him a few minutes inside, and then we move!"

"Since his escape, he's had enough time to collect a whole fucking arsenal," Robert muttered.

Stu watched Moon move quickly up the sidewalk and disappear through the hotel doors. "Even without a weapon, the man is deadly. But nobody, not even Moon, is indestructible."

CHAPTER

26

Thursday, December 17, 1988: 1800 Hrs.

Stu opened his gun case and pulled out the Freedom Arms .454 Casull, thumbing five rounds in the beefy cylinder. *Five shots, Redlam, so you'd better make 'em count*, he told himself as he watched Robert jog across the rain-slick street.

On a night like this, with everybody wanting to get home out of the rain, the end of the rush-hour traffic was light. It was a good thing. Stu had the feeling their battle with Moon wasn't going to end in the hotel, and the fewer people around, the better it would be.

It had been decided that Robert, Mike, Dalton, and Runyo would move in and try to make contact. Taylor had volunteered to take the back of the building and Stu had the front.

Stu stepped out of the Blazer, pushed the six-inch barrel of the gun into his pants, zipped up his thick fatigue jacket, and took his position at the hotel entrance.

Inside the musty hotel lobby, Robert brushed the rain from

his face and approached the desk. Mike, Dalton, and Runyo stayed by the door. A thin middle-aged man put aside the newspaper he was reading and looked up.

"A man, a big son of a bitch just came in," Robert said, flashing his badge. "What room is he in?"

The desk clerk studied Robert for a moment, then said, "Room two-ten. Second floor."

"Is there a phone in the room?" Robert asked.

The desk clerk shook his head.

Robert nodded at the detectives and all four hurried toward the stairs.

On the second floor, with guns drawn, they inched their way over the faded flowered carpeting, checking room numbers as they went. Moon's room faced west, overlooking the alley.

Not good, thought Robert. *Especially if there is a fire escape.* He tried to slow down his accelerated breathing as they paired up on both sides of the door, but he was filled with too many memories. He had gone through this with Neal Jessop, and Neal was dead. Sweat formed on his brow.

Runyo made wild motions, vigorously shaking his head, but Robert ignored him, getting into position to kick the door.

Just like you did it at the range, Robert told himself, starting to count. *One, two . . . Don't do it the way Neal did it. Three . . . Now!*

Robert hit the door and bounced off, pain shooting up his leg, momentarily putting him down on the rancid-smelling carpeting.

Immediately, a volley of gunfire from inside the room erupted, spitting through the old wooden door.

Just as quickly, Runyo stepped forward and screamed out, unleashing a brutal kick, spinning the door off its hinges. The muzzle of Moon's gun inside the dark room flashed another volley of gunfire as Runyo jumped clear, but splinters from the wooden door casing caught him in the face and eyes. Runyo grabbed at his face and cried out in pain.

Robert and Mike, coming in low on either side of the doorway, unloaded several rounds into the dark room. The return fire of six consecutive shots sent the detectives scrambling for cover.

In that split second, Dalton rolled toward the doorway and let go a deafening barrage of gunfire. The return of bullets ripped through his shoulder, rendering his right hand useless. Panic clamped down on him as bullets burned hot spots into the carpeting and floor around him.

Gut instinct and determination, and maybe even the same blind craziness that had sent Neal Jessop to his death, overtook Robert as he fed in a fresh clip and charged the room, rolling to the right as he squeezed the trigger until the slide locked. He heard the "whump" as the bullets connected. He could see the big man's silhouette as he staggered backward toward the window. "He's hit!" Robert yelled out, taking cover behind a chair.

Mike dropped the slide on a fresh clip and rolled into the room, aiming at the hulking man outlined against the window. And then the window seemed to explode with the weight of Walker Moon.

Taylor entered the alley from I Street and watched Moon drop from the fire escape, stumble, and then stand erect. Taking cover behind garbage cans and assorted boxes, Taylor bolted up the alley screaming, "Freeze, motherfucker!"

Moon whirled, raised his gun, and fired, just as Taylor got off two shots. Taylor crumpled to the ground as a searing pain tore through his gut.

Taylor's two shots had hit Moon in the forearm and shoulder, but the man didn't flinch. Grinning, he fired two more rounds at the fallen detective.

Out front, Stu had listened to the volley of shots coming from the hotel followed by the shattering of glass, but it wasn't until he heard Taylor yell that he realized that Moon had crashed out of a window into the alley.

And then he heard the shots, and heavy footsteps running

in his direction. There was no time for cover. All he could do was plant his feet, hold the .454 at full extension, and wait for Walker Moon to appear.

Moon hit the sidewalk at a dead run, looking neither right nor left as he started across the street.

Stu yelled out, "Moon!"

Moon stopped.

"You're under arrest, you lousy, fucking bastard. Toss your gun and drop down, now! I want to see your nose on the asphalt!"

Moon whirled, the Beretta in his bloody hands. "Fuck you, cop." He laughed, charging Stu.

The Casull coughed once, the sound of the shot echoing off the buildings. Moon spun, the round tearing off his left arm. Stu squeezed the trigger again and again, and yet again, until Moon finally fell to one knee.

Moon was still grinning when he brought the Beretta up, spraying lead all over the street.

Sirens wailed in the distance as Stu held his aim and let the final round go, exploding Moon's chest into a fountain of blood. Moon collapsed, face down.

Stu dove for a parked car, slid the empty Casull under the vehicle, and quickly reached for his holster, pulling out his backup .45. He then slowly approached Moon's motionless form. Gaping holes exposed bone and vital organs, and yet Stu found a pulse, though it was weak.

"This isn't over until you're dead, you bastard son of a monster," Stu yelled at Moon, backing away only after the pulse had completely stopped.

With shaking hands, Stu reached for his portable radio, even though patrol units were already screaming to the scene. "Ivy two-two-six. Shots fired, Franciscan Hotel. One officer down, possibly more. Roll code three ambulance."

"Ivy two-two-six. Do you want the air cleared?"

"Negative," Stu answered, hurrying down the alley toward his partner.

* * *

The street was ablaze with lights that included patrol cars, unmarked vehicles, ambulances, the rescue squad, fire trucks, the DA, the chief of police, the coroner, CSI, and every reporter in Sacramento County. Helicopters buzzed overhead while camera crews struggled to catch every detail and make their deadlines for the eleven o'clock news.

Robert stood beside Stu as white-coated attendants lifted Steve Taylor into one of the four remaining ambulances.

Pale and disheveled, Lieutenant Stanfield walked up to his two detectives and shook his head. "Jesus, God Almighty," he said, sucking in his breath through his teeth. "Who would've believed it would come down to this. Is Taylor gonna be okay?"

Stu nodded. "He's pretty mangled, but they don't think the bullets hit any vitals."

"Dalton took a slug in the shoulder?"

"Yeah," Robert said. "They've transported him already. Said something about the fact he might need some surgery, but he's tough."

"He's gonna be okay, too," Stu said, nodding toward the rescue truck where a medic was removing wood splinters from Runyo's face. He sighed. "We're all lucky to be alive."

Behind them, near the hotel entrance, a screaming blonde woman pounded on an officer's chest.

"Jesus, this sort of thing really brings out the crazies," the lieutenant said, moving off to talk to the DA.

The woman broke away from the officer and ran toward Stu and Robert. "Are you detectives?" she asked, tears streaming down her cheeks.

The officer was right behind her, trying to grab her arm.

Mike walked up then, and said, "It's okay, officer. I know the lady, and I'll take care of it."

The blonde stared at Mike. "You were with Detective Casteel that night, weren't you?"

Mike nodded. "This is Toy," Mike said. "The sweet, sweet lady who gave us the tip."

"Is . . . Is Detective Casteel . . ."

Mike managed a smile. "He took a slug in the shoulder, but he's gonna be fine."

Toy closed her eyes and whispered, "Thank God!"

After Mike had escorted her away from the scene, Stu shook his head. "She must really like the big nut."

"Well, we sure as hell owe her a lot more than a couple dozen roses."

"You going to the arraignment in the morning?"

"Wouldn't miss it," Stu said. "Maybe we'll pick up another miracle like Toy."

"Or we'll get to watch Smitovich walk. I'd sure as hell like to go to Neal's funeral knowing we got both of them. One without the other is like a half-written book. You read it and come away feeling cheated.

"You ready to roll?"

Stu nodded. "I'm gonna make a call first. Meet you at the Blazer."

In the phone booth, Stu dialed Julie's number. It rang once, and she was on the line.

"Hi," he said.

"Oh, God, Stu! I've been so worried! They broke in right in the middle of regular programming. They said some officers were injured. . . ."

"Three, but they'll pull through . . . Mind if I drive out?"

"Oh, Stu, of course I don't mind. Have you eaten?"

"I'm not really hungry, Julie."

"Then I'll put on a fresh pot of coffee." Julie's voice sounded full of tears as she said, "I'll be waiting."

Stu found Stanfield and handed him the Casull, then crossed the street. When he reached the corner, he glanced back at the hotel. "Fuck you, Dr. Market. We made it."

EPILOGUE

Friday, December 18, 1988: 0500 Hrs.

Stu bolted up in bed, covered with sweat. The nightmare had been so real it took him several minutes to calm his galloping pulse. Walker Moon had been in the room, laughing at him, holding up a bloody gun in one hand and Jenny Marshton's severed head in the other. He took deep breaths, trying to rid his memory of the dream. Walker Moon was dead, and he, Stu, was alive, with beautiful Julie sleeping beside him.

Walking into Julie's waiting arms after last night had been like entering a sanctuary where only peace and tranquillity existed. They had made love, talked, and then made love again, falling asleep in each other's arms. He hadn't been surprised by her compassion, but he had been surprised by her understanding. Julie was one in a million, and he wasn't going to let her get away.

It was early, only five o'clock, but a nagging restlessness took him downstairs and into the kitchen, where he made a pot of coffee. In only his shorts, the house felt drafty and cold. He turned up the thermostat, built a fire in the fireplace, and checked out front to see if there was a morning paper. It was right on the stoop, and he plucked it up, carrying it to the kitchen table.

The front page was full of the events of last night, with pictures of Moon lying under a tarp and of Dalton being lifted into an ambulance. There were even pictures of the shooting self, scowling at the camera.

The next page covered the case, which had finally been released to the media in its entirety, including the brutality charges Jack Smitovich and his attorney were going to file against the city. Because of it, the paper went on to say, the district attorney would more than likely drop the conspiracy charges against businessman Smitovich.

Stu shook his head. The man's business had been corrupt gambling and murder. He could almost live with the thought of Smitovich walking, because somewhere, someday, he was going to make a mistake big enough to either kill him or put him away for the rest of his life. Stu's only regret was that it couldn't be now.

Stu looked up as Julie walked into the kitchen, rubbing her eyes. She wore a fuzzy pink robe, and he pulled her close, burying his head against her soft body.

"Couldn't you sleep?" she asked, rubbing his neck.

"Not too well, I'm afraid. I kept thinking about all the paperwork ahead, the flack I'm gonna get from Internal Affairs, this mess with Smitovich, and then Neal Jessop's funeral this afternoon. I'll be on a five-day mandatory leave, and I have the feeling they'll be the longest five days of my life."

"Is there anything I can do to help?" Julie said gently.

"Just be here for me," he said, smiling up at her. "Just be ready to catch me if I fall on my ass."

Robert met Stu on the courthouse steps, and they walked into the large entrance area together. Neither detective wore a topcoat, because the sky was blue, the sun almost warm. They wore conservative suits, blending in with all the attorneys in and around the building.

"How did you sleep?" Robert asked, punching the button in the elevator after they had gone through security.

Several assorted men and women and a pretty girl carrying a stack of briefs pushed into the elevator. Stu waited until they had reached their floor before answering.

"I had one hell of a restless night," he said finally. "Being with Julie helped, but I kept thinking about this fucked-up case."

"Me, too," Robert replied.

Stu grinned at the young detective. "If I were you, I'd start to wonder who up there doesn't like you." Stu pointed up. "I mean, now it's four shoot-outs."

"And another mandatory leave. I seem to have time to burn. You know, I've been thinking. Maybe it's time for a change."

Stu raised a brow. "You mean get out of law enforcement?"

"No, I was thinking more like Homicide. I've enjoyed working with you, and I like the department."

Stu smiled. "Well, there's a vacancy in Homicide, and although I can't promise anything, I'll sure put in one hell of a recommendation."

Robert nodded. "Thanks."

They walked into the crowded courtroom and took their usual seats at the back. Stu nodded at Mike and Runyo, who were sitting two rows up, and had to stifle a chuckle when Runyo turned around. His face was covered in bandages, with only his big nose sticking out.

Robert poked Stu and nodded to the right. The reporters were grouped in the corner with undeniable excitement dancing in their eyes. They were like turkey vultures ready to swoop down.

At nine o'clock, the bailiff entered the courtroom, said his "all rise" speech, after which a tall, black, black-robed judge walked in, taking his seat at the bench.

With everybody seated again, the judge looked around.

"Looks like we have a full house here, Mr. Jackson. What's the first case on the calendar?"

The court clerk handed the judge the file. "The People versus Jack Smitovich, your honor."

The judge exchanged knowing glances with the clerk. It was obvious the clerk had pushed the Smitovich case to the front of the line, and this, in turn, would quickly clear out the courtroom, leaving the judge to deal with the remaining cases at peace.

The sleaze lawyer from Florida stood as a door to the left opened. Smitovich appeared, wearing the customary orange jumpsuit, and was escorted to the table and his attorney.

Deputy DA Boyes stood up. "Your honor, the People have been forced to drop all charges against Jack Smitovich. I'll write a full report to explain my actions."

The judge nodded, and said, "At the request of the prosecution, I am dismissing the charges against Mr. Smitovich."

Stu and Robert were already out the door before the judge brought down the gavel.

Outside, both detectives took in great gulps of air. It hadn't been a surprise, but the fact that it had actually happened left the taste of bitter injustice in their mouths.

They sat on a bench in the sun by the fountain and waited for Smitovich to appear, trying to ignore the media, who swarmed and hovered and laughed.

"They think it's a big joke," Robert muttered. "Maybe we should invite them over to watch the autopsy on Phoebe Baker."

One brave, female reporter, who recognized Stu and Robert sidled up to them and asked, "How does it feel to have your investigation go down the toilet because of a stupid cop?"

Stu glared up at her. "How does it feel to have a penis for a tongue and balls for ears, lady. Get the fuck out of my face."

The reporter quickly moved off, and Robert chuckled.

A few minutes later, a white stretch limo pulled up at the curb. Stu and Robert stared at it. "Christ," Stu muttered, "I don't believe it."

"The fuck is leaving in style. Bet you a cup of coffee Smitovich arranged it."

"No bet."

"You really want to stick around here and watch this shit?" Robert asked.

Stu shook his head and stood up, just as the courthouse doors opened, and Smitovich stepped out with two deputies and his attorney. He wore a snappy white suit and white shoes, the orange jumpsuit undoubtedly long forgotten in the holding cell in the courthouse basement.

The media storm-trooped Smitovich as he tried to make his way through the crowd, his pudgy face aglow from all the hubbub and attention.

Stu and Robert stood in silence while Smitovich laughed with his attorney and the media and began his walk to freedom.

Smitovich was at the halfway point, when the cab pulled up and parked behind the limo. Rachel Harrison emerged, quickly paid the driver, and headed up the steps toward Smitovich.

Stu and Robert stared at her, but it was Stu who finally blurted out, "What the hell is she doing here?"

Smitovich stopped and smiled at her. "Well, well, well," he said smoothly. "So I see you made it through the jaws of death without a scratch." He continued to smile. "Have you talked to Holly Anderson lately? I understand she lives in Oregon."

Stu saw it coming, but it was too late. It all seemed to be happening in slow motion; even Stu yelling out, "Rachel, no!" echoed like a cracked phonograph record playing at the wrong speed.

Rachel Harrison had pulled a .357 magnum revolver out of her purse, and the gun roared to life, blowing through Smitovich's head, splattering bone and debris all over his attorney.

Smitovich hit the steps and rolled on his side; death was instantaneous.

Two deputies hit Rachel at the same time, disarming her

and slapping her in cuffs, all in one motion, while people screamed and scurried around.

Stunned, weak in the knees, Stu moved forward. "Why?" he asked, as other deputies held back the wall of reporters.

Sobbing, Rachel looked up at Stu with anguished eyes. "Suzy was my sister.... I had to kill him, because nobody else would have. He wouldn't have paid, Detective Redlam. He would never have paid for what he did to her!"

Robert walked up to Stu as the deputies took Rachel away, and muttered, "And justice for all."

"And Rachel Harrison is going to pay for it for the rest of her life. Jesus, what a shame." Stu felt sick, and headed down the steps, oblivious to the mass confusion going on around him. He had gotten his miracle, if you could call it that, and Smitovich had made his mistake, underestimating Rachel Harrison. But what a shitty price to pay for glory.

Robert watched Rachel Harrison disappear into the back of a patrol car, and sighed, following along behind Stu. When they reached the sidewalk, he said, "After the funeral, I'm gonna go to Toomie's and hoist one for Neal, and then I'm gonna go home and ask Dana to marry me. Right now, I feel a real heavy need for stability in this fucked-up world of ours."

Stu looked over his shoulder one last time, catching only a glimpse of Smitovich on the stairs.